D0235513

AUG 2019

DONATION

Guardians of the Key

Guardians of the Key

Clio Gray

Love your local library,

long may they live

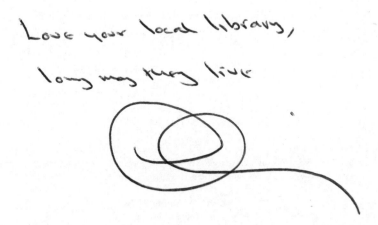

headline

Copyright © 2006 Clio Gray

The right of Clio Gray to be identified as the Author of
the Work has been asserted by her in accordance with the
Copyright, Designs and Patents Act 1988.

First published in 2006 by
HEADLINE BOOK PUBLISHING

1

Apart from any use permitted under UK copyright law, this publication may
only be reproduced, stored, or transmitted, in any form, or by any means,
with prior permission in writing of the publishers or, in the case of reprographic production,
in accordance with the terms of licences issued by the Copyright Licensing Agency.

All characters − other than the obvious historical figures − in this publication are fictitious
and any resemblance to real persons, living or dead,
is purely coincidental.

Cataloguing in Publication Data is available from the British Library

ISBN 0 7553 3104 4

Typeset in Bembo by Palimpsest Book Production Limited,
Polmont, Stirlingshire

Printed and bound in Great Britain by
Clays Ltd St Ives plc

Headline's policy is to use papers that are natural, renewable and recyclable products and
made from wood grown in sustainable forests. The logging and manufacturing processes are
expected to conform to the environmental regulations of the country of origin.

HEADLINE BOOK PUBLISHING
A division of Hodder Headline
338 Euston Road
London NW1 3BH

www.headline.co.uk
www.hodderheadline.com

Thanks, Harry

Contents

1

Mr Izod and the Unknown Pilgrim

UP ON THE spire the jugglers were throwing fruit in the air and dropping sugared nuts to the crowd of children below. The tiles were mossed and dashed with pigeon droppings, muffling the thuds of acrobats missing their beat and tumbling from their holds. The wire slung between St Anthony's and the Hall of the Innocent Martyrs swung and hummed in the wind, stung by the rain which intermittently fell. The drums got louder and louder as the crowd watched a dwarf being strapped to a crossbar mounted on a wheel. With a terrifying scream he was pitched from one end of the wire to the other, his arms scrabbling at the air, and the onlookers gasped and stepped aside every time he screeched overhead, expecting him to plummet the twenty-five feet below him to his death, smashed to smithereens on the cobbles at their feet.

Two boys, Thomas and Toby, took advantage of the distraction to slip sardine-like amongst the stalls, pocketing a few eggs or apples, a handful of beans, a bag of meat-scraps, chicken necks, a broken biscuit or pie discarded beneath the rag-bag of carts and trolleys, amongst a maze of legs. If the earth were flat and the air were clear, Thomas knew he could have seen the Mountains of Tibet, but today it was just boots and stockinged calves and trousers pinched at the knee, taffeta catching the weak light of the sun and flouncing over mud and spilt cockles, squashed pasties, horse-dung steaming in between the showers.

The boys skipped across the alley, round back of the church, choking on a bag of lemon drops they'd found dissolving in a puddle, and half a tub of sherbet fizzing up their noses, courtesy of the sherbet-seller into whom they'd accidentally run. It was dark in the shadows, distant, though they were only a few yards from the crowd. The noise dropped away when you moved from the square, the stones of St Anthony's holding back the noise like a harbour holds its arms against the sea. Over on the green, the geese had gone to sleep behind their wattle and the sheep had settled into eating neeps, nudging noses, scraping dirty wool against the rough wooden fences, scratching, somnolent, unalarmed.

Thomas rolled up a cigarette but it fell to bits as soon as the spittle hit the sog-line of the newspaper. Toby grabbed the doings from him with a superior sniff, packed it into perfect shape. The boys sat and puffed in turn, because one apiece was too much even for eleven-year-old smoke-hands like them.

One day, dreamed Toby, I'll have a room and all I'll do in it is smoke cigars from India and eat lemon sherbet and pickled crab.

It was Thomas's turn, and all he saw was a road, grey in the rain, and muddy, it was all he ever saw and it seemed to go on for ever.

★   ★   ★

Inside St Anthony's, Stanley Izod ignored the Advent festivities and hammered home the last wooden peg holding the repaired stanchion in place. It was England 1805, and Stanley believed such medieval pageants should have long ago been abandoned to the past where they belonged. For a moment, the coloured glass of the window shivered rainbows across the flagged floor before settling back into its frame. He huffed and slapped the dust from his thighs, began to collect up the scatter of chisels and hammers he had been using to shape the pegs just so.

A chicken pecked its way up the aisle, finding oat husk in the flagstone cracks, barleycorn in the corners of the pews. The bottom of the heck-door must have blown open again. He'd have a word with Father Ignatius, see if he wouldn't let him fix it the morrow before it got ripped clean off by the gales he could feel in his bones were coming. The oil lamps wavered as a breeze lifted the wall-hanging of St Dunstan pulling the devil by his nose, and rustled the corn doilies still hooked to the wall from this year's Harvest Thanksgiving. In the eaves there was a flurry of flapping wings as a pigeon detached itself from its perch and headed into the outside afternoon.

Glancing up, Stanley missed his bag, the chisel striking the stone with a clang, which died in echoes and sent the hen, pluffed and indignant, cock-o-laying back up the aisle. It reached the door just as the top half was pulled open and it had to duck through the pair of boots that appeared on the threshold.

A man, his tunic so ripped and dirty he might have been playing pig-in-the-punch, took a slow step in, blocking the light for a moment. He was lame in one leg and wore the badge of a pilgrim. Taking the north aisle, the man walked down the nave and into the chantry chapel of St Clare, where he took one of the crossed daggers of Gerald de Montrey, who had fought in the Crusades, off the wall above the small altar. He spat on the flat of the blade, gave it a quick sharpen with the soapstone he had taken from his pocket, then without a word he raised his head to the sky, closed his mouth to tighten the skin, gripped hard on the knife and slit his throat.

He stood for a few seconds gazing at the blue gesso and stars of the chantry ceiling, the knife-point still on his skin, then his arm dropped and the blood began to bubble over his collar, down his shirt. He sank to his knees, his head dropped. He swayed on to his side, the knife clattering across the flagging.

Izod heard the crack of the man's head hitting the floor, a gentle gurgle of life leaving, springlike, tumbling through a lazy day of leaves and moss and small, sun-warmed pools. He smelt the spilling blood, a slight steam rising. When he reached the chantry, the crash and clatter of his tools behind him where he had kicked over his bag as he rose, he leaned hard against the outer pillar, turned his head, retched up his dinner of pickles and cheese, retched again as he watched in disbelief the warm blood gathering momentum through the paving cracks, touching his boots, staining the wisps of straw being gently breathed on by the breeze, which seemed of a sudden as cold as ice.

2

The Wheels Begin to Spin

ACROSS THE SQUARE from St Anthony's church, Mabel Flinchurst poured some more tea into a china cup, glancing the gilt edge with the spout, setting off a wave of tuts and rolling eyes. She was distracted. She wanted to sit by the window and watch the children playing, see the acrobats atop the roof, clap with the crowds, laugh at the man on stilts as he wobbled up and down between the stalls. She loved the smell that drifted up from the animals' pens: the damp straw, the warm, wet fleece, the oily odours of leather and sweat, the underlying stench of stable waste. It reminded her of Labour's End, her father's farm out at Stonebury, where she'd helped milk the cows and goats with the rest of the girls, prepared the cream, patted the butter, forked the hay into the byres.

'Mabel, for heaven's sake, child! You're dribbling my finest Indian on to the gingernuts!'

For a few more precious moments, Mabel lingered in her daydream, remembering the scents of the oaks at Epping, the nuzzle of a lamb in her lap, the delicious aroma of bread baking in the vast open range of the kitchen. Then it was back to London and her great-aunt's living room, and the interminable twitter of ladies-of-station chattering about embroidery motifs, hat-beadings, whether button-up boots were better than laced, the latest in gloves, a new face cream, how Lady This or That was doing her hair and which eligible captains would be at the upcoming Christmas ball, on leave from the fields of Europe. Lady Haviscombe's ball was the primary subject of this meeting, the reason why Mabel was prevented from flinging on a cape, grabbing a maid and escaping into the carnival going on in the streets below to celebrate the coming of Advent.

'Pass that plate of curates to Mrs Witheridge, dear, or perhaps you'd prefer some shortbread?'

Mrs Flora Midweather-Etherington looked questioningly at Penelope Witheridge, her oldest friend. Seventy years ago they had attended each other's christening parties, played with each other's toys in the nursery, learnt to speak and stand as one is required to do, practised the gavotte together, gone to their first dance on each other's arm and left on the arms of prospective husbands. Twice they had been courted by the same men and twice they had swapped beaux before deciding which one should have which and who should marry whom. The only difference between them now was that Mrs Flora Midweather-Etherington had outlived all her ten children and her husband, whilst Penelope Witheridge still had two sons extant and, unfortunately, Mr Witheridge, who was getting more senile by the day. Still, Penelope had the joy of grandchildren to pamper and daughters-in-law to dominate or advise as she liked. It had been she who suggested to Flora Midweather-Etherington that if she no longer had immediate family, then her best plan was to find some members more far-flung. Hence the scouring of the countryside for distant relatives in whom to take an interest, and ergo the presence of Mabel.

She was the daughter of Flora's husband's sister's brother-in-law and it had been quite a struggle to wrest the child into her care. Her first missive to Mr Flinchurst, Labour's End Farm, Stonebury by Epping Forest, had been met with silence. She followed it two weeks later with a further letter stating her intent to visit 'the relatives of whom I have only recently become cognisant, and in whom I wish to make a tentative step towards introduction'. It hadn't occurred to her that such flowery language might not be immediately understood by the Flinchurst farmers and that it had taken the man a week to pin down the vicar in order to get the first letter translated into understandable English. By the time the second letter had been similarly translated, the visit was almost upon them, which was as well, as it gave neither Mabel nor her father nor any of the rest of the household much time to worry about the meaning of it all.

Flora Midweather-Etherington arrived on a dismal winter afternoon in a sable hat and cape, long silk gloves, shoes designed for a salon rather than a farmyard and a dress of watered silk which muttered every time she moved. Sidney Flinchurst was aghast at seeing this fine aristocratic lady arriving, the wheels of her hansom getting stuck in the slurry of the courtyard as soon as it had drawn past the gate. To his credit, he also immediately grasped the import of this visit: rich elderly relation seeking out countryside cousins with a view to patronising those who presented themselves well. Mabel and her two brothers, Ezra and Henry, were told to change immediately into Sunday best and give themselves a quick brush-up, whilst he and his men set to laying planks across the courtyard so Mrs Midweather-Etherington could approach the farmhouse with the minimum of dirt attaching to her fine attire.

Mrs Harley, the housekeeper, with the help of Betsy and Heather, the two scullery maids, whirled into the kitchen and whipped up an extra batch of honey biscuits and put fresh cream on the tea tray, hoiked the sugar lumps out of the pantry, spread a table with a cloth and gave the old silver teapot a quick polish. Up until the actual point of her arrival, Mrs Midweather-Etherington's visit had been treated with a mixture of suspicion and apprehension, with the general notion that 'no good would come of it'. A seedcake had been grudgingly prepared, along with some cherry buns, but it was quickly realised now that more would have to be provided and in a hurry. Mrs Harley, ever up to a challenge, was quick and efficient. She could whip up a vanilla sponge in ten minutes and have it served with warm custard in under half an hour. Brandy was put to mull on the stove with some spices, and the best packet of tea was retrieved and the pot put to warm.

By the time Mrs Midweather-Etherington had negotiated the makeshift pontoon across the muddy lake of farmyard cobbles, much that had not been done within the house had now been achieved. The fire had been stacked into a roaring blaze, the best chair quickly covered with a clean blanket, the coat rack roughly emptied so as not to sully her cape and hat. The house was filling with the scent of cakes and cooking, Mabel and her brothers were scrubbed to a nicety and Mr Flinchurst had even managed to throw on a waist-coat and thread his watch across it. The watch didn't work, but it looked good. And then, once comfortably settled and replete with tea, Mrs Midweather-Etherington laid forth her plan.

And so it was that Mabel was sitting in a fine dress in a fine drawing room, drinking fine tea and wishing all the while that she wasn't. It had seemed a grand adventure two years ago when she was fourteen. The village had held a farewell dance and she had been crowned queen. She'd said goodbye to her brothers and her father, tears in all their eyes. She'd hugged Mrs Harley and Betsy and Heather, and every single one of the animals out in the pens and further abroad in the field. She'd even hugged the chickens.

How stupid of me, she thought now, gazing at a piece of shortbread: not that she had hugged everything she could lay her hands on, but that she had let them all go. It wasn't that her great-aunt, as she had been instructed to call Mrs Midweather-Etherington, was unkind to her. Quite the op-posite. She'd been taught to write well, to sing, to dance, to draw, to embroider pictures in hoops, to walk in ridiculously tight bodices and shoes. She'd had her pronunciation brushed up, her hair brushed down and curled, her nails polished and buffed. The calluses on her hands had softened, her skin grown pale for lack of sun and overuse of parasols. She had the promise of being introduced to Society at next week's grand dance and yet she was discontented. She knew she shouldn't be. She knew her father was proud to have a daughter who might marry a lord and not a farmhand, she knew she was being selfish and ridiculous, but she couldn't help it. Mabel was miserable.

She was broken out of these thoughts by a commotion down in the square below. Not just the sounds of the fair and people having fun and bartering at the market stalls. This was a different kind of noise, more alarming. Police whistles were involved and there were feet running in all directions. Even her aunt and her stuffy old friend craned their necks towards the window, and eventually called a maid to find out what was going on.

'There's a man murdered himself in the church, ma'am,' said Elsa, the general maid, when she was asked.

'What do you mean "murdered himself", Elsa? Make yourself understood. Plain speaking is a virtue.'

Elsa blushed and hid her hands below her apron. 'Just that, ma'am. Everyone's saying he's killed himself in St Anthony's.'

'Killed himself?' repeated Mrs Midweather-Etherington. 'In the church? Don't be preposterous!'

She and her friend exchanged weary glances and decided to go back to more important topics, such as deciding Mabel's attire for the ball next week. Elsa withdrew, and Mabel begged to follow. She pleaded a headache, having learnt that ladies had headaches rather a lot, particularly when needing to leave a situation quickly, and cornered Elsa as she was ducking into the kitchen.

'Tell me all,' Mabel begged as the two girls sat conspiratorially huddled around the kitchen fire, and Elsa did.

3

Mabel Meets
a Mysterious Corpse

ELSA HAD BEEN sent out by Cook to fetch green vegetables for dinner, some best bacon and put in an order for next week's ice. As expected, she had lingered a little to take advantage of all the lively goings-on. She had bought a few hair ribbons for herself, and a pretty pair of laces, a packet of ornate buttons and a bag of broken biscuits. Just as she was heading back across the square there was an almighty clatter coming from over by the church, and she saw Stanley Izod coming round the side.

You might think it an odd thing that the church didn't have its doors facing on to the square, but as everyone knew, it was hundreds of years old and built on the old plan of facing east, the square having grown behind it, and the once main road to Bexley, on to which it used to open its doors, had now become a back street running along by the river. This meant that when Stanley Izod came out the door of the church he was standing quite alone on Church Lane, apart from the chicken, which was still picking and pecking in the dust nearby, and two boys sitting on the steps. He was

11

clutching his hat in his hand and descended the steps so slowly and in such a daze, he hardly noticed the two young lads sitting in the shade, sucking on lemon sherbet.

''Ere, mister,' said one of them as Stanley near trod on him, 'watch where you're goin'!'

Stanley nodded absently and continued past them, walking on towards the square. The two boys cursed him as he passed, then held their tongues. He was leaving footprints all the way behind him where the rain had cleared the cobbles, and what the boys saw was something they recognised from years of scabbed knees and scraped knuckles, nosebleeds and thwacks around the head by the beadle at the poorhouse.

They looked quickly at each other, then up they jumped and start scampering along beside Izod shouting, 'Mister! Mister! There's blood on your boots!'

Now it could just have been that the man was a butcher, and that he had been bleeding pigs for the evening sales, or carving up lambs for the spit, or chopping the heads off geese. But these boys lived on the square and they knew everyone in it, at least by sight if not by name, and they knew that this was the man who fixed the windows in the church and did all the odd jobs around and about, mending broken doors, or axles, turning new spokes for wheels. This was a man they often passed time with of an evening as they all sat on the river bank, he carving clogs for the mill workers whilst they tried to catch fish with a bent nail on a piece of string. He'd even given them some baccy one night, and a bottle of beer. So they came running after him, pulling at his coat-tails because he seemed in a daze and not exactly right in the head.

As they came round the corner into the square, the two ragamuffin boys were shouting about the blood on his boots and how Stanley had gone mad.

Stanley Izod stood amongst the scatter of people who turned around to look and saw the strange gaze in his eyes and the blood still dripping from his boots. He looked at nobody in particular and said it straight.

'There's a man just slit his throat in the church.'

For a few moments nobody said a word. Then there was a sudden sort of flurry as several men detached from the group and went running for the doors of St Anthony's. Within minutes there were shouts and cries, and the constables were sent for and the crowds gathered, and the stilt-man tumbled off his stilts and the dwarf up high on his wire had a narrow escape when his minders almost forgot to grab him home to safety so busy were they gaping at the commotion down below. The two boys took advantage and grabbed a few purses and a bag, and shoved in as much food as they could muster whilst everyone's attention was turned.

Elsa caught one of them by the ear as he was trying to lift the pack of bacon from her bag and she dragged him to the corner of the crowd and demanded explanation. She recognised the lad as one who came round regularly asking for pennies or a bowl of soup, and she knew Miss Mabel was fond of him and treated him well, so she boxed him hard around the cheek, squeezed him for information and let him go. Which is when she hurried back to the house to tell the news to Cook, who had already gone out on the street and got mingled up and lost in the crowd. And how

13

she had just got her coat off and scraped her boots when Mistress had called her upstairs, still a little out of breath – as she still was now, breathing the news to Mabel.

'So who was he?' asked Mabel in an excited whisper, 'the man who slit his throat?'

'No one seems to know him, miss. Stanley didn't recognise him so he can't be from hereabouts.'

'Would he know whether he knew him?' asked Mabel, who, unlike most people in the square, had seen a cow with its throat cut and knew what a mess it made.

Elsa shook her head slightly, not understanding.

'I mean,' continued Mabel, 'Stanley was in the church, which is quite dark, and in walks a man and just stands there and slits his throat in front of him. I mean, he'd certainly have fallen over. Maybe Stanley didn't even see his face properly, or at all.'

'Mmm,' replied Elsa, the pinkness in her cheeks getting a little paler as her imagination worked, 'I suppose.'

Mabel picked at a couple of crumbs she'd found trapped in her cuff. 'I think, Elsa,' her tone was decisive, 'we should find out. Come along!'

And with that, Mabel kicked off her shoes, put on a pair of boots that stood by the stove and rose to leave. Elsa was scandalised – those were Cook's boots and had to be at least two sizes too big, though Miss Mabel didn't seem to mind. In fact, Mabel had spent most of her young life growing into her brothers' boots, which were inevitably too big, until at last, when they actually did fit, they were only fit to fall to bits.

'Let's go and find Thomas. He's sure to know what's going on.'

Mabel had made up her mind and Elsa hurried to follow. If the truth were told, it was the most exciting thing that had happened to Mabel since she had arrived in London, and she was blessed if she was going to let it pass her by as if it were no more interesting than a plate of her great-aunt's shortbread.

Out in the square, the mêlée had moved round to the front of St Anthony's and Church Street was as crowded as the square was now bare. The atmosphere was still one of carnival and bated breath as Mabel and Elsa pushed their way into the throng. A constable stood guard at the door out of which another constable was ejecting the few men who were still inside the church. Stanley Izod stood to the other side of the door, twisting his cap and ignoring all the questions being shouted at him from the crowd. Then there was a collective cessation of noise and a hushed gasp spread through the gathering from the front to the back, like the sound of starlings sweeping through the night air.

A constable's back had emerged from the church door, carrying a makeshift stretcher. A pair of boots was clearly visible. The constable shifted his weight, being careful as he descended backwards down the church steps. As he did, the rest of the stretcher emerged and, visible to all, held up at the angle of the steps as if he was still in the act of falling, there was the dead man for all to see. His face was pale and shone like alabaster beneath a dark crop of hair. His eyelids were heavy but not closed and, like a flag at half-mast, showed only a line of white. From lips bereft of colour, a tongue hung, monstrously long, severed at its root where his throat gaped ghastly open, deep and dark, almost black with crust, fine white sinew glistening somewhere beneath, and everything about him from shoulder to knee was soaked in bloody gore. The smell of it had gathered over him and began to dissipate amongst the crowd. People who had been as eager to see the sights as shoot a fish in a barrel now stumbled backwards into their neighbours, horrified. Some clutched possessively at their own throats; most covered their mouths; all were silenced.

As the second constable downed the steps the hideous apparition was lowered to waist-height and no longer on display, and the murmurs began again, the crowd parting before the men, closing behind them, as a log will pass through a drift of leaves down a stream. Mabel had been right: this was not a man you would recognise even if you knew him. You did not want to get close up and poke and pry. His pilgrim's badge was hidden, as were his clothes; his unsteady gait would no longer be seen and recalled; the colour of his eyes was veiled, his face a pale mask as if it were already lost beneath the shroud and a ton of cold earth.

Mabel felt Elsa shudder as the unknown body passed them by and she was ashamed of her earlier curiosity, the tingle of excitement she had felt. What had given her a brief surge of life was someone else's death and a horrible death at that. She took Elsa's arm and steered her back through the crowd.

'Never mind Thomas,' she said to Elsa gently, 'let's get home. We can make some tea.'

Mabel's forehead glistened slightly with sweat and her hands were clammy. It was as if she had a foreboding then that something was going to happen. Something connected with that unknown man who had willingly made of himself a corpse. She shuddered as they re-entered the square and the sun shone for a brilliant second, then passed behind another scud of cloud.

As the two girls walked back across the square, neither of them saw the man watching them from the shadow of the church. His dark hat was pulled down over his forehead and he wrapped his cloak tight as the rain again began to fall. Just a light drizzle falling on the two girls ahead; just a light step as the man behind them smiled and slowly began to follow.

4

Taking Ariadne's Advice

LUCCA, JEWEL OF Tuscany, lying in the lowland brooch that was its walls. It is night. It is quiet. The moon traces a thread of streets that wind like spiderwebs between the dark and shadowed walls. A man climbs the steps of San Martino, puts his hand against its stone. He doesn't look up at the Duomo's grandly carved façade, is blind to Adam and Eve as they crouch beneath the Saviour's Tree; he doesn't see the mermaids or the dolphins, the monsters or the heroes, is oblivious to Roland, whose army fights again at Roncesvalles. There is a small part of the portico on the pier of the porch, anonymous, unnoticed: here he traces fingers over the ill-formed labyrinth. It is the shape beneath it which his fingers seek, below the maze that has been incised upon its boundaries, a map already ancient when the mason took his tools to chisel out the way to Jerusalem and salvation, to cover up the graffiti below. Did the mason know when he inscribed the words beside it? Did he know that what he chiselled was the truth? Did he know that his words echoed the first graffitist, that they would ultimately lead to the secrets so well hidden?

Here is the Cretan Labyrinth of Daedalus. Who went in, none came out, save Theseus, by the grace of Ariadne and her ball of thread.

The man moves his finger through the chiselled streets, feels the deeper lines behind. It is not Jerusalem he seeks nor a route to Paradise. His eyes are closed; he visions blackness, and the line his finger moves, and where it goes, a silver thread. He reads the map, discerns direction. He knows where he must go. He is one in a line of many and Aribert knows he must not fail.

He moves from the shadow of the Duomo and slips into the alleyways amongst the gutters and the rats. He knows where he is going. The walls around the city-state of Lucca hem him in but he does not worry. They are thirty metres wide and soldiers still march their tops to keep their city safe; the bastions at every door are guarded and the portcullis of St Peter's Gate is hard against the ground. There is no one to espy him as his form is lost in dark and narrow lanes, no one to stop the way he knows that he must go. He slips below the shadow of the Council Building, knocks twice upon the wooden door, soft but sharp like a dog barks in its sleep when it hears a tread upon the floor but does not wake. A wooden grille is slipped aside and he presses his face close so that he is seen, then the bolt is sprung and the door is opened and he descends into the labyrinths of Lucca.

Mabel wasn't sleeping well. She sighed and groaned and turned from side to side. She saw the face of the murdered man every place she looked. It disturbed her, this man who went against the will of God and took his life before his time. Her bed was too soft even though she had slipped a few boards beneath the mattress. Still she dreams of the hard grass beneath her back, lying on the gentle slopes of Epping Hill, her brothers' boots against her feet, the smell of ash from the dying fire, the scent of fresh-shorn sheep upon her face, the warmth of that old dog whose feet smelt inexplicably of cheese. She can see the stars arc above her, hear the geese gibbelling gently in the gleaning fields, the sentries shifting their weight from foot to foot as the rest of the flock tuck in their heads and snooze. And then of a sudden she's back on the church steps again, and there's the man with a body of blood, his worn boots poking from the sheet, accusing her, pointing her out from the crowd. The dark rent across his neck seems to sneer in a horrid echo of the silent gasp of his blue mouth and she leans across him to try to catch those last few words that nobody else has heard.

She sat up suddenly to find Elsa tiptoeing over to the window, her hands at the curtains, pulling them quietly open. Mabel hated sleeping with the window and curtains shut, so every night, after she had gone to sleep, Elsa came in and closed them up, then crept back in the morning to open them. It was a compromise they had come to after Great-aunt Flora gave her a big speech about encouraging no-goods and peep-toms and begging every thief in London to come and take their fill.

'Mmm, thank you, Elsa,' said Mabel, still fuzzy with sleep. 'What day is it today? I've quite forgotten.'

'It's Friday, miss,' said Elsa, pouring the hot water she had brought into a bowl and fluffing up a towel.

'Oh God,' sighed Mabel, pulling at the tangles of her hair,

'fish day. What a ridiculous custom. We don't do that in Epping, you know. We just have whatever we had on Thursday if there's enough, or whatever we're going to have on Saturday if there's not.'

'Very sensible, miss,' replied Elsa. 'Course, I happen to know that there's a bit of ham left in the pantry and some cheese and pickle and that it'd be ever so easy to do up a pack with some bread and butter and that someone might have thought of it already because it's mill day as well as fish day.'

Mabel crossed the room in two strides and hugged Elsa as she was going out the door.

'Thank you, Elsa. What would I do without you?'

'Starve, miss,' sniffed Elsa, backing out into the corridor, 'or run off back to Epping.'

Mabel laughed but Elsa had already closed the door. She put on her dressing gown and opened the casement window, went out on to the balcony, bare feet on the stone floor, leaned on the railings. It was a wonderful view, looking to the east, right across the square, past the church and over the river, far beyond, where the morning sun set the reed meadows on fire, and mist lay along the dykes and wreathed the feet of the long line of windmills, which stretched on to God knew where. She loved those windmills, loved that the city spires of London and St Paul's were only a smudge away to the west, and she was glad for the crisp beauty of the morning. She had finally persuaded Great-Aunt Flora to let her go with Elsa and James, the footman, to collect the monthly batch of flour from the miller, and she counted the windmills with her eyes, wondering which one it would be.

★   ★   ★

It turned out to be none of them, and also that they had two hangers-on. Toby and Thomas had latched on to the trap for the ride.

Mabel liked the boys, liked their cheek and freedom. Liked the way they always got by without a nod from anyone. Thomas in particular was often at the door, and Cook set him to polish boots for a bowl or two of soup. Mabel had chatted with him in the kitchen oftentimes when she'd escaped from sticking needles through hoops of fabric or threading loops of wool into tapestry screens, or doing breathing exercises so she could talk normally with a corset crushing up all her insides. She'd asked him once about his mum and dad but he'd shrugged his shoulders and said he'd forgotten, that he'd lost them somewhere or they'd lost him, 'or something'. He'd said it so easily that a lump came to her throat and she handed him another piece of buttered toast – probably just as he'd planned, but still it hurt her to think of him out there on his own. Except for Toby, of course. The two of them stuck together like fingers on the same glove. At least they have someone, she thought, and everyone needs that.

It was Toby who pointed out the man hanging around in the porch of the Hall of the Innocent Martyrs when they got back that night. Elsa and James were sitting up front together laughing, arms linked, sharing a bottle of perry. Thomas and Toby were leaning against the flour sacks, sucking the sweets Mabel had bought for them, primarily to stop the boys pinching them anyway. She'd also bought a penny-ballad sheet, and all the way home they'd been trying to get the hang of the fifteen verses of 'The Bonnie Lassie of

Dundee'. The boys couldn't read but were quick to pick up the tune and gist of the story, and before long they were bawling like vaudeville stars from the side of the cart, making up their own verses and interrupting each other's songs.

As they came alongside the river, up towards St Anthony's, Toby and Thomas grabbed their bundles and leapt off the still-moving cart.

'See yah!' they shouted, grabbing their sacks by the neck to keep in all the bits of dinner that were left and the extra loaves Mabel had bought them at the mill. She waved as the cart jogged on, pleased by the smells of evening smoke and rotting winter leaves, the wet slick of water, the first snap of frost she could smell in the air. It had been a great day, out of the town and the stink of dirty streets. The windmill had swooped and sung as the sloop-sails went by, and although it wasn't one she could see from her window, it didn't matter. Running through the long grass had been enough, paddling in the mill-pool, getting told off by Elsa for throwing water over the boys when they weren't looking and getting splashed back in the process, losing her bonnet, watching it sail over the weir and Thomas leaping in to get it and practically drowning and having to be dried off in the miller's kitchen. The sort of day you remember for all your life because it is just right.

As they turned the corner by St Anthony's, Toby came trotting back, tapping on the cart side with his fist.

'He's there again, miss,' he whispered as he flitted by. 'Told you he would be. You watch as you go into the yard.'

Then Thomas came running after Toby, dragging their two sacks; he nodded at Mabel, handed Toby his sack and they headed for the river and the bridge where they'd elected to have their kip.

The evening was well down, the sun behind them, the square in shadow. The chestnut seller was standing by his brazier, chatting to the man beside him selling warm gin. Mabel strained her eyes, staring between the pillars of the Innocent Martyrs. Normally she didn't pay it much mind. It had been a church once, but now was as empty as a turtle-shell after the soup's been made. All the pews had gone and the walls limed over. Sometimes it was used for temperance meetings, but mostly it just sat there quietly, making up its side of the square, unobtrusive, barely noticed. But tonight Mabel did notice, and she thought she did see something against the dark backdrop of the huge wooden door. A slight movement maybe? A shifting of black on black? She couldn't be sure, but she frowned. Toby had mentioned it once before, a couple of nights ago; said he'd seen someone following Mabel when she took an afternoon stroll through the square and along by the river. Said he didn't look quite right, that he'd seen him staring up at her window later that night.

Afterwards, when she was in her bed, she wondered if Great-Aunt Flora hadn't been right. Maybe she should close the window and keep her curtains drawn after all, at least for a while.

5

Learning to Weave

LUCCA; AND THE gate-man at the Council Building watches the man steer his way through the stacks of papers and folios, boxes and bundles tied up with lengths of string or faded ribbon. All the shelves have iron feet, which are set into rails in the floor so they can be moved back to back, side to side, but most of them haven't been moved in years and they've rusted in their tracks. The gate-man watches the visitor counting his way through the rows of records. Twice he comes back and starts again, but the third time he disappears down the bottom of the hall and finds the archway leading through to the older archives, and his lamplight climbs the keystone, then dims into darkness.

This is the second visitor the gate-man's had this week, and they've both gone the same way, both been anxious no one knew of their visit, both cornered him in the tavern and dropped him a hefty purse of coins to keep his mouth shut. Fine with him if they want to go poking about the stacks at night.

He doesn't read himself, but he knows that those who do seem to enjoy it. He's always meant to learn, but, well, the years slip by and there's work to do and a family to raise and it just gets left behind. Sometimes on his rounds, when he's obliged to walk the whole course through the record rooms to make sure no one has left a candle burning or fallen asleep after the gates are locked or left a door open to the Council Rooms upstairs, he's run his fingers along the side of the shelves, felt the papery leaves flicker past. He stops occasionally and takes down a bundle, looks at all the rivers of ink patterning the pages, wonders at the world of meaning closed to him. These are usually the nights he's taken in a bit much grog and is feeling sorry for himself and the world. It's happened more recently, since the French have started pressing on the city boundaries, changing all the export tariffs, making life difficult for the silk workers and olive growers on which everyone depends. The whole city is uneasy. They were used to being independent, had been a city-state, the Lucchese Republic, for so many hundreds of years they thought no one could touch them. They felt safe within their walls, buttressed in and divided from the rest of the world. And then Napoleon had ridden rough-shod over all the north of Italy, declared it his pet cisalpine state. But still the gate-man and his city felt protected and apart: no one had scaled their walls in three hundred years and no one was going to do it now. And then Napoleon declared himself President of Italy and said to his sisters, this is yours and yours and yours, and said to the oldest sister, 'Maria Anna Elisa Bacciochi, you are now a princess,' and when she had asked of where, he had said, 'How about Lucca?'

Down in the vaults, Aribert finds what he is looking for. He doesn't know that Taraborrelli has been there first.

Neither of them knows that they will crisscross the breadth of Europe in each other's tracks, that within days of one another they will reach London, walk the same streets, visit the same places, follow a line from Lucca to London and both would find Mabel at its end.

It was Sunday morning, exactly a week after the suicide, and Mabel had come to early mass at St Anthony's. It was just before six o'clock when she wrapped her cloak around her, strapped on her hat and carefully made her way across the cobbles of the square. It was icy, small pools frozen in the dips, cracking over like spiders' webs. The sky was still dark, but there was a luminescence over to the east that silhouetted the lines of windmills and large oak trees on the other side of the river. The water itself was the colour of tarnished pennies, glinting here and there as the moon caught a ripple when the dark blue clouds cleared its face. She came round the corner and put her hand on the stair rail, stopped a moment, her face lifted towards the rising sun, feeling a slight breeze on her cheeks, listening to the birds beginning to rustle and sing in the hedgerows of the fields beyond the water. Another day, she thought, and was grateful, as mornings like this always made her feel. Then she went in through the open door, nearly tripping on the chicken, which always seemed to be there for the purpose, and saw that Father Ignatius was still messing with the thurible, and Stanley was having trouble with the lamps.

Mabel settled herself in the second pew from the front. She nodded to Widow Brackman, who was already kneeling on her hassock, mouth moving in silent recitation, rosary clicking in her restless fingers. It didn't stop her looking up to note who was coming in. Stanley and Father Ignatius were having a muttered conversation about there being a new hole in the roof, and to prove them right a sudden gust of wind blew out the few lamps Stanley had at last got lit, and from out the spire hatch came a barn owl, arms outstretched as if it were falling from a cliff, white as plaster, eyes dark as heartwood. Father Ignatius swore and dropped the thurible, Stanley crossed himself and Widow Brackman clutched her rosary so hard the string broke and all the amber beads clattered and spun against the stones. Mabel stood up and was entranced as the beautiful bird swooped once around the church, then came to rest on the gable above the back water-stoup, folded up its feet and feathers and went to sleep.

The echoes of disturbance died as Mabel and Stanley helped gather the widow's spilt beads and Father Ignatius picked up the thurible and hung it on its hook. He straightened his cassock, adjusted the alb, then mounted the lectern stand and opened the clasps of the Bible with a click. He looked up at the owl as the back of the book hit the wood, but the bird didn't stir. Unlike Stanley, he didn't think it presaged death and gloom, and rather liked having it sitting there, another member of the congregation, which was always rather paltry at first mass. Of course, no one could deny what had happened in the chapel and every person who passed it stepped a little lighter, looked for dark stains on the stones, leant slightly away or poked their noses forward to see what they could see. It had been a shocking time and had put some people off coming to the church during the week, where the tragedy lingered on unseen. Each time he glanced into the chantry he saw the scene, as he imagined it, unfold again. How much worse, he thought, for Stanley, who had taken to sitting on the edge of the outermost pew near the sacristy and could get no further away without passing miraculously through the solid walls.

Father Ignatius looked up and surveyed his parishioners fondly – Stanley and Mabel, Widow Brackman, the owl, that blasted chicken. He waited a few more minutes, shuffling his feet, clearing his throat, in case the gin-seller came in as he sometimes did, or Mankby, the grocer, or Dibbleworth, the caretaker of the Innocent Martyrs hall. No one came, and he began. The antiphon of approach to the alter, the Iudica me psalm, the prayer of penitence. It was the best time of his day, almost a private mass for himself alone. He often thought that was why the other few came too. It was a quiet, holy time without intrusion, excepting a gentle croaking from the chicken, a scratch of its claw upon the stone of the floor. At least it had been until then.

The door banged wide open, the top and bottom hitting the wall one after the other, hinges creaking as they rebounded, the *floof* of the barn owl unfolding its wings and taking off through the hatch into the hollow spire, the clatter of iron-heeled boots running down the side aisle. The thurible swung in the sudden breeze from the open door, the scents of cinnamon and frankincense hung in the air, Widow Brackman's beads chattered in her bag and her knees and neck creaked as she turned to look from her hassock. Stanley blanched and swallowed hard, seeing other things; Mabel caught the father's eye as she turned and saw what everyone saw: that little urchin boy who was always sitting on the steps, forehead white as suet, beads of sweat runnelling down the sides of his nose. He was clutching something in his hand and came straight up to Mabel, who stood up and caught him by the shoulders.

'Thomas,' she said, her dark eyes concerned, her cheeks slightly flushed as she saw the boy look as if he were about to vomit, his hand shaking as he reached out to her.

The paper folded in his fingers was grimy, creased as if he'd screwed it in his hand while he ran, fast as he could from the bridge, along the road and up the steps. He dropped his hand suddenly and the twisted paper fell to the floor by his twitching feet.

'They've took Toby,' was all the boy got out before he slumped against Mabel's waist and, for only the second time in all his life, began to cry.

They'd moved into the sacristy and the priest had barred the doors. He knew it was a sin, but thought, for once God probably wouldn't mind. The chicken did, and immediately started pecking at its base, a faint grumble in its gizzard amongst the half-digested seeds.

'First thing, we need to go over the square and tell your great-aunt what is going on. She can get the authorities. They'll know what to do,' Father Ignatius said, pouring them all a small cup of unblessed communion wine.

'They said not to say anything!' wailed Thomas, not for the first time. 'I told you what they said! They wants her and that's that!'

Mabel cupped her hands around the boy's face and forced him to look at her. He didn't want to. He was ashamed of the tear-streaks on his face. He put his hands on her wrists to try to pull them away but she stayed fast.

'Look at me, Thomas. I'm not going to let anything happen to Toby. He's a good boy. Why would I want anything to happen to him? But you have to understand it's not that simple. We've got to know who these people are and what they want.'

But to herself she thought, it really is that simple, though, isn't it? The scribble on the paper had been hard to understand, but what Thomas had said was not. They'd come down to the bridge where the boys had been sleeping. They'd surprised them but both boys woke immediately, struck out and fought. They'd been attacked under the bridge before. But this was different. The men had grabbed at them, caught Toby by the arm, twisted it till he screamed, then flung a blanket over him and bundled him up. Thomas had been going to run but a man caught at his ankle and he fell crashing on to the crates they used as tables. The candles they'd saved so carefully went rolling down the bank into the mud.

'Listen,' the man had growled into his ear. 'Don't move and we won't hurt you. But we will hurt your little mate if you don't deliver a message for us. That missy you hang about with, the one from across the square – tell her she's to come to us. Tell her the old place, and she'll know where. And give her this.' Then he'd put the paper in Thomas's hand and whacked him across the back of the head.

Thomas had passed out briefly and when he'd picked himself up, they'd gone. And Toby had gone with them. The paper was clutched in his hand.

He'd scrambled up the bank, skidding and sliding on the frost. He'd fallen twice as he ran along the road. His head felt dizzy. His stomach was beating like a drum. He thought his heart might suddenly stop. But then he saw the steps of

St Anthony's and he'd flown up them and through the door. He knew who they meant by the missy. He knew she'd be here because somewhere in his dreams, which seemed a week ago but can't have been more than a quarter of an hour since, he knew he'd heard the bell toll for early mass, and that Mabel always came to early mass, and the missy the men had meant was Mabel.

Mabel was still shaking her head. 'I just don't understand. What did they mean – the old place? What does this mean?' She slapped at the paper again, which had been unfolded and lay on the table between them. She kept trying to uncrease it with her fingers, but it just seemed to stay the same.

Father Ignatius said, 'Well, we know it's in Italian – I recognise some of the words from Latin. The first words here, *Custode Corrente*, mean Present Custodian or Keeper. And this is obviously your address, Mabel. Or rather your father's and then underneath, your great-aunt's. I really do think we should go over there right now and speak to her. It's possible she knows what this is about.'

He was at a loss. He dealt with infidelities, greed, sloth, minor thoughts of malice – people who spoke a lot and confessed a lot, but didn't do very much. He didn't like what had happened only a week ago, with that strange man in his chapel. He didn't like what was happening now. He wanted to take it all outside and put it somewhere else, let someone else deal with it, let him get back to the way things were. He liked the way things were. He didn't want them to change. He wanted to potter around with Stanley Izod and discuss mending this, repairing that, wondering who was on the list for his visits that day. He didn't like that big things seemed to be coming his way.

'Your aunt will know the proper course of action,' he repeated.

'My great-aunt,' said Mabel automatically. 'She never gets up till eleven on a Sunday. It's her rest day.'

Stanley never said much. Had said even less since the incident in the chapel. Even the coroner, appointed by the King, couldn't get more out of him than, 'He just came in. I saw him go into the chapel and that was that. That was just that.' And that was all Stanley said to anyone that asked. If he never spoke about it, maybe it wouldn't stay so keen in his memory. Maybe that smell of warm butchering would go away; maybe the stains on his boots wouldn't be there next time he looked. He hoped so. He couldn't afford a new pair of boots. Even a new old pair.

He was troubled by what had just happened; especially because the barn owl had come out when it had. The barn owl never came out excepting there was a death coming. Everyone knew that. Stanley worried over what the paper said, what the boy said, what the girl would do. What was a girl supposed to do? She was supposed to stay at home and keep out of trouble and cook dinners and keep pleasant company with her family, that's what. She was not supposed to get involved in things like this. Whatever things like this were. He made up his mind, waited a moment, then spoke right as everyone else was still talking and Widow Brackman was starting another noisy prayer for protection of the good and righteous. 'Take it to Mr Stroop on Eggmonde Street.' He didn't speak loudly, but they all heard him.

'Stanley?' said Father Ignatius, hoping he was hearing divine intervention.

'Mr Izod?' said Mabel, surprised that the man had spoken at all.

'Eh?' said Thomas, pulling the cup from his lips, a fine red skein of wine winding down his hairless chin.

'Mr Whilbert Stroop of Eggmonde Street,' Stanley repeated. He took off his hat and rubbed at his head, but didn't lift his eyes from the paper on the table. 'He sort of looks into things for people. He finds people who are missing and such-like.'

'Ah!' exclaimed Father Ignatius. 'Yes, indeed!' He'd never heard of Mr Whilbert Stroop before, but liked him already.

'How can he help?' asked Mabel, but already she was feeling more confident, the ground beginning to firm beneath her feet.

'I know where Eggmonde Street is!' Thomas jumped up from his chair, sending it skidding across the floor and into the small cupboard Father Ignatius kept his vestments in.

'But it's so early . . .' Mabel made a vague protest but knew she'd made her mind up. 'Me and Thomas will go. No need for you to trouble with this. It's our trouble, isn't it, Thomas?'

'Oh, but,' said Ignatius, trying to hide his relief at having them go.

'I suppose,' murmured Widow Brackman, 'and I do have to get back. My sister, you know . . .'

'I'll come with,' said Stanley Izod and stood up, 'far as Crouch Street wise. Make sure . . .'

'Thank you,' said Mabel, and they went back through the sacristy door, up the aisle, unbarred the doors, and away across the square. First they would stop at Mabel's. Elsa would be up by now and they'd leave a message telling Great-Aunt Flora where they'd gone in case they weren't back by the time she was up.

Mabel wondered what she would say, as she took Thomas by the hand and he dragged her across the square.

Stanley Izod came on behind them, his hat on his head, his hands clasped across his stomach, his eyes pricking with the cold. At least, he hoped it was the cold. He had a horrible feeling it was fear.

6

Making Maps

WHILBERT NATHANIEL STROOP was awake when he
heard someone ringing the bell. It was shaped like a
rat with a long tail curled down on a spring. It always made
him smile when he heard it, to think of the person reaching
up to set the bell going, seeing the rat as it turned its head
and gazed down at the visitor, its whiskers set twitching by
the movement.

He had been working on his Sense Map of London. He
had started close to home, noted what kinds of trees and
plants grew by the riverside, along the roads, in people's
gardens. He marked out which trades were on which street.
Next to each one was a neatly printed set of symbols. Each
of these indicated a certain type of smell, or an impression
of colour, or the type of ground underfoot, or what could
be seen to the left and right. In this way he had spiralled
out from his home to within one and a half square miles
and he had had to divide his map into areas because it was
too large for the single sheet he had begun with, laid out
on his table. Now, each wall of his map room was covered

with paper, cordoned off into squares, indicating faithfully the immediate radius in each direction from his house: north, south, east and west. He considered it immensely fortuitous that the original architect had sited the house so as to exactly coordinate with the cardinal points, otherwise his task would have been far more complicated than it already was.

At the moment he heard the bell, he was busy transferring a set of markers from his notebook to the area around St Anthony's Square. It had been a part of his map neglected up till now, but when news of the sensational suicide came to his ears and he checked his walls for the exact place, he had been dismayed to find the paucity of facts this area of his map supplied, and had immediately set out to remedy the situation. Now he had the area from the goose green to the bridge practically finished. He had all the dates of the occasional fairs – such as Martinmas, Michaelmas, or the one that had just passed, marking Advent – and the cloth markets. He had segregated the permanent traders from the temporary market stall holders who drifted from place to place. He knew the names of the gin-seller and the grocer, of the baker, the chestnut-roaster, the priest of the church, the warden of the Hall of the Innocent Martyrs, the ironmonger, the salt-seller and the ice and fire-fuel men who came around every week. He had been intrigued to find that the doors of St Anthony's opened not on to the square as might have been expected, but on to the road running along by the river. It had set him on a four-hour search through his library for the history of the place. He had discovered that it was not named for St Anthony of Padua, but the much earlier Anthony of Egypt, who spent most of his apparently very long life in the desert creating the strange paradox of a community of hermits. He also found that Gerald de Montrey had taken the cross and the first name of Gerald, after hearing Gerald of Wales preach for the Third Crusade. He also came up with the interesting if irrelevant fact that Giraldus Cambrensis, as the Welshman signed himself in his many writings, had made one of the few references to beavers in medieval literature, which in turn led him to find out far more than he ever wanted to know about the use of the beaver's anal scent glands in curing headaches and dyspepsia.

He answered the door himself, his boy, Jack, having already left to get bacon and pies for breakfast. Stroop believed in a good breakfast prior to taking his satchel and notebooks and setting off to tramp the streets. He glanced out of the window before he took the stairs, saw the top of a soft-rimmed hat, and a young boy. When he opened the door, he saw a young woman, pretty but unremarkable, her felt hat sliding to one side, her cheeks red. The boy was skinny and unkempt and had bruises developing on his face. Stroop glimpsed a movement on the street corner and, to his surprise, thought he could make out the handyman from St Anthony's retreating rapidly down the street.

'Apologies for the early hour, Mr Stroop.' It was the girl speaking. No hesitation, or embarrassment, perhaps a touch of worry. 'But we really need your help.'

They were all sitting around the kitchen table. Jack had returned and was filling the morning with a sizzle of bacon and the smell of mutton pies heating in the oven, and eggs coddling on the stove. A huge pot of tea sat on a spirit warmer, surrounded by incongruously tiny cups standing on a pot-rest made of a stack of slate sheets on which scribbles of chalk could be seen on the bits that protruded.

Whilbert Stroop was studying the mysterious piece of paper and consulting a dictionary he had culled from his library for the purpose.

'Definitely Italian, and the first words certainly read Present Keeper, or Custodian. Followed by your name, Mabel Amelia Flinchurst. This is your address?' Stroop pointed to where a line of writing had been crossed through and a smaller scribble put below.

'That's my father's farm out at Epping,' replied Mabel, pointing at the crossed-through address, 'and this is where I live now, with my great-aunt. Well, she's not really a great-aunt, but she is a relative. We live just across the square from St Anthony's.'

'Ah, yes,' murmured Stroop, 'St Anthony's.'

He leafed rapidly through the dictionary, jotted a few words down on a second piece of paper, sucked the end of his pencil. Mabel poured the tea and passed it round, trying to keep herself occupied and not ask questions or interrupt the man's train of thought. Stanley had been right to send them here. Whilbert Stroop had an air of calm about him, the sort of man who enjoyed every moment of every day but would not complain if it all came abruptly to an end tomorrow. You could tell he had a head full of facts just by looking at his dark eyes, which sparkled and seemed to focus some way just behind your shoulder as if his mind was always on the verge of wandering off and leaving you behind. His hands were strangely scarred, burnt maybe, crisscrossed with thin white lines across the palms, obliterating the lines of life and heart, where you could read nothing, except perhaps a game of solitaire marked with the burnt end of a match.

'Tell me, Mabel, what do you know about the man who killed himself in the church last week?'

Mabel was startled, not that he knew about it – practically everyone knew – but that he thought she might know something about it, presumably that others did not.

'Nothing. Well, I mean, me and Elsa did go across the square to take a look. We didn't stop, though. We saw him but so did everyone else. Then we just went home.'

'Aha,' said Stroop, stroking the side of his nose. 'Did you know that he wore the badge of an Italian pilgrim? A shell incised with a crucifix crowned with thorns, and underneath the word "*Libertad*". Liberty. I'm still trying to trace the emblem. But it does seem a coincidence that this note is also Italian, does it not?'

Mabel and Thomas looked at each other, not sure where the man was going with this.

'This note is a riddle, at least to me. It implies you are the Custodian of something important, something religious. It actually names you. Someone has found out where you have been living and where you are living. It is instructing the Guardian of the Custodian to watch over you and remove you if necessary out of harm's way. It is very specific that you and yours are valuable to them. It speaks of you as a link in a chain that must not be broken, particularly now, for the reason that – and this is as close as I can translate it – "those things most precious to us are about to be recalled".'

The only noise in the room was Jack taking the eggs out

of the pan. He seemed not to take the slightest interest in the mysterious note and what it meant.

Mabel could only shake her head. 'I don't understand,' she said. 'How is this going to help us find Toby? It doesn't make any sense.' She gave the table a small thump with her fist.

Stroop raised his eyebrows. 'You have absolutely no idea what is being referred to in this letter? No family secrets passed down to you? No valuable heirlooms?'

Mabel shook her head again. She could feel tears prickling at her eyes and swallowed hard, pinched her palms to stop herself from crying. Jack put plates before them filled with crispy bacon and eggs and mutton pie. Mabel pushed hers away. Stroop pushed it gently back.

'Eat,' he commanded, 'a brain needs a body and a body needs food. And we need all the brains we can get.'

An hour later, Mabel bitterly regretted obeying Whilbert Stroop. The eggs in particular could be felt arguing about which one should come up first. She, Thomas and Stroop had left the latter's house and walked a way along the front of the river to Dismal Cobbett's. He kept a sort of makeshift mortuary in a large shed, which backed on to the ice house and had the river running below it. It was the coldest place you could get if you didn't want to tie your legs to stones and lie on the bottom of the river. Dismal Cobbett himself was a tidy man, apart from being constantly covered in wood-dust from making coffins for the dead. He also made sideboards and tables, as a rough wooden board leaning against the side of the shack declared in flaking black paint. It seemed he and Stroop were old friends, and also that Stroop had been here not that long before, taking a good look at the suicide stranger that no one wanted to claim. Now he'd made Mabel and Thomas take a look. They were just in time – another couple of days and the body was to be buried outside the *poor church* boundary wall in the suicide pit before it began to split and stink.

Mabel and Thomas sat on the bank while Stroop and Cobbett talked. Stroop was asking if the corpse had come direct to Cobbett from St Anthony's, to which the answer was yes, directly. Did you remove all the clothing yourself? Yes. Was there anything in the pockets or secreted on the body? Hesitation. A prompt from Stroop. A coin passing hands. Then Dismal Cobbett went over to a collection of drawstring-flour sacks in one corner and poked about, eventually surfacing with one. It was marked 'XSU24', meaning Unknown Suicide Unclaimed number 24. Stroop briefly congratulated Cobbett on his notation, which was concise without losing precision, and Cobbett responded by giving Stroop the sack.

Mabel heard all this going on but it sounded a mile away. What she actually saw was the yellow sagging face of the man who hung from a hammock on the wall. One among the many forms hung one above the other, shrouded with stained sheets. He didn't look so different from when she first saw him on the steps of St Anthony's, except the skin had discoloured and lost its substance, as if the muscles had all drained away with his blood. And he was naked. Dismal Cobbett hadn't given the unknown man any propriety and had just folded the sheet back right to his toes. Stroop had then made him take it away completely. Thomas had stood slightly to her side, on tiptoe to get a better look.

45

Mabel had been utterly dismayed by what she saw; she had seen plenty of slaughtered beasts being hauled from her father's shed on to the butcher's cart; she had skinny-dipped with her brothers in the river and seen her father taking a piss behind the cowshed. She wasn't shocked by his nakedness being on display. What made her draw her breath was the lividity of his skin where the bruises lay across him in stripes. Quite clearly the man had been repeatedly beaten, probably with a length of wood or pipe. His feet and ankles still held the impression of his boots where the swollen skin had forced its turgid face upon the leather; one elbow was obviously dislocated, his right knee had been smashed, the splinters of bone could clearly be seen where the puckered purple skin had slid to one side, stretching the rest tight. Several ribs dipped and the hairs upon his chest could not hide the cruel marks that lay in a cross upon his sternum, cracking across the place where his heart must have been. It was a miracle the man made it up the steps and into the church, and if he hadn't finished himself off, he must surely have died soon after anyway. There was a rigid bulge against his side where the blood had leaked from his liver and bowled in his guts.

He hadn't been a handsome man. He had long dark hair tied back from his face. His fingers, now clawed and crooked, had been long and smooth, free of calluses. The inside of his thighs were strong and chafe-scarred, indicating he'd been accustomed to riding, most probably a horse. He'd been neither fat, nor thin, probably fit, though the flaccidity with which death afflicted him made it difficult to tell; he'd been most likely in his thirties and smelt very faintly of oil –

spiced oil, or maybe an oil in which rosemary or basil had been steeped. Mabel closed her eyes, not to forget the man's face, but to try to fix every detail so that she would never forget.

Thomas was tugging at her arm. He was finding it hard to keep still, especially now. He understood the marks of a severe doing-over, recognised the impress of pain and punishment, feared every moment more and more for Toby, had awful phantasmagoric visions of Toby and torture, which were as fleet as they were frightening.

It might've been me, he thought, and was immediately ashamed.

Stroop came out of the shed, shaking Dismal Cobbett's hand, giving him another coin. He held a small paper package and whistled to them both to come on. Jack suddenly appeared with a pony-trap and they clambered past an old mongrel, who growled and bared his miserable teeth, then wagged his stumpy tail and settled on Thomas's feet, allowing his matted ears to be tickled and tugged. At least it cheered the boy for a few moments, thought Mabel, and wondered what it would be like to have nothing and nobody, with nowhere to go, nothing to share and nobody to share it with anyway. That's Thomas and Toby, she thought, they're all the other's got. Take that away and there's nothing.

Stroop nudged her gently and she shuddered slightly, letting the thought go, turning to see him looking not at her but at the little bundle he was busy untying on his knee.

'This is what I got from Dismal Cobbett,' he said. 'He wouldn't part with the clothes themselves but I've had a good look at them anyway. Good quality but badly worn and obviously blood-soaked. Still, Cobbett knows women who can wring the dirt from a ten-year-old skillet and sew a slaughtered rabbit back together, so I'm sure he'll make a profit somewhere. He's also got the boots. We, on the other hand, have this.'

And he peeled back the cloth upon his knee.

7

The Dead Begin
to Open Their Mouths

IT WAS A BOOK. A small dark-bound book. It gave off the faint smell of ammonia that Stroop always associated with dog-skin. He had several large indexed volumes at home that made note of such things. Where a gap in his knowledge existed, he got on the track of the missing element at once and found it hard to rest until he could fill in details of the missing entry. Cow-skin, rabbit-skin, horse-skin, calf-skin, and dog-skin, all common enough types. Although the usual leather derivatives came from cow, calf and horse, there was always a gap in the market for cheaper alternatives. Or more expensive ones. He also had examples of shagreen, otherwise known as shark-skin. And of course there were beaver and badger, but they came under different cross-referenced categories, being associated with hats or brushes rather than gloves or books, which oddly had much in common with the types of material with which they were associated. He also had a volume of murderous confessions reputedly bound in the skin of the executed criminal who had penned them. Stroop had no doubt this was a forgery and made with nothing more exotic than dyed and boiled vellum, but he kept it as a curiosity and leafed through its blurred, red-inked pages every now and then when the weather was foul and leant itself to morbidity.

This book now on his knee was sadder by far than the boasting of a criminal who deserved all he got. It had been strapped to the belly of a man who had been beaten so badly his guts had practically burst from his skin, and yet who had felt compelled to drag himself inside a church and slit his gullet before it slit itself. Dismal Cobbett had been very disappointed to find its pages scrawled over, as if by spiders, in words of nonsense, or 'foreign filth', as he declared anything he could not readily understand.

What he did understand, though, was that personal effects unclaimed belonged by rights to him. Once a body passed through his door, only a proven relative could relieve him of its burden and occasionally its profit. The authorities didn't appear to have searched the corpse apart from going through his pockets and finding nothing. Any money he had was long gone by the time he'd got to Cobbett's. He'd guessed the filching fingers didn't delve more deeply because of the undeniably copious spill of blood, which covered the man from nape to boot. The booklet had been strapped by an underbelt below his clothes, tight against his skin. It was still warm when Cobbett unclasped the buckle and peeled it gently away. He'd hoped for a hidden stash of bonds or notes or gold coins taped to a scrap of leather. Still, at least the man Stroop had paid him well for its removal, and good luck to him.

Stroop squinted over the tiny pages with his glass held close to his eye.

'Italian again,' he murmured, 'just as one would expect.'

He continued his careful examination while the pony-trap bumped along the street, and Thomas stroked the old dog's head, and Mabel held tight within her hand what Stroop had told her was a pilgrim's medal. It was similar to the badge Stroop had described as being sewn on to the dead man's clothes. The medal, though, was much smaller, made of beaten gold, but the crucifix was there and the word '*Libertad*' again appeared below the Saviour's feet. It also had the faint outline of a building incised behind it, obviously a church of some sort because the spires and bell towers could clearly be seen. Somewhere quite grand then, she thought. The metal was very thin, so insubstantial it had bent to the shape of the man's body where it had been slotted into the back cover of the notebook, hidden from even Dismal Cobbett's view. Stroop had shown her the book after having carefully rubbed off some flaking brown scraps she knew to be blood. It seemed somehow wrong just to let them fall to the bottom of the cart or be scattered one part from another on the wind as if the man's life had meant so little that even these last remaining scrapings could just be thrown away and lost.

Mabel carefully picked up the handkerchief that Stroop had dropped and folded it once then twice again and slid it into her pocket. She didn't know what she would do with it. Maybe she should bury it later, although even as she thought it, it seemed utterly ridiculous.

'Aha!' shouted Stroop without, however, lifting his head from the pages.

I wonder if he suffers from a stiff neck, thought Mabel,

remembering the dull ache punctuated by twinges she'd incurred after several hours at the embroidery hoop.

'Jack, take the road that goes towards the Corn Mart building at Barnehurst and head straight down towards the river by Erith. It may take us an hour or two, but there is a house nearby I think we should track down.'

Mabel looked over eagerly at him and Thomas leapt to his feet and almost kicked the dog out the back of the cart in his eagerness. They managed to haul the poor thing back on, despite the wobbling caused by Thomas's sudden movement, and it soon lay its head back on the nearest set of feet, which happened to be Mabel's. For a second or two both Mabel and Thomas held poses as though they were agawk on a pantomime stage, but Stroop kept his head down and carried on examining the paper.

'Mr Stroop.' Mabel could stand it no longer, and Thomas had a hard grip on her arm, which was making her wince. 'Mr Stroop!' she said a little louder. 'Please! Please, if there is anything there, please tell us.'

She had modified her voice but the tone was insistent and Stroop did look up from his letters. He pointed the glass directly at Thomas, who had subsided on to a seat.

'You said the man under the bridge told you to meet him at "the old place", is that right?'

Thomas nodded. He didn't want to move in case Mr Stroop's concentration broke and he threw them all off the cart and went home to do something more sensible.

'Is it possible what he actually said was, "at Aldo's place" or "Aldo's house"?'

Thomas felt a whirring in his head as he tried to recall

the scene exactly, that big face looming down at him through the dark light of dawn, the pain in his upper arms where he thought the man might snap his bones like you snapped off a rabbit's feet when you were pulling it from its skin. He remembered that behind the man he had seen the river gliding by unconcerned, that it had been a strange metallic grey backlit by luminescent blue, which must have come from the setting moon. The man had smelt of sausage and strong cheese. His front teeth were crooked, his moustache greased. His eyes glinted like marbles sinking in a pool of mud. And he had spoken with an odd accent that Thomas hadn't remembered before. It was like dredging through a box of fuzzy wool only to prick one's thumb on a sharp pin, and he suddenly recalled everything the man had said and how he had looked and smelt and what his voice sounded like.

'Yes, yes, yes!' he cried excitedly.

'Very well then,' said Stroop, looking back to the book, 'let's be off.'

The clock of St Wilfrid was striking the half of four and it was almost dark when they turned the corner by an old wool warehouse and into Wattlebottom Lane. It was a gentle street, the cobbles old and worn almost flat, the houses quiet, washing strung from window to window, creating a gentle breeze as it wafted in the upper wind. The air was almost sweet despite the over-running gutters. It seemed there was an enclave of tilers and pot-makers at the end of the lane and their continual use of water to moisten the clay before it was fired, added to the constant wood-burning fires of the kilns, took much of the noxious stink from the streets and hid the smell of the stables nearby. No children littered the doorways of the houses, most of which seemed residential apart from the pie-maker, whose shutters were drawn. The clip-clop of the trap and trundle of wheels echoed from the high walls and not a soul was to be seen, besides a scrawny old arm leaning out of a doorway scrubbing at a step with a brush, sounding like the suck of the sea.

Mabel and Thomas held their breath, Jack whistled loudly and unconcerned, Stroop looked up from the booklet and scrutinised the walls as they slowly advanced.

'Stop, Jack,' he said as they had just passed the pie-maker's, and out of the trap he leapt. With Mabel and Thomas scrabbling behind him, Stroop strode across the street and knocked sharply upon an unpainted wooden door.

There was no answer.

He knocked again.

Then Stroop put his hand in his pocket, withdrew a large set of keys and began inserting them one by one into the lock.

8

Behind the Tapestry

THE CASTRACANI HOUSEHOLD, in the Italian Quarter of London, was built with an Italian façade and leant against the small canal as if it were in Venice. The fine pillars were peeling slightly but the yellow stucco of its face withstood the beating of the rain. Petrus Castracani had just returned from a most extraordinary meeting of the London Lucchese Council, of whose Second Circle he was a rising star. He had hopes of gaining access to the Inner Circle within the next year or two. He was prosperous enough, by God, and had credentials anyone would have been proud of. He was directly related to the famous Castrucchio Castracani, who had flown from London to save his native Lucca from humiliation and defeat several hundred years before.

He eyed the embroidered silks hanging from his walls – every Lucchese of note had these to remind them of their past, to heed them to their future. He had a particularly fine collection, which had been augmented by the family through the years, and contained historically important altar frontals, amice cloaks and orphrey strips of finest woven gold and split-stitch threads. He had been obliged to donate several of them to the Council to secure his passage from one circle to another, and at last things were paying off.

He returned from the cabinet in which he housed his drinks, sorted primarily by colour, which was his passion, whether in silks or drinks or paintings. He had the finest Canalettos this side of Italy, the oils seeming to live and ripple within their frames. Having selected a not-too-lurid selection of liqueurs, he placed the tray upon the table and asked his guest his pleasure. Despite them both having been born in London, they spoke Italian, as all Lucchese did. Over the years the accent had subtly changed and become a dialect all its own, slightly less lilting, flatter somehow than its continental cousin. The real Lucchese said it was the weather that did it: all that rain and wind and the clouds constantly covering the sun.

'So,' Castracani broached the subject as the other swilled a pale strawberry shrub around his glass, 'I am flattered the Council has need of me in its business. Of course I will do whatever I can to aid you. Can I assume it is to do with the matter touched upon in the meeting this morning, and not to do with the Guild?'

He was burning with curiosity but knew that Bertolucchi Sandrini would not be hurried.

At the earlier meeting of the Council (Inner and Second Circle only) they had been given uncomfortable and potentially disastrous news. It had been confirmed that Napoleon had seized their native Lucca for his own, and although the citizenry was not in immediate peril, their independence had been compromised and repercussions would undoubtedly follow. Lucca was rich in many things, particularly olive oil and silk. If the French severed the trade links between London and Lucca, both communities would lose not only their independence but their livelihoods. The London Lucchese would be left without their most important commodity: the finest silk in Europe. Certainly they could import silk from elsewhere but it would not have the stamp of quality associated with Lucca. Much of its business came from the King's court. If they could no longer offer Lucchese silk, their advantage would evaporate and other traders would move in quicker than rats to a carcass.

Back in Lucca, things would be as bad. Without the direct government of their own resources, the City would lose its pride of identity; foreign traders would move in, native traders move out. Their great families would become diluted, and dissolve as if the city had no walls and no history.

Castracani was uneasy, as was everyone. They recognised the threat but knew not how to combat it, either here or in Lucca. That duty fell to the Inner Circle of the Councils of both communities. That was the onus that lay on their shoulders, the cohesion that had made both communities so strong in the past and today. They had a single purpose uniting them, and a leadership that straddled the continent between them. Castracani was confident that they had a plan.

'Before we know it,' Sandrini had said at that earlier meeting, smouldering with anger but never raising his voice, 'we will be ruled by a pornocracy of French pretenders and their courtesans. Lucca will be submitted to a yoke of foreign tyranny not felt for five hundred years, and by proxy we too will be subdued under an alien foot. Steps have been taken in Lucca and we have our part to play. Only a few of the Inner Circle can know the true extent of our plans, which is for the safety of Lucca and of ourselves. However, I can tell you that it involves the repatriation of something precious to the city of our birth. Lucca is the cradle of our community. Some of us have never been there; some of us, like myself, wish only to return. I can tell you something else: there is treachery in our midst. There are those who care nothing for their country or their countrymen and would sell them like pigs at market to further their own ends. Some of you will know what I mean. To others, I say beware and guard your secrets well. There are certain duties to be performed and those of you who must perform them will know. For the rest, we must wait, and watch the tapestry unfold.'

Sandrini had looked slowly around the room at the fourteen men gathered there who between them represented the most powerful families of both Lucca and London: the Crivellis, Castracanis, Uccellis, Sonninos, di Rudinis, Siccardis, Mansegnas, di Cavours, Gadis, Salandras, Badoglios, Roncinos. Some belonged to one family only, others were direct descendants of two, or three or more. They had kept the power within their own circles for centuries, marrying, creating ties, merging businesses. His eyes lingered on each Council member, nodding slightly at one or another, his dark eyes gazing at each one in turn as if he might seize the soul of the traitor he knew to be there even if he didn't yet recognise his face.

Sandrini had finished his second tiny tot, this time an apricot liqueur, commenting appreciatively on the subtle orange blush of its colour in the glass. For once, Castracani brushed the praise impatiently aside and attempted once more to move the conversation on.

'You flatter me, sir. It is only a small hobby, as I am sure you are aware, and cannot compare to the import of Council duty. Do I gather there is something that perhaps I can do for you and the Council?'

Sandrini put his glass on the table and stood up, which took a little time as he was a stiff and crooked man, dependent on his silver-topped canes. Castracani knew better than to offer help. Once he gained his feet, Sandrini began to walk slowly around the room, looking at each painting and tapestry in turn. He stopped by the one that hung above Castracani's writing bureau.

'Ah, the Volto Santo,' Sandrini's voice rose slightly as he gazed at the image on the wall above him, 'how strange to think that this could be the very image of the Lord Jesus, that I could be looking on the human face of God.'

Castracani had moved to a respectable distance by Sandrini's side. He too looked up. It was his favourite tapestry, very old. It was a depiction of the most precious relic of Lucca, the Holy Face: a crucifix carved in one piece by Nicodemus, who had looked on the dead body of Christ and had brought the aloes and myrrh with which He was anointed, and the linen in which His Body was bound.

'Do you believe it was really brought from the Holy Land in a ship that steered itself?'

Castracani was shocked. Of course he did! The whole identity of Lucca was bound up with the Volto Santo. It was the one place on earth Christ had entrusted to guard His actual image; it made the Volto Santo the most Holy of things, apart from the relics that came with it. For hundreds of years, thousands upon thousands had pilgrimaged to their town to be blessed by the very sight of it.

Sandrini droned on, 'Do you visit often the replica we have here in London?'

Castracani was momentarily taken aback. The replica in Old St Thomas's was the focus of the London Lucchese community. It too had been a site of pilgrimage since medieval times, and was the centre of Lucchese civic pride.

Sandrini went on before he had time to answer, 'Of course you do. We all do. It is the heart of us here in our exile and yet it is just a shadow of the one that was actually carved in the Holy Land. Imagine whose hands have touched it! Maybe even the Mother of God. So how much more does it mean to our homeland? If lost, would Lucca be lost with it?'

Sandrini went back to his seat and Castracani stoked up the fire. They talked long and did not notice the evening drawing dark, or the rain that came and went, that the wind began to sigh through the chimneys, that the rooks and pigeons became uneasy in the rising gusts and lifted from the buildings and window ledges and left, crawing and flapping for home.

Sandrini told Castracani of the menace that Lucca was now facing, of the treachery they had discovered within. They discussed the old stories, and the new ones, and how they were linked. He told Castracani of Aldo Santorelli, the Guardianship, the legacy bound up with the girl, the awful significance of Santorelli being missing, his suspicions that their time was running out.

They didn't know that there was smoke gliding up the walls of the coal cellar, that it was feeling its way through the cracks in the doors, that the floor of the kitchen was getting warm and the plaster beginning to crack below the sleeping cook's feet. They didn't see it creeping along the halls, pushing through half-open doors, skimming up the thick carpets of the stairs, curling the corners of the tapestries, clouding the Canalettos, moving like a shadow across the painted water.

9

Meet Thine Enemy

STROOP AT LAST found the right key and, with a bit of jiggling and the aid of his silver toothpick, the lock at last gave. The bolts on the inside were lying undrawn, and the door moved slowly open as he lifted the latch. The hall was thin and musty, the floors were bare boards but swept and clean. Behind the door was a coat-hanger in the shape of a pineapple, looking shockingly like a human head in the gloom. Stroop struck a flint and lit the oil lamps hanging from hooks on the walls; they revealed the hallway stretching to two back rooms, and the stairs climbing up almost directly in front of the door. With Mabel and Thomas treading on his heels, Stroop lifted one of the lamps and made his way down the hall.

The end door opened on to a small kitchen. There was a loaf, the knife still partway through a slice, the bread going mouldy on the table. Some cheese lay crumbled on a plate, surrounded by tiny mounds of mice droppings. Milk curdled in a jug, a coffee pot sat next to it, and a cup stood in its saucer, half full. Aldo had clearly meant to return here when last he left, and obviously had not meant to be gone so long. Stroop stood still a moment and surveyed the scene. Mabel wrinkled her nose. The smell of mice was strong and, coupled with the rancid milk and stale coffee dregs, the air was distinctly unpleasant.

Thomas poked at the cheese and licked his finger.

'Don't!' said Mabel, and gave his hand a light slap.

'Bit of mouse shit never hurt anybody,' Thomas replied with the assurance of experience, but nevertheless he wiped his finger on his trousers and withdrew. There was nothing there of interest that he could see. A moment later he was out of the kitchen and had his hand on the knob of the second door that led from the small hallway, and half a second after that the others heard his surprised voice.

'Blimey! Come and look at this!'

Stroop had finished his brief examination of the deserted kitchen and was already moving, but Mabel, being behind him, got there first.

Blimey indeed, she thought, and heard her great-aunt's voice telling her to mind her lip, but looking through the door-frame gave her the feeling she was about to step into the inside of an egg.

The ceiling was white, as was the lime-washed floor, and the walls a vivid orange yellow even in the dim light and lined with a single strip of tapestry which went the whole room round as far as the window bay. The colours of the silken threads were easy to distinguish though the tapestry was obviously old. Parts of the reinforced edging, which housed the runners, were frayed and there were holes here and there where a nail had come through. Stroop came up behind Mabel, put his hands around her waist and lifted her in one move to the side. At the time, she hardly noticed, and only later did it strike her as an odd thing to do. Perhaps he had spoken to her and perhaps she just hadn't moved. She had been blocking the door, after all. She remembered the pressure of his hands on her waist. They had been gentle, and smooth against her dress. All that scar tissue, she thought, I wonder if it hurts.

Stroop was walking the walls around, glancing from the notebook to the tapestry and back again. Thomas was busy poking amongst the papers on the desk in the centre of the room. He found half a cheroot and put it in his mouth. Mabel moved to the large windows, which were obscured by curtains. They weren't made of a heavy material, more like several sheets of voile, which filtered the outside light but didn't stop it altogether coming through. Stroop stopped her as she went to pull them aside.

'Any light will damage the tapestry,' he said, 'and it really is the most remarkable thing. There is mention of it in the notebook, and see here?' He pointed to a part of the tapestry near the door. 'Does this look familiar?'

Mabel came up beside him and gave a small gasp.

'Why, yes! It's the building in the medallion!' She brought the thin metal disk from her pocket, inadvertently dragging out a corner of Stroop's handkerchief. A flake of dried blood fell unnoticed to the floor and Mabel stepped on it as she came closer. 'So where is it? What does it say?'

Stroop told her the tapestry held a story, a history. It was a form of pictogram enlightened at intervals with Latin words.

'The building appears to be San Martino, the Cathedral

of St Martin's, and look at this: there is a Tree of Life, and what is this? Yes, mermaids and dragons, the months of the year and their labours. Fascinating!'

'That there's a bear,' said Thomas, who had squirmed his way between them and put his grubby finger on part of the tapestry they were looking at. In his mouth he still had the cheroot, which fell to the floor as they all heard the noise simultaneously. The front door creaked and they heard footsteps coming down the hall.

'Well, well,' said a voice, dark with smoke and a soft unrecognisable accent, 'together at last, and how nice: you've brought company.'

Mabel, Stroop and Thomas were herded into the middle of the room while the man stayed leaning in the doorway, his pistol raised and levelled.

'This is all very simple; no need for things to be hard. You have what my master wants, and he has what you want.' The man held up his hand as Mabel opened her mouth to speak. 'He is hidden. Give me the map and you will get him back. You saw what happened to Mr Santorelli. We can do much worse to the boy. Santorelli was strong. He even escaped us for a short while, but the outcome was the same.'

He waited expectantly, but the three people in the middle of the room were slow to respond. After a few moments, Mabel spoke, softly but with resolution.

'I don't know what you want. I don't know a Mr Santorelli and I don't have a map. Why can't you just let Toby go? He's only a boy.'

'My dear girl,' the man wheezed out a laugh, 'I have been

your shadow these last few days, but the time for games is over. You say you don't know Santorelli and yet you are right here in his house! You are looking at La Lucchese Tappezzeria Storica. Your name is Mabel. How can you not know?'

At that moment Thomas, who had by now crept below the table, suddenly launched himself across the room, screaming, 'You give me Toby! You tell me where he is!'

Startled, the man took a step backwards through the doorway, swept his pistol around the room and released the shot. Thomas stopped where he stood as Stroop groaned and fell to the floor. Mabel was immediately kneeling beside him, and the man in the doorway started forward. Thomas charged right at him and caught him in the gut, but the man merely picked Thomas up by his collar and hit him across the head with the butt of the gun, sent him sprawling across the floor, rolling like an orange till he hit the wall. The tapestry above shivered and sent a stream of colour rippling its way round the room like a rainbow. Momentarily off guard, the man had no time to react as Stroop drew a dagger from his boot and sent it whirling through the air. It caught the man in the shoulder and stuck, quivering, the man blasting off his second shot as he tripped backwards and fell through the doorway. Within moments he was on his feet, tugging the dagger from his wound and throwing it back without expertise across the room. It clattered and spun on the planking.

'My master will not be pleased at this.' His voice was low, the pain keeping it harsh and short. 'We will get what we want, we—' He stopped, cocked his head, heard the outside door open, heard people running in the street.

'I will find you again, do not doubt it, and then my master will find you.' The man stood sideways in the doorway, his hand tight on his bleeding shoulder, and he looked right at Mabel, saw the confusion in her brown eyes; kept his words soft and sharp. 'And he, little girl, is the one you should fear.'

Then he was running down the hall, pushing Jack roughly to one side as they collided in the doorway. With the street door flung wide, the three of them, dazed and confused, realised there were people running up the once deserted lane. There were shouts and screams, clogs battering the cobbles, the rumble of carts and clatter of ponies' hooves hitting the stone too hard.

Then Jack picked himself from the floor and appeared in the doorway, his head bleeding, complaining that he'd been thrown off the buggy and that . . . But he never got any further. He rushed forward and lifted Stroop into a chair, fussed at him, dabbing him ineffectually with a dirty neckerchief. Mabel gently pushed him to one side and had a quick glance at the wound. Stroop had only been grazed along his midriff. His jacket and shirt were torn and a streak of blood beaded his pale skin but apart from the shock, he was fine.

Thomas, only momentarily concussed, was soon wobbling his way up the wall, tears streaking his face, ashamed, frightened, unable to stop himself shaking. He didn't understand anything that was happening, but he knew that he would never see Toby again.

And thank God he never did, for there wasn't much left to see.

10

London's Burning

THE SILK QUARTER was in uproar. The conflagration had spread from the Castracani Palace and was gutting the houses to left and right. Several fires seemed to be breaking out at once all along the street. Everyone had stockpiled for winter, their cellars were filled with wood and coal. The canal behind the street dulled the sound of masonry as it collapsed into its sedentary skirts. Castracani was screaming from his turret. He'd had time at last to see the flames licking below the doors; had dragged Sandrini up from his chair, thrown his canes aside and took him on his shoulder. Together they had mounted the garret stairs, Sandrini soon unconscious with the smoke, and now they stood upon the gable of the roof. There had been a garden here, still was. The lemons never fruited, nor the orange, but the pomegranate stood tall, and the tamarisk, shielded from the wind by a woven screen, grew but never flowered. Castracani stood like a devil, framed against a dimming sky as the sun sank below the thick grey clouds. The smoke caught in his throat. His clothes were torn from the stone of the walls as he'd scraped his way up the bare-slabbed steps to the roof. All the way, he had held Sandrini to him like a child.

'For God's sake, help!' he screamed across the rooftops.

'For God's sake!' he cried as he sank amongst his mustard and his melons, which hung around him in broken trails. So many years he'd had sacks of dirt brought up here. The best of dirt, the finest dirt, long lain in barrels and garden heaps. He'd hoped he would grow cantaloupes one day and maybe figs. He'd cared for his rooftop garden with raffia hedges and screens of wattle. He'd harvested his own strawberries up here in June. He'd had walnuts from his dwarf trees in November. But now it was all noise and heat and smoke and fear.

He no longer cared what Sandrini had told him of the Council and its plans. He no longer cared for his homeland and his pride. All he wanted was his skin and to be going on living in it for a few more years. He forgot the Canalettos and his cabinet of colours. He forgot the all-consuming interest in his family name and the history on which he had traded for so long. He no longer cared whether his boots were polished in the morning or whether his cravat was stiffly shone. He never cast a thought on his wife, who had died so long ago and never been replaced, the children he had never had but thought about each day. He forgot about the cook who was being slowly roasted in the aggravated fire. He stood upon his rooftop and wept and when the flames had chased him through the turret stairs and he felt the roof begin to sag under his own weight, he hesitated but a moment, then he picked up Sandrini and threw him from the turret, took one deep breath, took two yards back, then ran and hurled himself across the cornice and out over the edge.

When they reached the doorway, Jack helping Stroop, who was telling him he didn't need help, and Mabel trying to help Thomas who didn't want any help from anyone ever again, they could feel the heat from the conflagration on their arms and legs and faces. The whole skyline was alive with sparks and a heavy tumbrel of deep black smoke rolled across the rooftops, some of it sinking in between the houses and creeping like a thief along the ground. Streaked with dirt and blood, they made their way up the street, the fire casting shadows about them, making walls and doorways jump and shift, and ordinary objects jar like demons working the kilns of hell. The air was filled with the crack and crash of stones and homes, the appalled ululation of families watching their houses collapse to their knees, the scream of men and women as children leapt from attic rooms and missed their parents' wavering arms, the awful stench of burning wood and fur and linen and cloths and melting metal and pantries of food and the skin of those who had slumbered to sleep in the smoke while the flames licked at their boots.

And above all was the cackle and crackle of fire as it ignored them all and clawed its way up the street, tile by tile, brick by brick, room by room, sneaking down chimneys and winding through windows, creeping through halls and tunnels, across carpets, behind pictures and hangings and skirting boards, sometimes on its belly, sometimes racing the height of the wall and slinking across ceilings, seeking cracks and tiny holes and forcing its way through and through and on and on until it had taken possession of every house in the street and emptied each and every one of them from the outside in and the inside out.

Mabel stood amongst the crying crowd and felt as if her heart was being torn to pieces. She knew it had all started with the man in St Anthony's, taking that dagger off the wall. She knew what Stanley Izod had felt amidst the stench of blood that wasn't his own. She knew that somehow she was involved in the trouble of it all, that other people's lives had become her own.

She felt an arm around her shoulder and Stroop was guiding her away and pulling her with him, and then without warning, she found herself slumping to the cobbles, which were littered with cinders and smouldering embers, and Thomas was sat beside her, his grey eyes gaunt and looking at her and a hundred years old.

'This is not the time to cry,' said Stroop, as he put his hands below her elbows and tried to pull her to her feet.

She didn't even feel like she was there. Too much had happened in too short a time, and nothing made sense any more. Jack was at one elbow, and Stroop at the other, and she found herself standing once more, amidst the ruins and devastation and back in a world she didn't know.

'We have to go,' said a voice, warm against her neck, 'come on now, before it's all too late.'

Mabel saw Jack grabbing hold of a halter rein and bringing a rearing pony back to calm and reason, and seeing the animal settle and gain his wits, knew she had to do the same. She brushed off the hands that were around her and breathed hard and deep of the fractured, burning air. She stood, tripping on her skirt, but knew she was once again her own.

'Where?' was all she managed, and then the trap was alongside her and Thomas was already in and Stroop was helping her up, and she wondered what had happened to the dog.

'It's not ours.' It was Jack who had spoken, and for the first time Mabel properly looked at the lad's face and saw that the skin against his neck was taut and sallow, crisscrossed with white webbing like Stroop's hands.

What happened to them? she thought, but was answered as if she had spoken out loud.

'The Silk Quarter has been set on fire.' It was an answer, but not the one to the question she had asked. Not that it mattered. Then there was Stroop: she was sitting beside him up on the trap that wasn't their own, no blankets below the seats where they had been, no dog to warm her feet; the pony drawing them was brown not dappled grey.

'We have to go,' said Stroop again. 'I believe I know where they will go next.'

It was a terrible journey through mist and drizzle and the awful choke of smoke that smelt of the slaughterhouse, pushing past people who huddled under blankets in the rain. The falling cinders pursued them for almost half an hour, but perhaps too soon they had left the burning streets behind them and were driving through the evening, their one lamp still burning to show them the way. At Woolwich they hauled a ferry-keeper out of his hut and argued until he took them over the river.

'Too high,' he had muttered, 'the water's up far too high. And the trap, that'll mean taking up the barge.'

But Stroop had bartered and persuaded, and the grumpy ferryman had gone and got his mate from out the pub, and they'd loaded on the trap and the barge had been clipped to its girdle wire and they'd gone across the mud-brown river.

While they stood on the deck, they'd looked back across the water, saw the dull dome of orange sky from where they had come. The sun had long past sunk, and the moon still rising in the east.

Mabel didn't know where Stroop was taking them, didn't ask. She found it hard to take her eyes from the quarter of Erith that still burned and smouldered, the smoke like a cloak above it, blotting out the stars.

11

Mabel on the Move

'THERE ARE THINGS I must ask you,' said Stroop, and the goosepimples rose again on Mabel's arms below her sleeves, which draggled like dead ducks.

She had been leaning on the rails, watching the black water sneak below the prow, emerging triumphant white the other side. She'd hoped for the flash of silver fish but all she saw were the idle tides of scum suck together as they passed.

'I don't know anything.' She was weary as a world that had long since finished forming and had no place to go. She wanted to rest her head and forever sleep. Stroop stood beside her. She turned her face towards him, hoping everything had gone away. But it hadn't. His jacket was still torn, and she saw him shiver as a whisper of wind blew by them with their passing.

'What am I going to tell my aunt?' It was pathetic, she knew, but still she paused and it suddenly occurred to her that she had told Elsa she would be back for Sunday supper at four and that time must now be long gone. She had been missing all day and not once, not once had she thought of Great-Aunt Flora or how she would be worried, or how many hours had passed or how many miles Elsa must have gone to try and find her. But no, Elsa would first have gone over to the church, and Father Ignatius would have told her about Toby, and Stanley would have given her Mr Stroop's address. But no one would be there! What would they all think? That she had been kidnapped? That she had . . .

Stroop interrupted. 'I sent a boy earlier with a message, right after we left Dismal Cobbett's. I explained you might not be back until evening; I said it was,' Stroop looked faintly embarrassed but carried on, 'Church business; I signed for your wellbeing, told them I would return you as soon as possible. I also sent a message to your Father Ignatius explaining the ruse. Hopefully he will back me up if asked.'

This had been the longest day in Mabel's life. She gazed at Stroop as he looked off into the water. How was it this man she'd met only this morning seemed to know more about her life than she did? How long was it since she'd rung the bell which had looked weirdly like a rat and he had opened the door? How long since she had linked her life with all of these unknown people and caused so much despair?

'Where's Thomas?' she asked, ignoring his earlier enquiry and her question and his answer.

'He's with Jack, in the steering house. They're pretending to be pirates. I paid extra for that.'

Mabel didn't mean to, but she smiled. She couldn't think of anything to say.

'The notebook —' Stroop supplied — 'I didn't have much time with it, and I'm afraid with all the fuss I must have dropped it sometime after we left the house of the man we now know to be Aldo Santorelli. I had it in my hand when we were looking at the tapestry, and I thought I had picked it up when we went. Probably it fell from my coat as we gained the cart. Still, what's gone is gone, and at least I have studied some of it and what I read is what I know. And, as I said, there was the tapestry.'

Involuntarily Mabel grimaced at the black water. It pained her to think she'd broken into someone else's house, walked through the room the unknown man had walked in, riffled through places she had not been invited. Great-aunt Flora was a stickler for etiquette and Mabel had studied hours of the tedious stuff – don't lift this knife before that spoon, or that glass before this one, and do this before you do that or don't do this before someone else has done that. She knew she'd been almost sick with the silliness of it all. But she also knew that what belonged to her was hers and what belonged to someone else was theirs, and that only a few hours ago she had confused the two.

Her elbow was on the rail and a hand was laid across it.

'There's more in that journal I haven't told you.'

Mabel shook herself, took herself back from black oblivion and the water that sluiced below.

'Tell me.' Her voice came out of her and she heard it as if it were someone else's because she knew she shouldn't want to know, but also that she did, and, like the eyes she'd seen in Thomas before he was playing pirates in the steering house, he was about to tell her something that would make her feel about a hundred years old.

★   ★   ★

They'd crossed the river and taken the pony as far as it could go. They were all tired, and Thomas's head had begun to bleed. They'd got as far as Woodford Bridge when Stroop told Jack to stop the trap and they pulled into the yard of an old inn. The thatch was a barber's nightmare and the sign had dropped to one side, showing a swan swaying dizzily on an ancient pool. The pony was taken out back and watered and fed, and Stroop instructed the stable boy to wash her down and find a blanket to rub her warm afterwards.

Once inside, Whilbert Stroop sat them at a private table and ordered pigeon pie and plum sauce with dumplings. There was a small objection from the landlord about having women on the premises but he'd been overruled by extra coins and the food was soon on the table with a pitcher of warmed wine. It had been an age since breakfast's mutton and eggs and they tucked in like the living dead.

Between mouthfuls, Stroop enlightened them as to what he knew, which wasn't much, but was surely a start.

Santorelli's notebook, like the original note given to Thomas under the bridge, had been written in Italian, but Stroop had picked the bare bones from the midden of unknown words.

'What it amounts to is that Mabel is part of a historical secret that goes back many years.' Stroop was carefully picking a small bone from the pie that steamed upon his plate. 'She has what our assailant described as a map.'

'But that's ridiculous.' Mabel swallowed too quickly and started to choke. She took a gulp of clove-scented wine and carried on, 'I'd know if I had his blasted map.' She heard her great-aunt again but carried on regardless. 'Don't you think

I would have given it up if it would have brought—' She stopped abruptly, glancing at Thomas, who kept his head parallel with the table and slowly wiped a piece of bread across his plate but didn't lift it to his mouth. 'I mean, if I had it – which I haven't – don't you think I would know?'

Stroop filled her cup placatingly. 'I didn't say it was an actual map as such. It is a key to the location of a particular thing of which I admit I don't yet know the nature.' Mabel kept quiet and Stroop carried on. 'Apparently it has been passed down for generations from your mother's side. Incidentally,' he spooned a little more plum sauce from the communal bowl on to his plate, 'is your mother called Mabel too?'

The spoon she'd been holding slipped from her hand and fell to the floor. As she stooped to retrieve it, Mabel informed them brusquely that her mother had died when she herself was six, after her youngest brother was born. The unnamed brother had been blue and buried below blankets in the cot beside the bed. He hadn't lasted the day. She had a brief vision of her mother lying with a pink eiderdown right up to her neck, the hair that had always been trapped in a bun lying in a horrid spray across the pillow, framing her thin grey face. Mabel was ashamed that she had so few memories of her mother and, even worse, that the blankness she represented had just been known as Mother, and that Mabel had never thought to ask her name.

After some unnecessarily prolonged cleaning of the spoon Mabel simply said, 'I don't know.'

Stroop was silent. Thomas, on the other hand, looked up brightly.

'My mam was called Isabella Rose and she told me stories every night. That was after she'd given me a piece of chocolate. She did that every night too.'

Mabel was too astonished to reply, but Thomas wasn't about to be stopped.

'And she'd leave me a candle on the table with a glass of milk and later I'd hear her and Dad talking in the next room. I had three brothers and two sisters and we all slept in a huge bed and when she'd said good night and kissed us, we'd sit up together and tell each other jokes and what we'd done all day until we were all so tired we went to sleep.'

He looked up from his plate at last and glanced around the table, which admittedly was agog. 'The woman at the orphanage place told us that if we said things often enough they might come true. Me and Toby used to talk about it all the time. He'd tell me about his family and I'd tell him about mine. You can make up anything you want. That's part of the rules.'

Jack was the only one who spoke up. 'Seems a funny kind of game. I'd rather have been a pirate.'

Thomas looked thoughtful. 'Yes, a pirate would have been good too. Maybe I'll have to make up a whole new family.' He paused a moment, then almost shouted, 'We could be brothers!'

Jack looked immensely pleased and went red as a beet. He took the last dumpling out of the bowl and put it on Thomas's plate and Thomas started chattering about how they could have been shipwrecked on a foreign island and been rescued and brought back to London by a man with a beard that came down to his knees and a chest filled with pearls.

Stroop dipped his head towards Mabel and softly asked, 'Are you sure you don't know her name?'

'I'm sorry,' was all she could say. 'We'll have to ask my father when we get home. That's where we're going, isn't it? To Epping?'

She had recognised the route from when she had first come to Bexleyheath, knew that Woodford Bridge was halfway between her father's and her aunt's, between her old life and her new.

'That's where we're going,' Stroop confirmed, and Mabel had just nodded.

She was tired. She didn't want to think about why they were going there and not back to Great-Aunt Flora's. She didn't want to think about anything any more. She was glad of Stroop, felt a strength in him and a comfort, knew that any thinking needed to be done he would do it, and for the moment that was enough.

They slept at the Swooping Swan that night – Jack and Thomas and Stroop in one of the small damp rooms provided, and Mabel in another. She'd been able to wash in the small bowl provided and then had shivered between cold sheets and blankets that had holes as big as her fists. She had lain a long time gazing out of the unshuttered window. There were no stars and she imagined she still saw the dying shadow of that awful fire on the dark horizon. She heard geese flying low over the marshes and thought of home. Real home. With her dad and her brothers and the dog with his bad breath and stinky-cheese feet. All the chickens she had said goodbye to. The memory made tears prick behind her closed eyelids as she willed herself to sleep. She had never once been back after she had gone away that day, though she had thought about it often.

'Your home is here now,' her great-aunt had said the afternoon she had arrived. That was after James had helped her out of the coach as if she were already a great lady, and after Elsa had taken her upstairs and helped her undress. It had been embarrassing having someone else taking off her clothes and help her on with new ones that didn't quite fit. Elsa had pulled off her head the little bonnet that Mabel had worn to church every Sunday for as long as she could remember, at first too big and then just right and then too small. Perhaps that hat had been her mother's. She couldn't imagine where else it could have come from.

'Goodness!' Elsa had said as she tried to run her fingers through Mabel's thick brown hair. 'We'll have to do something about this!'

There had been a set of brushes on the little boudoir in her bedroom. Elsa had picked one up and said, 'Twenty strokes in the morning and twenty again at night and we'll soon have you fixed.'

And Mabel had started slowly crying with no noise. Just sat looking at herself in the mirror, with someone else brushing through her hair, and wishing she were still at home. Elsa had stopped her brushing and opened a drawer. She'd picked up a tiny lace handkerchief, which smelled of lavender.

'Don't cry, miss,' she'd said. 'Madam's really very nice and she's awful kind. And you can come and have tea downstairs with us if it all gets a bit too much. Don't you worry. All things turn out for the best, you'll see.'

But Mabel lay between her cold sheets shivering and thought of the horrible day that had just been. She knew with awful clarity that Elsa had lied and that some things never turn out for the best, no matter how hard you tried. She tried not to think of Toby, or her mother, lying under that pink eiderdown. She hadn't really recognised until that moment that when she saw her mother that time, she had been two hours dead. She tried to think again what had been her mother's name and cursed herself bitterly for not knowing. Her last thought before she slept was of her father and the farm she had known so well, and the mother she had hardly known at all.

12

Home

CASTRACANI SWEPT HIS numb arms through the black water and searched in vain for Sandrini, wondered where he was beneath the cinder-surface, if he was already sunk to silt and forever asleep. He lay panting for a few moments on his back, watched his little part of Italy disappear in angry roaring smoke and flames. His eyes wept from the waste and the stench, and then he turned his body and made for the other side.

Many hundreds of years before, the Lucchese had moved to this place, made this outer little village of London their own with all their silk mills and sewing shops, the vats of dye, the skeins of thread. Street by street they had conquered and changed the architecture, built fortunes and façades, erected pillars and laid courtyards surrounded by high walls. The richest merchants moved their shops to the City, but they still elected to live right here where they had first begun amidst this alien world. Canals had been dug and lined with stone and brought the water to power their factories, soak their silk, prepare the merchandise for which they were famous, franchised them by the guild. Their silk was the best in all London, in all England, and kings and queens fought to buy their goods and expertise.

Castracani dragged himself up the opposite bank and lay panting for breath and life, his throat scorched, his skin peeling from the heat and sudden immersion in the cold of the river. Ice laced the water of the bank and hardened the mud at its sides. He felt dizzy and exhausted. He felt pity and elation at having escaped. He forced himself to scan the dark uncaring water for Sandrini's body amongst the smouldering planks and flotsam that had once cared for him and covered his life with luxury. He knew the fire had been no accident, knew without forming the actual thoughts that this had been the attack Sandrini had foretold, that the traitors were ruthless and sought only to cover their tracks and extinguish the Council and its secrets, to forestall the nemesis they knew would soon be on their trail.

Castracani swore an oath as he gathered his limbs to his body and shivered, seeking the warmth of the fire he had fought so hard to elude.

'They will not succeed in their goal,' he said out loud, though there was no one to hear. 'I will avenge Sandrini and the Council. I will seek the secret out and gain it by whatever means. I will find the girl and reunite what was lost and give Lucca back its birthright.'

He repeated the words over and over, then at last he found the strength to pull himself to his knees and begin to crawl up the bank. The pain in his lungs did not deter him but rather spurred him on. The remnants of his clothes clung to him and together they clawed a way to the towpath. Castracani looked one last time at the ruins of his little palace. He thought he saw several coloured bottles swirling in the debris, then, like his ancestor before him, he set forth to right the wrongs being done to Lucca, vowing to return what belonged to the homeland he had never seen.

They left the Swooping Swan at early doors, the dawn light seeping over the marshes like a septic wound. Barely had the sun lifted its head when the clouds crossed it over like a blindfold and covered the day in dreary mizzle. Mabel sat on the open cart, getting damp and depressed. Three hours over potholes and wheel-ridged roads, but as they closed on Epping and the smell of wet trees saturated the air, Mabel lifted her head and watched the hedges and the fields and saw the low-slung houses scattered through the wet grass and finally felt the pull of recognition and, at long last, of home. To make things better, the drizzle ceased as they jolted up the rough track that led from the village to her father's farm, and she forgot she was cold and damp, and the dourness began to lift.

Thomas was sitting next to Jack up front, and Jack was teaching Thomas how to hold the reigns and make the pony go left and right and how to make him stop and start. Neither Stroop nor Mabel showed impatience at their games; the boys had hardly ceased their chattering since leaving the inn and the simplicity of the scene lifted her beyond measure.

Stroop had stopped asking her questions about her family. She had explained all she could and knew it wasn't much, had related the small kinks of life that had brought her to where she was and where she had been, and now was bringing her back.

They came to the gate at the top of the track and found it already open and propped with a stone. They could hear the geese and hens clattering about the plot behind the house. Mabel wanted to leap down there and then, and run across the slurried yard and shout to everyone that she was home. No one appeared, and she guessed her brothers were in the fields, seeing to the sheep, and her father would be out checking the winter fodder crops or maybe shedding a sick cow or checking the coppicing and the wood for winter. She saw the rough pile of planks that had been shoved to one side of the lane and recognised them as the same ones that had formed the pontoon to the door to let Mrs Midweather-Etherington, as she had been before she properly became Great-Aunt Flora, before she crossed over their threshold and carried Mabel away to change all their lives. The hope of the planks left there awaiting her return brought those annoying tears back to her eyes, but she swallowed hard and kept herself firmly figured on the peeling white-washed walls of the house. The roses were drooping from the first frosts and the honeysuckle leaves were withered, but the ivy clung firm as ever, threatening to take hold of the roof. She'd have to mention that to Dad when she saw him. That ivy always needed keeping back a bit and chopping down this time of year.

She was faintly surprised no one had come out to greet her, but she wasn't at her great-aunt's now, and visitors were the exception not the norm, and people on a farm always had things to do. That had hit her hard the first few months in London – that not having anything to do. There was hair-brushing and dressing right, but nothing that demanded the strength that once she'd had. She knew she'd greeted laziness with a smile, and for the first time worried about the flabbiness she'd seen in her once taut arms. But then the pony pulled them through the gate and Thomas jumped down unbidden, kicked away the stone and pulled it firm behind them. Jack leapt down beside Thomas and together they started pulling at the pile of planks, laying them out across the mud of the yard.

Before Mabel got down from the cart, Stroop put a hand on her arm.

'There's things we need to know, Mabel, and it's you will have to ask.'

She registered that it was the first time he had called her by her name, at least that she remembered. He'd hardly spoken at all during the entire journey from the Swooping Swan after he'd finished asking his questions. He seemed all the time to be looking at his feet or over her head or else gazing somewhere far off.

Mabel had been too full of her own things to pay him much mind and had spent hours deciding what she would tell her father and how she would laugh to see her brothers and how they would laugh at her to see her in her fine get-up, although admittedly it wasn't as fine as it had been when she'd left for church the day before. She noted the large charcoal smudges on the amber skirts and the hint of Stroop's blood on her fingernails. Her gloves had long since gone, as had her hat. She couldn't even remember if she'd worn a cape. It didn't seem to matter now she was where she was, and the blood rushed to her cheeks as she stepped from the running board on to the plank bridge and made her way to the door. Thomas and Jack stayed with the cart and Stroop came behind her like a ghost. She was dainty as she could be, treading across the boards, so that Mrs Harley and Heather and Betsy would be suitably impressed by her return.

Mabel wondered why she couldn't smell the bread from the ovens – it was surely well past nine and her dad and brothers always came in for breakfast when the village church bell tolled ten. Betsy was always laying the table by this time and should have seen her through the window.

There were three yards to go to the door when she knew something was wrong. The window to the front room was broken and the door, though never locked, was tipped unevenly on its hinges. She started running and the planks gave under her unruly weight, tipping her into the mire, but she already felt the coldness in her veins as she sucked her boots from the dirt, and without stopping she ploughed into the door and started shouting her father's name and for her brothers.

She threw the door aside and it shuddered against the coat-hanger, knocked the line of working boots over one by one.

'Daddy!' she screamed and was at once in the room that when she last saw it had been swept and cleaned and laid out with honey buns and good cheese for her precipitate departure. She saw him as she'd never seen him, and she couldn't comprehend it.

She called for her brothers, though she knew she called in vain, for here they were altogether, her family, tied to chairs she didn't know they owned. She tripped on the rucks of carpet and scattered belongings that were strewn about the room. She knelt by her father's chair and wept. She hadn't recognised his face as his own. It was a massive yellow bruise like a greengage that has missed its summer, but she knew his legs and she knew his arms by the patches she had sewn, and even as she cried she fought to drag the wire from out his wounds. But it was too much and too hard, and when Stroop came up behind her and scooped her from the floor and took her outside on to the step, she didn't stop her weeping or protest. Just tried to rub her eyes hard enough to take away the awful things she had seen.

Jack and Thomas, who had been fussing with the pony and running up and down the planks, pretending they were on a ship, stopped their games and crossed to Mabel, Thomas sitting silently at her side, Jack pulling at the ivy around the door, waiting for someone to tell him what to do. But no one knew what to do. Not even Stroop.

He'd caught his breath the moment he'd stepped across the threshold and smelt the smell of drying blood. He'd known the man cruelly bound to his chair by fencing wire was dead but he forced himself to place his fingers at his neck. Then one by one he'd picked his footing across the littered floor to the two boys, laid his hands upon their cheeks, found them cold. He couldn't begin to grasp the enormity of this scene, not for himself, and certainly not for Mabel. It was one thing to see the dead lain out in neat hammocks at Dismal Cobbett's, stripped of clothes and humanity and the last vestiges of their lives, but these were people who had names and only yesterday had been feeding chickens, picking out horses' hooves, whistling as they axed logs or pursed their hands against the warm udders of milking cows.

91

Here were the brothers Mabel had talked about only the night before, whose trousers she had worn when they got too small, who stamped her feet into their old boots and mended their clothes, who got angry with them for treating her like a little girl, who'd mussed her hair on Sundays right before she put on her hat, who'd kissed her goodbye and had never seen her again. God knows, they wouldn't have wanted her to see them like this.

Stroop struggled to remember their names. Ezra and Henry, he thought, though which was which he couldn't have said. They looked too horribly alike: as their father, both were tied into immovability, a rabbit noose of wire tight about their ankles and wrists, one to each limb of the chair. Unlike their father, whose head had been pulled back across the neck of the chair, the two boys hung forward, chins on chest, and for that small mercy Stroop was grateful. He had no doubt they would be as bruised and beaten as their father had been, that their eyes had disappeared behind the blue billow of swollen flesh, that their lips were split and their mouths hoarse from crying and missing the teeth that were scattered in the gore around their feet. Stroop had a strong urge to flee and retch but there was something else he first must do.

He cast his eyes around the dim room. Every box and trinket had been smashed and lay in pieces on the floor. The drawers had been ripped from the writing chest and the few shelves had been swept clean of books and pipes, of pewter tankards and plates and pictures and tobacco pouches. The fire was dead in its grate, although the poker stood ominously straight by its side. He covered the floor in several quick strides and passed the open door.

Mabel was shuddering on the step. He felt her sobs deep within his chest and was almost overcome by the pity of it all, but he went on and opened the door into the scullery. The scene was no prettier and this time Stroop had to cover his mouth with both hands to stop the gag. It was perhaps the ordinariness of the scene that hit him worst: the elder woman whose name he couldn't recall, was leaning over the cooking range. Facing her, on the other side of the table, two younger women sat, one still holding a rolling pin, the other with her hands on the edge of a pie, her fingers apparently still fluting its edges. From behind, where he stood, everything looked perfectly normal except that nobody moved. You could smell the cooking – a pork pie and its jug of spiced aspic, both of which he could see on the long table, a leg of ham half-sliced still stuck with its cloves, a joint slow-roasting in the oven. But then when you looked closer you saw that the hands were paler than the pastry and that pieces of rope hung down the backs of the seated women. The woman cooking at the stove was caught on the hooks that hung her pans and it was her arm that was slowly been seared on a hot-plate still fired by yesterday's wood. The other hand was swollen with pooled blood by her side.

Stroop had no doubt that this was a scene from the previous evening. This was supper in the making; the plates and cutlery for dinner were piled at one side of the table. There was a jug lying cracked on the floor in a pool of spilt mead, the smell of its stale fermentation happily masking many others that must have been hanging in the air. This time Stroop could not manage to touch these women. He closed his blue-veined eyelids for a moment, then turned and left. He knew these things had to be reported. There were things that needed to be done, people to be told, but right now, at this moment, all Stroop wanted was to get himself out and gone. And obeying his instincts, at last he left.

13

Time to Tell

THE CHURCH OF St Thomas stood within the streets of the Silk Quarter, its square blocks blackened by the smoke, its stone-tiled steeple and massive mounted cross squinting down into the dying flames. It had feet of granite, a defensive skirt of walls, square and solid, still immovable half a millennium after the first piling had been laid. Above and against it leant the less aggressive additions of later years: a quieter line of sandstone chapels, a dome that housed a solar line, a spire that soared like a swan's neck into the sky.

Castracani now sat in the cool arm of St Thomas's transept, interrupting the calm with his coughing, rubbing absently at the burns that ran the length of his arms and legs. He had crawled along the towpath until, aided by passers-by, he had reached a friend's house, been bathed and covered with ill-fitting clothes that were not his own. All the while his anger never left him and he would not allow himself to be nestled into bed and sleep. Rather he sent messengers here and there to assess the damage, gather the news, alert the Lucchese and bring them here to St Thomas's.

He sat gazing up at the crude reredos, a Tree of Life in battered oak trellis, his eyes fixed on the surmounting figure, a Christ on the Cross carved in ancient wood, which was a replica of the true Volto Santo. Fashioned by his ancestors in medieval times, the London Volto Santo had been revered from that time to this, and brought their church and their community the wealth it had needed to establish itself and strengthen itself, to build its home on the outskirts of London, nestling by the river along from Erith. Just as in their homeland, the Volto Santo had funded their industry and buildings, taken care of them, allowed them to tear down the grim English houses and substitute their own. Castracani stared intently at that enigmatic face, its worn wooden lines shifting in candle-glow, mellowed by the smoke of incense and the prayers and lips of the faithful. He wondered if it could really be that this was the Face of God. Not the apocalyptic Judge of the Old Testament who smote you dead with flames if you so much as glimpsed his feet, but the gentle face of a God made human, the face of a man who was truly great and good. It struck him that perhaps the Lucchese really had gazed on God and that was why their streets had been burned to the ground, but he knew that was preposterous. This holy image had been here for over five hundred years, protecting them as they cared for Him.

Castracani was roused from his stupor by someone tapping him gently on the arm.

'They are here, sir – at least all that are able to come. We have made ready the room. We will use the upstairs gallery, if you feel able to take the stairs?'

It was one of the young oblates who had interrupted his

thoughts. Castracani allowed the boy to help him up and creaked his way from the pew along the aisle to the steps. He could hear the heavy tread of people on the boards above and the agitated undertow of voices. His knees cracked as he began to climb the steep stairs. The sudden darkness as he rounded the corner frightened him, and he heard again the roar and sear of the fire at his back, felt the weight of Sandrini on his shoulder and in his arms, the scrape of the smoking walls, which were warm as they grazed first his clothes then his skin. He shuddered, but then the light of the boy's candle reached him as he stood momentarily on the wide bay of the turning step. He pulled himself together and felt the anger surge in him again that he had come to this, frightened to climb the dark staircase of a church just because the afternoon light could not reach him, and with a last few determined steps he gained the lip of the gallery and flung open the door.

The skeleton of the London Lucchese Council stood before him, a clucking bunch of old men standing around the pot-bellied stove. Of the Inner Circle, there was only one representative. Two were in the nearby Caritas hospital with severe scorching of the lungs and throats, another was so badly burned he wasn't expected to last the night, and Sandrini – whose body wouldn't be found until dislodged by the opening of the sluice gates almost a week later – was presumed dead.

Castracani wasn't a member of the élite, not yet, but Sandrini's visit had confirmed what he had hoped – that he was about to be admitted, on completion of a certain task and the retirement of an Inner Circle member. That Sandrini had now retired was not really in doubt and Castracani was more ready now than ever to take his place, although he would have wished with all his heart the circumstances had been different. Still, there is was. *Cosi ha valuto il fato,* as his father always said: thus is the will of fate. Sandrini hadn't managed to tell all he had to tell, but Castracani knew most of the secret the Council had been hiding for all these years. He had had the time, whilst struggling along the bank on his hands and knees and later lying, skin screaming, in his bath, to make some sense of the afternoon's events. Even on entering the gallery he knew that this was his time to act, that though he had lost his house, his belongings and many of his friends, this was the time for his star to rise and the gaining of all he had ever hoped to gain.

Some men sat like old women on the benches, their heads in their hands; a small knot of young bloods stood hotly to one side, gesticulating and whispering wildly. Most stood with their hands behind their backs, some with bandages or arms in slings, cuts and grazes stitched but still bleeding, clothes and hair and skin and boot leather still impregnated with the horrid tar and acridity of smoke. Castracani realised that without the Inner Circle the snake had lost its head, and without another moment's thought, he strode across the room, held up his blistered, burn-blotched arms and called for them all to take a seat, pour him a glass, and listen.

'I have a tale to tell, and though I don't know all, I know enough.'

He glanced at Bostannito, the single remaining member of the Inner Circle, and as such things would have it, the oldest and most frail. Several years before, he had lost half his tongue to a cancer, making his speech difficult and hard to understand. His authority was not in dispute, but his effectiveness in this situation was minimal, and of that he was shamefully glad. He loved his homeland as much as anyone in this room, and understood only too well the gravity of what had happened – not only that Lucca had been given away like a bauble by a Corsican who had no right to give it, but here too, in the heart of their London community. He had been on the eve of retiring anyway; had already nominated Castracani in his place with the backing of the other members of the Inner Circle. And now, with that backing or without, he nodded at Castracani, and with it ceded his authority and the future of Lucca to the younger man. He prayed God he had chosen rightly – believed he had.

Castracani was now the mouth of the Council, he understood that, had agreed to take the millstone on his shoulders, and began again to speak.

'Gentlemen, we are under attack; these fires were no accident. Each one had been carefully laid in the cellars of the Inner Circle Members, and in my own home – no doubt because it was known Sandrini would be spending the afternoon discussing various matters with me. They were laid and lit in our coal cellars and woodpiles, one by one, working down the street, and left to do what damage they would do. Two were discovered, but only one in time to be extinguished, and thus we can thank God we still have Inner Circle member Bostannito with us. The only Inner Circle member whose safety is vouchsafed.'

There were murmurs, there were angry shouts, but Castracani held up his arm again and carried on.

'It is also surmised that pouches of gunpowder had been left at strategic intervals as we have had reports of explosions, which some at the time took to be musket fire. Someone set out to destroy our community at its very heart; to burn down these fine streets and houses we have made our own, and to set to the stake the Council by which we live.'

Castracani paused several times to clear his throat of soot, and now he could not stop the spasms that racked his chest. Great gobs of black phlegm came up and ruined the handkerchief that had been thrust in his hand. The men began to mutter and shift in their seats. A glass of brandy was poured down Castracani's inflamed throat, and then he lifted a hand for silence, croaked his way onwards.

'There is black treachery at work, both here and in our home town, and the time for secrecy is past. Listen then to the tale of our countrymen, who have protected a great treasure, and then I will tell you what we must do.'

Dámaso di Rudini sat in the small café on the corner of Via Canale and Via di Tessitóre. He had always loved the way the Silk Quarter had clung to its Italian ways. Beneath each street name put there by the city authorities, the Lucchese had affixed a second plaque in their own language. How much better to walk down Strada Panettiere than Baker Street, or peruse the exquisite finery on display in the shops of Via Copertura than stroll down Cloth Road. He dropped another sugar lump into the already over-sweet coffee he was drinking. He stirred the glass, watched the film on the surface of the liquid disrupt and dissolve. He couldn't shake the sights he had seen, the smell that hung over the quarter like a pall, made everything taste of burnt tar. After the meeting at St Thomas's he had avoided the company of his peers, who headed straightaway to the nearest tavern to discuss the evening's affairs. They were eager, excited to be doing, to be investigating, to perpetrate revenge. Dámaso di Rudini had brushed off their invitations.

'I've a bad headache,' he had said. 'It is all the smoke. I need to sleep.'

That had been almost true. He did have a headache. Worse, he had lost two friends who had fought the blaze and not come back, tried to salvage what they could from the shop and been burnt alive like ancient saints for their care. He himself hadn't lingered to try to save the paintings or the people trapped inside the burning building. Like most, he had been out on the street in a moment, mouth dropped in horror as the quarter seemed to go up all at once as if it had been doused with over-heated oil, acrid smoke terrible in his throat, obscuring the destruction happening right before his eyes. He hadn't thought about his colleagues or his work, but had run like a rat before gas to reach his home, had found his mother and his sisters safe; his wife at a neigh-bour's, propped up in a corner, yelling for their children name by name, unable to move, her belly big and quivering in the colours of the raging fire. He had touched her cheek, stood immobile as a tethering post only for an instant, then run like the devil to the school.

It had stood in the cul-de-sac at the end of Vicolo da Macellaio, the street once used by butchers but now a green lane lined with trees backing on to the street by the canal. The few leaves left on the trees were seared into curlicues

by the heat or crunched into cinders on the grass, which
was grey with ash. His blood had boiled within him as the
smoke cleared and he saw the school, roof on fire, gable posts
collapsed into the atrium, hearing the screams and groans of
brick and stone straining in their traces, swaying under the
pressure, collapsing into rubble. But thank God he saw all
the children gathered like pre-migrating geese on the green
that served as their playing field, frightened, not knowing
where to go, crowds of parents engulfing the small space,
blinded by smoke and by each other's bodies, cracked voices
crying for their offspring. For Dámaso, it might have been
the end of the world.

The thought of it made him swallow hard and deep. His
own children had been found, clinging to each other's hands,
shaken, smoke-smudged but unharmed, yet still the stink of
the air disturbed him deeply, reminded him of a charcuterie
where the charcoal had been fired beneath the cuts of pork
and slices of red sausage.

He could still smell it, sitting here, despite the strong fumes
of the coffeepot before him. He could not get used to it,
could not ignore it. The faces of those they had lost rose up
at every breath. He smelt their slow destruction in every
moment. He had seen people run back into burning buildings to rescue what they held most dear. The unlucky ones
died an abominable death, trying to save a brother or a son
or a box of money or a dog or a daughter or a deposition
or a deed or whatever they thought their life would be
nothing without. There had been no quarter given. Even in
war, people were given the chance to bury what was left of
their dead. But here? These streets were piles of rubble and

there was no choice but to pile them up and burn down further what was left. Everyone knew the dying brought their own diseases. Everyone had tales of battle-torn bodies killing their comrades when the war is done with the touch of decay, of cholera, typhus, and God knew what else. Great bonfires burnt all over the quarter, razing anything half-razed, disposing of the bodies of cats and caged birds, dogs, cooks, geese, rabbits hanging in the pantries, those men and women caught before they could escape. They had to protect those who were left.

And sleep? Sleep? He didn't believe he would ever know that again, not while he had these thoughts crowding in upon his mind, begging to be noticed, clamouring like children shouting, 'Look at me! Listen to me! *Me! Me! Me!*'

He could see the canal across the street, passing like oil beneath the bridge. The surface was sheathed in black rainbows where the pitch from ruined roofs pooled and spread as the water moved below. The banks shivered with the outline of pots and pans, broken planks, cracked tiles, crumbles of plaster, bits of bedding, shoes, broken-backed books. Dámaso looked away and closed his eyes, replayed in his mind several of the scenes that would give him no rest.

He recalled the day his second cousin Veza Gozzoli had turned up from Lucca those few days ago out of the blue.

'Veza! I haven't seen you for . . .' Dámaso had struggled. It had been too long – since they were children, he thought – though he had recognised instantly that large round face, the unembarrassed smile of crooked teeth.

'It has been twenty-one years, my friend. I have been counting!'

Veza Gozzoli had slung his arm around his cousin's shoulder and dragged him out of the shop. Struggling half-heartedly against the strong grip, Dámaso had turned to his workmates and shrugged, and they had grinned their approval.

'Go, go!' they had encouraged. 'He is your family and you have not seen him for twenty-one years. You must drink and talk, and drink some more!'

And that is precisely what they had done. Veza had taken Dámaso to a large inn on the edge of the quarter, where the Lucchese mixed with merchants coming out from the City of London and the docks to discuss, purchase and trade; where exporters mingled with sailors and struck bargains; where women hung at the bars and slender young men skulked in the doorway leading out to the small enclosed courtyard garden. Dámaso had been surprised at the venue but Veza had waved his hand and raised his voice.

'Here we can talk and drink with no one to worry us, without being interrupted every second by your inquisitive neighbours wanting to know who I am, how long I am here and what is the news from Lucca. I should have exhausted myself answering questions about the war and that bastard Napoleon stamping over our country in his big boots. But here,' he waved his arm again, 'this place, it is a world of its own. Nothing disturbs us. It doesn't matter who you are or what you do. And besides, I have a friend here who wants to meet you.'

Dámaso had raised his eyebrows. He couldn't think who on earth Veza would know who would want to meet Dámaso di Rudini. He might work in one of the better art gallerias in Via Ganimede, but basically he just framed pictures and hung tapestries, sometimes in the finest houses, for the best families, but still . . . any deals would have to go through his master. But by the time Veza's friend had shown up, Dámaso had been pretty much drunk.

Veza had introduced them: 'Dámaso di Rudini, meet Pietro Tarrabombi, writer and visionary extraordinaire; Pietro, meet Dámaso, one of my oldest and dearest friends.'

Pietro was a dark young man, that much Dámaso could remember, also that he said he was researching a piece for his newspaper on the London Lucchese for back home. He had been very interested in the workings of the Council, and Dámaso had explained it as best he could, though he had slurred a good deal and got a few things muddled up.

'We are very much like the Lucca system, based on it, obviously, though from many years ago. We have the same thing of all the families being listed in The Book, with genealogy and trade and marriages and everything. There are seventy-four families I think at the moment . . .'

Dámaso had tapped his chin with his thumb. He ought to know this stuff. His father was senior clerk at the Archives. The drink was fuddling him, but Veza and his earnest friend urged him to carry on. The friend kept scribbling notes.

'Um . . . right. Every two years, each family elects its own representative to stand for them at Council meetings, which are held every quarter. News is given of what is going on in Lucca, of the state of the silk industry, of anything important that is going on in the community and so on. Everyone gets a chance to bring up grievances or make announcements of engagements or new business opportunities or whatever. After two years, the outgoing representatives elect from amongst themselves thirty candidates whose names are given to the Inner Circle members. They choose twenty of them to make the Third Circle of the Council. These people effectively run the guilds and so on, but because there's a change every two years, it means no single family gets to dominate. We have to co-operate to continue, as the saying goes, get on together to get anywhere.'

Dámaso had laughed. He was getting bored with all this. Also, he was getting dry with all the talking. Veza's attention had wandered. He took advantage of the brief lull in his cousin's lecture to get up and go to the bar. Veza could have called one of the waitresses over, but Dámaso didn't notice. He could feel his head drooping.

Pietro had leant over and caught his arm. 'You need a little air, my friend?' His voice was solicitous and he had spoken in fluent English.

Dámaso realised he must have been swapping from Italian to English throughout his little speech. It often happened, particularly when he was drunk. He had flapped Pietro's arm off his own and said, 'No, no, no, no.' He was feeling very kindly towards Veza's friend. He remembered going to stay with Veza over in Lucca one summer many, many years ago. It had been the most wonderful time. They'd gone fishing in the crystal-blue river, helped stamp grapes, gone out to the hills with the goats and chewed grass, made whistles from bits of twigs. He'd got drunk then too. His first time ever. How sick he'd been, and how Veza had laughed!

'The Council, right,' he had wagged his finger in Pietro's face, 'the Second Circle, they're picked by the Inner Circle. Richest men, or most powerful. Fifteen of them. Second

Circle. They like oversee the Third Circle. Make lots of important decisions. But the Inner Circle, now they're the thing.
There's five of them and they elect themselves. 'S always
been like that.'

He'd heard himself slurring everything he was saying, but
the man had been so interested, and so on he'd gone.

'They carry on till one of 'em pops off or gets sick or
something, then the rest of them pick someone else to take
his place. From the Second Circle, see?'

Veza had come back then, and refilled his glass. Dámaso didn't
remember much after that, except Veza and his friend on either
side of him as they cavorted down the streets shouting and
singing. And if that had been all there was, he wouldn't be
sitting here in this café feeling sick. But he *did* remember something else. He remembered them weaving through the streets
and Pietro asking, Which one? And, house by house, Dámaso
had pointed out the Inner Circle, named their names, told this
stranger where they lived. And then had come the fire.

Mabel was too distraught to leave Epping immediately, despite
Stroop's insistence that they must hurry back to town. He
had been back into the house and searched the place from
top to toe, seeking whatever it was that Mabel was thought
to have in her possession. Then he dispatched Jack and Thomas
to take the fittest horses from the paddock and ride back as
fast as they could manage; they must alert Mabel's great-aunt
to the possibility of unwelcome visitors.

Obviously, the man they had met at Aldo's house had
taken Mabel at her word — that indeed she did not know
the thing that he desired. He had come to her home to try

and beat it out of her father, had tortured his sons in front of his eyes, made him listen to their screams and watch the blood streaming from their battered faces on to the floor. They had stolen into the kitchen first and noosed the two maids around the neck. There must have been more than one in the attack to have accomplished the thing so tidily. The cook had been next, pushed back against the stove and garrotted amongst her pan-hooks. Then the men had returned for their breakfast and found the strangers waiting insolently in their home. They had been overpowered and tied to chairs with ropes and wires, and beaten about their heads. The attackers would have screamed abuse and threats and the boys would have wept with fear to watch their father having the hot poker thrust against his skin and up his nostrils and against the pulled nails of his fingers. The younger boy had vomited, and the curdled yellow bile soiled his trousers, as did the stain of urine long since cold.

Stroop gagged many times as he made his way around the room, then climbed the ladder into the loft and went through their sleeping quarters. There was nothing he could find, no hidden boxes, no secret drawers or hiding places, no hint of where Mabel's inheritance might be. He did find a faded pastel portrait of a woman, whom he took to be Mabel's mother, wrapped in a faded piece of satin in the father's wardrobe. Mabel had the point of her chin, the straight line of her nose, the dark curve of her eyebrows. He turned the picture over, loosened the pins of the frame and removed it. He squinted at the line of writing he saw squiggling across its base: '*Per Rosa Mabellina, anniversario delle nozze 1763.*'

So, not Mabel's mother. More probably her grandmother;

a portrait made for the day of her wedding. Italian again, he thought, inescapably Italian. He put the picture back in its frame and wrapped it up, slipped it in his pocket. There was nothing else he could find. He stood for a moment looking through the small arrow-aperture that allowed the only natural light into the room. He could see Mabel walking across the yard, carrying a pail. She was making a light chucking noise and strewing seeds for the chickens and geese who dipped greedily at the ground, following her as if drawn by a net. She looked quite peaceful, apart from the redness around her eyes and the entanglement of her hair. Her dress, he noted, was completely ruined, ripped in places, darkened with blood and soot, encrusted for a good six inches at the base with drying mud. And yet there she was, completely at ease, chucking to chickens as if she were not ten yards away from the slaughtered remains of her family. He watched her carefully close the gate to the yard, having rounded the last of the birds up and secured them within.

She went into the milking shed, but only a few minutes later the back door of the shed opened and Mabel appeared again, leading the cows out into the pasture. This must mean that someone had had time to milk them the previous evening but not to have let them out again at dawn. Perhaps the two serving girls – Heather, was it? He couldn't remember the name of the other one – and shuddered at the thought of those cold backs with their plaits of ropes. Perhaps they had heard some commotion in the kitchen and come back in to see what was what. Or perhaps they never let the cows out till later. Stroop didn't know much about farming and admitted defeat.

Whatever had happened, it had happened last night. It had been bloody and brutal and, judging by the complete destruction, it had not been successful. It was a desecration brought about by anger and frustration. He was sure that whatever the attackers had sought, they had not found it. They must have assumed Mabel's father knew of her family secret, but it was becoming apparent, both from the present situation and the notes in Aldo's diary, that whatever the thing was, it was handed from mother to daughter and was kept strictly between them. But Mabel's mother had died before she had the chance to tell Mabel anything, and if Mabel didn't know where or what was the cause of all this – and Stroop had no doubt at all that it was the cause of everything that had happened, from the man in the church, to Toby, to this – how on earth where they supposed to stop it?

Enough, thought Stroop, and began down the ladder. We've got to go, like it or not. And so he called to Mabel and together they unstrapped the pony from its harness and led it out into the field, selected a stronger one and got it yoked to the cart. Apparently it had been a recent acquisition, for Mabel didn't call this one by name, as she had done the other animals. Even the chickens, thought Stroop absently, I'd swear she was calling to them one by one. Mabel didn't complain or stall for time. Apparently now she had checked on the animals and fed them and found them fine, she was willing to leave her home, no doubt knowing that someday soon she would have to come back and sort out whatever was left to be sorted. But the urgency of Stroop's manner had caught her and she knew she couldn't stay, that things weren't at an end yet and that somehow she had to go on.

Just as they were closing the gate, Mabel had a sudden stab of thought, knew she had missed something. She ran back around the house and out to the old shed where they kept the straw for the winter and the bales of beet. She struck hard at the door and called out loudly, and with an overwhelming sense of relief that left her weeping so hard she had to kneel down, she saw the old dog lying in his basket, struggling to get up and greet her. He was stiff at the joints and creaked as much as the wicker he was trying to leave, his eyes were dark blue pearls, but he managed to crawl across the floor to Mabel and sniffed her face and licked her hands, whining softly. Laughing, something an hour ago she thought she would never do again, Mabel picked the ailing dog up and carried him out into the afternoon air, all the way across the yard and into the cart.

'Old Bindlestiff,' she whispered as Stroop hauled at her arm and helped her up, 'good old Bindlestiff.' And Stroop left her in the back of the cart and steered the pony down the lane. He could hear her crying into the old dog's muffling fur and had to swallow rather too hard himself, and blink a little bit more than was necessary in the weak winter sun.

14

Darkness and Light

JACK AND THOMAS rode like devils, driving the horses along
the rough lanes, past hedges bared down to their bones,
birds' nests crumbling in their frozen branches. It was just
gone noon when they launched themselves into desperate
flight, glad to be gone from the smell and sadness of it all.
Thomas knew how to ride, despite his upbringing. He'd
spent some early years in keep of a farmer who ran him and
Toby like mules, shuttling goods from farm to town, getting
goods to market and getting his barters back. Thomas had
been only eight then, which made him light on a horse;
kept the produce surplus high.

He and Toby had been valued until they hit the age of
ten and got a little heavier than their competitors from the
orphanage. But by that time they didn't care and had chosen
not to go back. They would be brothers in their adversity.
They weren't to be bound by other people's rules. They
would tell each other their stories and not be held down by
things they didn't know.

But those were more thoughts than Thomas chose to

remember. Instead, he kept tapping at his pocket to make sure the missives Stroop had given him were still there. They had already dropped one off, having detoured into the village. They had been instructed not to stop, nor speak to anyone, which might delay their departure, but to find the manse and drop the letter off. In it Stroop had briefly outlined the nature of the disaster at the Flinchurst farm, given his name and Mabel's great-aunt's address and warned that the sight was not pretty. The villagers would no doubt take some time to gather, then set off to Mabel's father's farm. There would be horror, disgust, outrage, anger. There would be arguments about what to do and how to proceed and who to blame. A contingent would set off for the city to seek Authority and Advice. Stroop knew that he and Mabel did not have the time to stay and explain and take part in the theatrics of murder. Events were unfolding too fast, and there was no time to waste. So Thomas and Jack were to get to London as fast as they could. Epping lay less than thirteen miles north of Bexleyheath, but the roughness and bend of the roads made the going much further. Even taking the most direct route and using the most advantageous ferry, it was a journey of several hours on horseback, and two more with the cart. Still, despite the urgency, Stroop valued the time it gave him to try to get all things in order.

He was not the man of action this situation seemed to require. He was a man who sat in his study and wrote things down, who countered mystery by logic, who translated the rough edges of life into an understandable pattern so they could be measured with a string and rule. He must make his mind recall every jot that he had read in the suicide's notebook, line up his facts in soldierly order and prepare to march forward. Mabel must be forced to give up every scrap of information she had, even if she didn't know it was there. For a while he let her be, let her sink her head into the old collie's fur. He needed a little time to prepare his interrogation. And further, his nose, as he sat on the cart, twitched very slightly. He thought he caught a slight undercurrent of cheese, and it disturbed him.

It was, however, Mabel who interrupted Stroop rather than the other way round. She scrambled over the board and sat next to him, dragging the old collie across her knees. Stray dog-hairs covered the front of her dress, detaching every now and then as the air was stirred with the cart's passing.

'Mr Stroop,' she spoke quietly but with an assurance belonging to someone much older, 'I'm sorry for having got you into all this. I will quite understand if you don't want to go on with it. It was Stanley – Mr Izod at St Anthony's – who thought you might be able to help, but I'm sure you usually get paid for your time and trouble. And obviously this is trouble. And equally obviously, and I'm sorry I never thought about it before, I've no idea how I can pay you anything. Maybe I can ask Aunt Flora when we get back. Although just thinking about explaining things to her makes me . . . well, I'm not sure how I'm going to be able to explain anything at all.'

Mabel closed her mouth and was quiet. She'd thought about her speech for the last half-hour and it hadn't taken her as long as she had expected. She didn't know what else to say.

Stroop said nothing. If she'd looked at his face at that moment, she'd have seen it more animated than it had been for years. Surprise was the nearest thing to describe it, and an odd amusement. He even smiled, which was something he didn't often do. His hands carried on holding the reins and for a few minutes, all they could hear were the horse's hooves clipping at the loose stones of the track, the metal-rimmed wheels cracking against the mouths of potholes, sparks spitting from striking old nails or flints.

'What do you think I normally do?' Stroop eventually asked. He glanced at Mabel. She had her head down and her hand stroked slowly at the Bindlestiff blanket, which gave out small whines and snuffles and happy sighs. Stroop spoke on. 'I'll tell you what I normally do. People come to me and ask me to find things. Usually their daughters or sons, occasionally their possessions or a valued servant or even a horse. Then I collect all the facts. I question the household, the local shop-holders, the urchins in the streets, explore the nearby taverns. I gather gossip, I listen at doors and through windows. Then I go home and pour myself a stiff brandy and sit at my desk. I open my notebooks and write down everything I have learned in an orderly manner. Then I read it and think about it and write it all down again in a yet more orderly manner. I may get up and consult my books. I may send Jack out to check on this or that and add to my notes, in which case I have to rewrite them all over again. I may do this several times. Occasionally I have spent days doing it. At the last, I have a definitive set of facts, and from this I am able to deduce the answer. At least nine times out of ten, I am able to tell the father or mother that their daughter has run off with a visiting glove-maker or that the boy has set off to sea or that the horse has been set on by ruffians from the glue factory or that the servant has been poached by one of their cousins who visited last month.'

Mabel had stopped stroking the dog, who had fallen fast asleep, paws twitching, snoring gently. Her hand lay across his warm side, comforted by the rise and fall of it and the regular draw of his breath. Stroop paused briefly. It wasn't often that he spoke for so long at once. He could feel the girl looking at him, and he felt embarrassed but on he went.

'And then yesterday morning, you arrived at my door and since then I have hardly had time to think, let alone gather any notes. I have travelled from Bexleyheath to the silk mills to Woolwich to Epping. I have been shot at, had my cart stolen, seen half of London go up in flames, stolen someone else's cart, and seen today what I never hope to see again.'

He paused and cleared his throat, then finally looked down at Mabel and shook his head. 'For this, I do not want payment. All I want is to stop it happening again, particularly to you and the boy. And above all, I want to know why what has happened has happened. I do not have the sort of mind that can walk away from a tale half told. I don't care if the story is the worst in the world. If I have heard the beginning, I must hear the end.'

Stroop stopped abruptly, then added, 'All right?'

Mabel smiled. 'All right.'

They were quiet for a few moments. Stroop gave Mabel the knapsack he had brought with him from the farm. He hadn't liked to do it, but he'd gone back into that kitchen and into the pantry. He had stuffed the knapsack he'd found hanging by the door with food. There was ham and bread and some unidentifiable pickle, a small flask of what he'd hoped was wine but which turned out to be walnut oil. They dipped the bread in it anyway and sliced the ham. They stopped for a large bottle of beer in one of the inns they passed but always they went on. They talked as they ate. Stroop asked questions. Mabel asked questions. They went through everything that had happened since the morning of the spectacular suicide in the church. They did not skip over anything, although they stopped eating when they talked of Toby, and they spoke in allusion when they reached the tale that told of the farm that had once been Mabel's home.

'Whether you know it or not, Mabel, you are the key to all this,' said Stroop. He had shown her the portrait of her grandmother. He had skewered her through and through about her mother. He had found out precisely nothing. He had asked her mercilessly about her family, where they had come from, what they had done, tried to find how far back went her name. She knew nothing. He had talked about the farmhouse. Had she left anything that might have been called hers alone? Had her father had some keepsake he was supposed to send to her? Had her mother left some enigmatic message? But at the end of it all, Mabel knew no more than he, and probably less. He at least had looked at the Italian's diary, and had an inkling as to what secrets that diary possessed.

By the time they rolled wearily into Bexleyheath, it was

past six and very dark. Between them they had come to the following conclusions.

The man who had killed himself in the church was called Aldo Santorelli.

He was Italian and lived in the so-called Silk Quarter along the river from Woolwich.

He wore a pilgrim's badge and had been severely beaten before he got to the church.

He considered himself the Guardian to the Keeper of the Secret.

He considered Mabel to be the Keeper of that Secret.

He was not alone in this belief.

Someone else was after Mabel and her secret.

These people had kidnapped Toby and killed Mabel's family in the attempt to locate the whereabouts of Mabel's secret.

Mabel was a family name, passed down from mother to daughter, and very probably her family also had some Italian connection, as indicated by the inscription on her grand-mother's portrait.

This connection was almost certainly from her mother's side of the family.

Their final conclusion, reached as they came alongside the river and saw St Anthony's just ahead, was that Mabel had no idea what the family secret was, and that it was of para-mount importance to ascertain its nature as soon as possible. To this end, they would go through every scrap of paper, every trinket, every pocket of everything that Mabel had brought with her from the farm. They would need to inform Mabel's great-aunt of the situation and warn her of prob-able danger. It was even possible that she knew what this great family secret was, that Mabel's father had entrusted it to her, assuming her mother had entrusted it to her father before her death.

At that moment, as Mabel and Stroop were returning to Bexleyheath, Great-Aunt Flora was standing by the window in her drawing room while her friend Penelope Witheridge looked at the note. Great-Aunt Flora was not used to these feelings of agitation; she liked an orderly life, a predictable one. She had suffered the loss of those dearest to her, had kept her grief within her like a stone, coped precisely by carrying on in the manner she had always been accustomed to do. If she continued to have tea at four p.m. every afternoon, China tea, not Indian, if she ate two biscuits and one small slice of cake, if she talked of nothing more important than an upcoming dance or the latest marriage or birth, if that was what she did every day, then nothing would harm her. She feared upset, she feared more loss. She didn't think she could bear more loss.

'Ah!' exclaimed Great-Aunt Flora with unusual force. 'Here comes that girl at last!'

She turned away from the window, her eyes fixed on the door. She had made out the form of Elsa slipping across the square. She had been unsatisfied with the note from this Mr Stroop. She had never heard of him, and neither had Penelope. Who was he that he had taken Mabel on some unspecified errand? Glory to God, he had kept the girl out overnight! Flora Midweather-Etherington never blasphemed, but she couldn't help the thoughts that flitted across her mind. She had summoned Elsa, interrogated her. She knew that Mabel and Elsa were of an age and closer than servant and mistress should be, but she wasn't a tyrant. She turned a blind eye. She knew it hadn't been easy for Mabel these last two years, although she hoped the girl was grateful. More than that, and she would hardly admit it even to herself, she hoped the girl was growing fond of her; wanted the girl to grow fond of her. Great-Aunt Flora rarely permitted feelings to disturb the course of her life, but she knew she liked the girl, had grown used to her, knew without a doubt that she was worried for her and, God forgive her, worried for herself. To be alone again was something she would not permit if it was at all in her power to prevent.

She fixed her eyes on the door, but Elsa didn't come. What was wrong? She'd heard the yard door, and the door to the scullery close. How long did it take a girl to tidy herself up? She'd only been over to the church to talk to Mabel's priest, to get some answers about this Stroop. Confound it! Great-Aunt Flora started forward to the door, intending to go to the girl if the girl didn't see fit to report directly to her mistress. But something stopped her. A scuffling on the stairs, a muffled noise, a voice? Penelope had carried on pouring her tea – her hearing wasn't too good these days. Great-Aunt Flora decided to take charge again. She would not worry. She would not be afraid. She walked to the drawing-room door and pulled it quickly open.

15

Castracani Tells
of Cats in Cradles

A MAN RUNS DOWN the Via Calderia, his footsteps soft against
the stone, his sandals slipping in the rain-skelped mud.
His hair is wet against his head, his clothes sculpted to his back.
The sky is dark as oceans' depths as the clouds bank in from
the west. The few stars uncovered by the shifts of wind weep
their poor light upon him and several times he slips and stifles
a cry, shoulders crashing into walls he cannot see. Every moment
he feels a grain of sand drop from one glass to another, every
second lost is to an enemy gained. At last he recognises the
junction with the Via Pescheria and his hands reach out for
the corner stones, worn by time and dust into curves and
gargoyles. A grim smile creases his lips. His feet skid as he
wheels the turn and at last is at the back door of the palazzo.

Three times he thumps hard upon the door. The sound
must be heard throughout all Lucca, or so it seems. But all
are asleep and only a cat scowls through the night air, the
early frost beginning to trace its ownership on its dismal
tongue, which is soon quiet. The door is opened. The man
is panting, can hardly say his name but is admitted.

'They are waiting,' says the servant, and takes the man's wet cape, thrusts a goblet of warm wine at him, lets him catch his breath before showing him to the stairs. 'Pray God the news you give them is good.'

It is 1247 and Lucca is proud and rich, but the strong defensive walls that mark its name today are yet to be built. It is vulnerable and the Inner Circle of the Lucchese Council knows it. The Florentines are jealous, the Ghibellines are at its doors. There are many who wish to adopt the city's wealth for their own.

Fortified but still breathing fast, the man finishes the wine and forces himself to take the stairs one by one. He is nervous. He never wanted to be a spy but he knows the money and the prize are good. Knows also that the news he brings is bad, and is afraid to tell what he knows. He reaches the palazzo's great chamber and knocks stoutly on the door. Now is the time to prove his worth. Now is the time to be accepted, to make the months of treachery earn its own. It hadn't sat easy with him, pretending to be what he was not, pretending to be ready to sell the secrets of Lucca to the highest bidder, be they Ghibelline or Florentine or someone else. He had listened to the fantasies and far-fetched plots of bitter and greedy men who lived on the edges of Lucca, who believed less in Lucca than they did in their souls. But this last thing he had heard, picked up with his ear straining through the noise and dirt and smoke of a tavern outside the city walls, this last design had been one that was no fantasy and was already on the move. And so he had run through the streets at midnight to deliver his news, given his password at the gate, sped through wind and rain to tell what he knew, and hoped it would earn him a reprieve from that life that was only half a life.

'Come.'

He is summoned and he opens up the door. The room beyond is warm, girded with rich tapestry, the fire blazes despite the hour being late. Before him sit the Inner Circle members. The five great families of the Lucchese Republic are seated before him at a great oak table. He knows his grandfather made that table, but he never thought to see it surrounded by these men in their fine brocades and gowns, and the pride of his ancestry stirs him with fire. They are silent, these men, seated around his grandfather's table. They were talking when he hit the door like thunder, but now they are silent, waiting for him and for what he has to say. He glories in the moment, no longer afraid; he knows pride in his mission and his message. He is partaking of the history of his birthplace and his nation. He knows this is the moment that will earn him his mark.

He crosses the room slowly, lightly, tries to keep his muddy footprints from the floor. The candles in their sconces flicker as he makes his way across the chamber. He nears. He drops to one knee and bows his head.

'It is true. The rumours we have heard are true, and this last one is unlike the others. This last is meant to be carried out,' says he, but does not raise his head. 'If we must act, we must do it now or we will be done for by our enemies.'

His name is Sandro Santorelli and he means to marry well. To the daughter of one of the men sitting here, which is why he has done what he has done, despite the risk. And although he does not know it, his name will ring through generations because of what is to be decided here and now, and because of what he has done and what he will be asked to do. His name will reverberate through the years until ended on the cold flagstones of the chapel of St Clare, a thousand miles and half a millennium from here.

He does not know that many centuries later, the Council of Lucca will meet again in this same place because of what he has done. They will wait once again for their messenger to bring the news that they dread. It will not be a Santorelli at the door. It will be Aribert Ugonello, a man who might have been born a soldier to save a little time. As it was, he was five years old before he could nock an arrow into the bow and seven when he started struggling with the soap-stone, learning how to sharpen his father's sword. At thir-teen he would follow his father into the guard house and pledge his life and honour to Lucca, enlist as a soldier to its service. He would sweep barracks, polish boots, strip down pistols and apply the oil they needed, mix gunpowder, make cartridges and bullets. By sixteen he will skirmish with the Lucchese Guards, protecting the boundaries of their land. For twenty-seven years he will serve his homeland and earn the right to stand where Santorelli once stood so long ago. Beyond the door of the Palazzo Pretoria in the Via Pescheria, the Inner Circle of the Council of Lucca will sit and wait.

Sandro and Aribert are not so different: both had been honed in the service of their homeland and lived their lives in the honour that their service gave. They were hooks spaced out on a fishing line strung between the banks of a river, holding between them five hundred and fifty-eight years of the history of Lucca. Sandro's grandfather's table still stood where it had stood before. The Council members' ancestors were long gone, as was Sandro Santorelli, but the duty that was laid before them was still the same. This time the man they had chosen was Aribert Ugonello, and the fate of Lucca was his alone to protect.

'Stand.' It is Alberto Mansegna, and he has pushed a chair back from the table, motioned Santorelli to sit. 'You cannot tell us what we have not already guessed.'

Santorelli raises his head, sees every countenance upon him. His bad knee cracks as he stands and walks the two yards to where he has been motioned. A glass is put on the table before him, on his grandfather's table. Its rim is gilded; the chair he sits on is upholstered in crimson and gold. He wonders he has ever got so far. He wonders what more they can want of him, what other demands they might have. For an awful moment he imagines they will throw him on the fire and burn their secrets with him. But they are old men, and the moment passes. He knows they are dependent on him – on Sandro Santorelli. And that whatever is about to happen will change his whole life.

It is two minutes past three in the early morning when Santorelli leaves the Palazzo Pretoria. He crosses to the Via Beccheria, past the churches of San Giusto and San Giovanni. The night seems darker than before, quieter. The rain raises a gentle song against the stones and tiles, falls in rhythm with his fleeting feet, and then drizzles to a stop. His breath is pale in the black air and he wonders again at the uncommon cold, feels akin with the Council that it has come as a sign. There have always been many things he has wished to know, has always wondered at the workings of the Council, wanted to take them apart, the cog from the wheel, to see what would happen. But tonight, he knows what would happen. Take away the heart of Lucca and the city-state would surely fall. When he sought the hand of Petronella, when he asked her father, pleaded with him, swore he would do whatever he could do, he had surely not foreseen this.

'Go into the abode of our enemies and seek out their wiles. Find out what they plan against us. Then you may seek us out. Then we may give you what you desire.' Such was his ache to rise from his station, to take Petronella into his home, that he had no need to think.

'I will go.' That was all he had said and the plan, already made, was laid before him. They had known all along that he would go, had picked their man many months before. It all seemed so absurdly simple and for a while he had mistrusted them, had thought himself duped as a fool. But then he had discovered what they so desperately wanted to know. He had endured many nights drinking in many taverns with many men whose company he couldn't stand, but he had unearthed their plans, and now he would reap his reward. In truth, he did not think much of duty or of loyalty at the start, but over the long months of his exile he had come to see Lucca with foreign eyes and recognise its greatness, seen how it was the flower of the Tuscan plains and witnessed the jealousy that grew against it. He had forgotten Petronella and been seized by a righteousness that his homeland would not be pillaged and overtaken by the pigs who snuffled around it as about a midden. He would not allow the most precious parts of Lucca to be stolen away and used against those who had protected them for so many years. He knew that was the plan of Lucca's enemies. He knew that plan was meticulous and advanced. He knew that, with the Council, he would not allow it to reach fruition. He would do whatever the Council asked to prevent that happening.

Such were his thoughts as he left the palazzo that night and crept through the deserted streets. At last he knew what it was to be alive. He understood that the wheel would only continue to turn if he could push it on.

He comes to the Piazza Antelminelli, painted in white marble by the moon. For a few moments Sandro Santorelli stands and holds his breath, looks about him, makes sure he is not seen. Emboldened, he takes a few quick strides across the square and is soon in the dark safety of shadow. San Martino's shadow. The façade is a cliff before him, hiding its features in darkness and stone. He traces his hand down the cathedral wall as he swiftly runs its length. He clutches the keys which hang on a thong around his neck.

He finds the small door that leads to the bell tower. Rather than take the thong from his neck, he crouches down to insert the larger key. The smaller one he does not want to be parted from for even a moment. He will obey to the last Mansegna's exhortation to keep it always with him.

The door swings inward, taking Santorelli with it as he hugs the wood. The inside of the tower is darker than a stormy night, and the ancient beams creak and breath in their old age. The bones of the cathedral have rested here since the sixth century and although the most part of her bulk are recent prosthetics, here in the bell tower is the ancient and original rib from which the rest has grown.

Santorelli moves with care through the winding corridor, counts off the doors as he passes them with his fingertips. His heart is an animal rattling in its cage, spurred on by the secrecy and excitement of his fear. He opens the last door, as he had been told, and finds himself behind the altar, staring up at the great pillared roof as if he were in the hold of a ship. The moon is playing patterns through the glass and throwing shards of light on to the floor and seats, and etching weird patterns on the walls. Sandro braces himself a moment and genuflects, makes the sign of the cross, says a quick prayer. He has the blessing of the Council, but not the permission of the Church, and though he does what he does for his homeland, it does not make the violation any less.

He moves down the choir aisle, past the bishop's seat and down the altar steps. He takes a few paces into the east transept and there it is, right before his eyes. The statue of the Volto Santo has been taken down and laid against a heap of satin cushions, ready for the morrow. For it is the thirteenth of September and once a year the Volto Santo is taken down from its height and laid out for all to see and touch, and then, when dusk begins to fall, it is processed by torchlight through all the town, blessing every citizen within the city walls. And in this, its immediate presence, Sandro has never felt so blessed.

He crosses himself, reaches out his hand but does not dare touch the recumbent figure who truly does seem asleep. Many times he has seen it, but tonight there is an intimacy that almost makes him sob. He is alone with the fortune of Lucca and entrusted with its safekeeping, and the responsibility is almost too much to bear. The gilded collar and crown have been dimmed by moonlight and the gilt of the skirt is softened and seems to billow below his hand, the wooden chest to rise and fall beneath its pectoral. Sandro breathes deeply, crosses himself once more, then places his hands on the Holy Body and raises it gently from its bed.

Sandro Santorelli takes the thong from his neck. This time he has no choice but to remove it to see what he is doing. The small brass key has a halo in the thin light and seems to shine from within. Sandro knows this is nonsense, but all the same he sees his hand shake lightly as he slips the key into its lock. The back of the Volto Santo hides a box and as the key is turned the mechanism releases a spring and the panel slowly leaves its base, gives enough space for Sandro to insert a finger and lift the back fully open. The cavity is dark, yet he can just discern the glimmer of line and shape.

A strange odour reaches his nose: it is musky, like ambergris or civet, even a little of Hungary water, which is stilled from the leaves of rosemary. For a moment it enchants him and a pure contentment threatens to immobilise him, but his knee begins to protest its contact with the cold stone and he opens his eyes, unaware that he had closed them. He takes a pouch from his pocket and pulls open the neck. He dips his hand into the back of the Holy Body and grallochs it of its contents. The precious items are hot against his fingertips and he thinks he should have worn gloves – is suddenly stricken by the fear that he is touching these most sacred relics with his bare skin.

They are each wrapped separately in different coloured silks. He guesses the larger green bundle hides the part of the Crown of Thorns, the smallest brown one, the nail. The soft purple package he takes to be the sudarium that Christ wore around His neck on the way to Golgotha, which lay against His skin and veins and drank the sweat up from His Body. The smaller blue one he assumes to be the clippings of nail and hair taken by the Virgin Mary and tied in a corner of her veil. And there is the scarlet silk, which can house only the precious vial, and in that vial is the most holy thing the earth can offer heaven: actual drops of the Saviour's Blood.

Sandro Santorelli transfers each to the pouch and tightens the string. He places within the Holy Body a single scrap of white silk. On this is the outline of the labyrinth that will be the sole reminder of how to reach the history of this removal, the document that will tell the tale of how Sandro Santorelli saved the holy relics before they were stolen from Lucca and sold to the King of France or whoever would pay the highest fee. He feels nothing but contempt for those who would steal the heart of Lucca, carve it out from the Holy Body and cut Lucca off from her prosperity. Without the relics given by God, there would be no blessing upon their land, there would come drought and flood and their precious crops, their olives and mulberries, would be destroyed. Without the constant influx of pilgrims there would be no income to maintain the defences that had kept them safe for all these two hundred years. Without the gift God had expressly given them, Lucca would return to being just another town with too many churches, and the wolves would come down from the hills and take the town into their dominion. The Volto Santo was the Body of Christ, the relics the entrails within. It was their protector and their prosperity. If they could not protect the Protector, what then? It would mean the end of trust, the end of the blessing of God which had smiled on Lucca for so long.

Santorelli closed the wound he had opened in the Volto Santo's body. He rubbed the break with wax and dirt to disguise his entry, laid the ancient wooden flesh gently back upon its crib. He placed the thong around his neck, hiding it below his shirt, and grasped the pouch, laced its strings tight around his wrist. He retraced the steps of his desecration till he reached again the altar; here he stopped on the first step and genuflected twice, repeated his pleas for understanding, his need for absolution. He glanced behind him before he left by the door behind the altar, saw the glitter of the Holy Body, the closed eyes, the tired face, the smooth surface of the cheeks, which bore the shine of two hundred years of Lucchese lips and the breath of two centuries of whispered supplications. The moonlight fractured his vision into a soft mosaic, then turned its face from him, wound the cathedral in a sheet of darkness. His skin tingled with sudden fear and he turned and fled, running softly down the passageway and easing open the final door, sliding the key into its lock to hold it shut and quiet.

As he leant forward he twined a wisp of hair with the key as he snapped the locking mechanism home. He pulled sharply away, left his hair lodged in the metalwork, lifting in the slight but rising breeze. He pulled his hood hard over his head and rounded the base of the cathedral, then ran briskly up a side street. The rain beginning to break from the sombre moon-ringed clouds, tiny droplets of water pittering down on him as, with a sigh, the wind began to raise itself and run alongside him through the empty streets.

Santorelli wound his way through ginnel and snicket and got himself to Via del Fosso. This was where the men from the Hospitallers Order were lodged by decree of the Council. For two weeks they had been lavishly entertained, given private mass, shown around the orchards and silk mills, fêted and feasted by the best families the city had to offer. It had been a long journey for them and they deserved this rest; they had gone from Acre to Jaffa, sailed from Cyprus to Crete, called at Malta and at Sicily and of course, at Rome. From there they had gone the pilgrimage way through Italy to visit their various shrines, eventually to land in Lucca. It took little to persuade them to prolong their stay a while, to ease themselves and take solace, both spiritual and otherwise. The Council insisted they stay until the city's Holiest of Days, when they would be honoured to lead the procession of the Volto Santo through the streets of Lucca, a task for which many, the world over, would have wept with the honour of it.

These hard men from Acre and Jerusalem told tales of battles against the wicked heathen; they exhibited with pride the awful sickle-shaped scars which had sliced their arms in two, dislocated knees and elbows, severed half their scalps from off their heads. Their dark brown skin boasted years of sun and sand and ferocious fighting in baking deserts; their tonsured skulls attested to the silent endeavours of their still strong faith. People came from all the outlying citadels to hear their stories, to kiss the hands of men who had trod and fought for the land of Christ. Boys who knew nothing but how to squeeze an olive for oil or knock oranges out of trees queued up to take their vows and return the way the Hospitallers and soldiers had come, to go and fight the Holy Wars in far off lands.

The older men had seen all this show before, knew an enlistment rally when they saw it, tried to warn their sons and tell them not to go and throw their lives away in foreign lands. Santorelli sat amongst the old men in the taverns, saw the fervour in young lads' eyes, and grieved for their innocence. They set off in droves from Tuscany to join the lost Crusades, seeking blood and adventure, tagging to the backs of the others who had set off before them all the way the Hospitallers had trod. Women sewed red crosses for their backs and watched their sons and husbands march off with shouts and songs under banners that were too soon stowed and packed once the minuscule army was underway to join the other foot soldiers tramping their way to Jerusalem, claiming victory or death. Their timing was wrong; their leaders were weak; victory had gone before they even arrived. But still those men marched on.

Santorelli was not one of them, though he was fired by similar fervour. He was enthralled by the old Crusaders' stories, but knew his mission was much deeper. He tied the pouch around his waist, wore it in an old leather purse against his skin. He proceeded with the entourage as they left Lucca. He crossed the Alps and went through France with them, to the port of Calais and into London, sailing down the Thames as if he were a king.

16

In the Arms of St Anthony

As Mabel and Stroop crossed the deserted square, the noise of their pony's hooves echoing amongst the pillars of the Innocent Martyrs, they felt tired but content. They had worked through all the information they had at hand and at last had a sort of plan, minimal though it was. It remained now to get Mabel safely home and lay the whole plot before Great-Aunt Flora. From there, they felt sure, they would find a way ahead. It was a good feeling, which made its fleeting nature all the worse.

Stroop got down from the trap and led the pony through the ginnel into the yard behind Great-Aunt Flora's house. He glanced at the windows, five of which were lit, and wondered how Thomas and Jack had been received. Badly, he thought. From what he knew of great-aunts, though he had none of his own – had no family of his own – he was fairly well aware that two ragamuffin boys riding sweaty steeds would most likely not be in great favour, and probably not lightly be let into the yard, let alone the house. Still, he saw no sign of them, and noted that the stable doors were closed. With any luck, they had got the stable boy to take the letter into the house and the great-aunt had let them into the kitchen.

Mabel was still sitting on the trap, didn't want to wake the old dog from its sleep, didn't want to face what she must have known would be next.

'Hold still,' said Stroop. 'I'll see who's about,' and Mabel nodded, stayed sitting in the trap, now divested of the pony, who mooched at the hay that was hanging in a net on the stable yard wall, slurped at the water straight from the trough by the pump.

Everything was very quiet, and Stroop wondered why nobody had come to see what they were about. Maybe the stable boy had gone home for the night, or down the road for a few jars. Either way, the pony was content to stand, and Mabel content to sit, and the dog still slept.

The yard was lit by a lamp sputtering above the kitchen door. Stroop crossed and knocked. There was no answer. He knocked again, wondered how the other half lived. Knew he couldn't live that way himself. He liked to answer the door himself and see what he was facing. Or he had done until he acquired Jack. Now that was Jack's job, to open the door, and it was more than Stroop's life was worth to take such a job away from Jack.

There wasn't any answer so he lifted the latch and pushed at the door. But Stroop could not move. Of a sudden, he knew what was in there, and it was somewhere he knew he didn't want to go.

Mabel was sitting in her cart, draped with dog and feeling warm and safe. She knew she was in the yard of Great-Aunt

Flora's house yet had the feeling that the whole world had slowed and was ceasing to spin, that time hung like a chain, suspended between two points. She saw the pony drinking from the trough but heard no sound. She saw Stroop standing by the scullery door, his hand resting on the latch, the door only opened by an inch. It seemed that she was all alone in Bexleyheath, that she was the fulcrum of the world and all reality was falling away from her and that soon, the whole of London would disappear and then the church and the square and the house and the stables and all that would be left would be Mabel, and then there would be no air to breath nor light to see nor things to feel or touch, and she too would cease, and that at last and at its right time, everything would be at an end.

Stroop had pushed open the scullery door and taken a step inside. Mabel watched him absently, felt herself removed, but gently rolled the old Bindlestiff from off her knees. She made him comfortable on the few sacks in the back of the cart. Slowly she sat on the wooden edge, then swung herself to the ground. She said nothing, hardly breathed, walked across the yard and put her hand on the stable door. A dark stain ran the length of its foot, the culms of protruding straw looking limp and black. She pushed against the door, but found it would not open. She sighed deeply, put her shoulder against the wood and shoved; remembered doing just this to a cow who baulked at the milking pen, her nose next to the stink of its tail, her face scratched by the warm bristle of hairs on her flank. Then she remembered that this wasn't the way it should go, heard the faint querulous carping of the hinges. She removed her shoulder, took a step back and pulled at the door.

It opened in a sudden sweep, nearly taking her off her feet. The momentum was too great but Mabel didn't even think to wonder why. She saw Edward's arm roll out towards her and his head crack against the stone. The black gape of his neck grinned up at her, deep and dark and evil. His face was hidden by mud and spoiled straw, and she was glad for that. She didn't move him, just propped the door with a stone to stop it banging back against his broken head and stepped over the body, which she knew would never have call to rise again.

It was so dark inside that she had to stand and wait, her eyes flicking around black corners and walls, trying to make out pinpoints of light where the brass of the tack glittered as it hung from the wall, the pale lips of metal buckets, the straight backs of rakes and shovels. There was a movement so sudden and loud that Mabel swayed at the interruption. A horse whinnied and snubbed its nose against the side of its stall. A shiver of life began to stir in Mabel's body and she took a quick step forward, felt for the shelf to the right of the door and found the stub of candle and the flint. It took several goes to get her cold fingers to strike a spark but at last the candle was lit and its glow suffused the dim interior. Mabel held it in front of her, slightly above her head, trying to pour as much warmth and light as she could into the gloom. She saw a recumbent outline, took it to be a sleeping horse, even saw four legs. Then it occurred to her that it was all the wrong shape and that, anyhow, horses didn't wear boots and trousers. She recognised the dip of the head where it seemed to slumber in the night. She knew the torn jacket and the discarded cap. It was all familiar and yet somehow wrong, but Mabel was quite numb. She had felt too much and now felt nothing, as if she were buried in snow.

'Thomas?' she called quietly, but no voice came from her to break through the air. She tried again, and this time the name of Thomas whispered across the stable and stirred the small body lying in the heap of straw.

'Thomas?' Mabel called again, louder this time, setting the candle flickering horribly as she took a step across the littered and sticky floor. She heard a sob and took another step, knelt down, put out a hand. She felt a body lying low on its back, stretched out upon the straw. Another smaller one was lying across it and there was something else. Something tall, angled, unbending. She ignored it for the moment, could not think what it could be. Instead she gently laid a hand on the boy's shoulder, for surely she saw it was Thomas who was slumped across the other body, which she assumed must be Jack.

'Thomas.' She kept her hand steady on his shoulder, felt a faint movement as of water pulling up and sand seeping gently away. She shook him very slightly, put the candle down and reached her other arm over and lifted him slowly by his shoulders. Suddenly, fiercely, he dragged one arm away and slammed the crook of elbow against his face, hiding his eyes and nose, leaving only his mouth gasping.

'Just leave me alone!' If he had been a dog it would have been a whimper but one on the edge of a bark.

'It's me, Thomas, it's Mabel.'

The light had shifted because of where she had laid the candle, and the slight breeze from Thomas's sudden movement caused the shadows to shift. Mabel saw now what was wrong about the picture; she saw with clarity the shaft of the pitchfork stretching above them, quivering very slightly as if it were an eel on a vertical rack. Mabel at once assessed the situation and found no time to be repulsed or fearful, felt no prick of tears.

'Thomas, move away. You must move away. Let me see if I can help him.'

It was the tone of Mabel's voice rather than the words. The curtness caught him like a slap across the face and Thomas put down his arm and stared at her. His face was swollen red where he had wept and had a violent bruise butting like a blown egg under one cheek. But he moved. He rolled his body to one side and sat behind the candle as if shielding it from the wind, although there was none.

Mabel knelt forward, placed her ear against Jack's chest and her finger at his wrist. The boy still breathed. The third and fourth tines of the fork had stuck him through the neck and stabbed him to the packed mud of the stable floor. As she listened, Mabel could hear his chest creak with every shallow breath, an oar drawn through the water, rusty on its rowlocks.

'Can you hear me, Jack?' She almost breathed the words into his ear. Thomas was rocking slightly. The small flame flickered with his movement, ran up and down Jack's pale face, water on a beach.

Mabel saw his lips twitch and she lowered her head, brushed back her hair. Jack croaked. No words could be made out but Mabel imagined he had said Stroop's name, not once, but twice, in slow and deliberate succession. She glanced up at Thomas and nodded to one of the horse-pails.

'Go and get some water. Can you manage that? Can you go and get some water? And get those old sacks from the back of the cart. Don't mind the dog.'

Thomas looked yellow as the moon but he got to his feet, picked up a pail and, without a word, stepped over Edward's cooling body and out into the yard. Mabel was busy packing straw around Jack when Thomas returned. He put the pail down at the door and took a deliberate hold of Edward's feet, dragged him to one side and bumped him unpityingly into the dark of the corner. He brought the pail over to Mabel, then returned with the blanket. He went back out one more time and returned with old Bindlestiff.

'He can keep him warm.' It was the first time Thomas had spoken properly and his voice was water-weak and cracked with strain.

Mabel smiled. 'That he will,' she said, and called the dog over, snuffling at his muzzle with her hand, got him to lie down next to Jack. The old dog lifted his head and lolloped it over Jack's stomach, gazed at Mabel for a moment, but closed his rheumy eyes as soon as Mabel pulled the sacking over boy and dog, and went to sleep. Mabel rocked back on her heels and looked over the candle at Thomas. She saw but half of his face, whey-wan and cold as cheese.

'We'd better find Mr Stroop,' she said, feeling stronger now she had done something practical. She hadn't done much, couldn't do much, but Jack seemed more comfortable. He could breath, which meant the fork hadn't gone through his windpipe; he wasn't bleeding much, so it had missed all the big veins; he'd managed to swallow some water, so she hoped things couldn't be too bad. They needed help and light to

143

do more, but it wasn't the time. She didn't dare pull the fork free of his neck just yet: it could be pulling the cork from out the bottle. She'd get Stroop to look at him first. Stroop would know what to do. He always did.

'Are you ready?' said Mabel to Thomas as she stood up to leave. 'You can stay here if you like, keep Jack company, but I've got to find Mr Stroop.'

'I'll come with you,' said Thomas, his voice stronger than he felt.

'Right then,' said Mabel, and went to the open door with Thomas following behind.

They stood for a moment looking across the yard, then Mabel took Thomas by the hand and they set off to where the light flickered above the scullery door. They both knew what they would find as they advanced towards the old house, but they were already too full of feeling, and had no room for more.

17

Cats Have Claws

THE CLOCK ON the table was in the shape of a cathedral, with a façade made entirely of Murano glass. Castracani, sitting back in someone else's chair, in someone else's house, hands laced on his lap, was focused on the curious cathedral. Its body was made of smoked blue glass, the spires attenuated to green, the bell tower housing a white-enamelled face with hands of gold tipped with ivory. He considered the result a monstrosity but marvelled at its creation. He thought of the glass-makers at Murano, exiled so the poisonous fumes could not harm the general populace, so they arrived there as apprentices, became journeymen there, brought their wives there, had their children there, and rarely ventured anywhere else.

He knew a little of what they felt. He was born here in London, as was his father and his grandfather, and his grandfather's grandfather before him. He might have been called Baker, or Glover, or Johnson or White. But his name was Castracani and he was Lucchese. He felt it in his bones, he saw it in his face, he knews it when he walked the streets and heard people bartering in the shops, or chatting on street corners, or drinking grappe in the bars. All spoke the Italian he wore like a second skin. Whenever he had call to visit the city, or go to neighbouring settlements along the Thames, he found himself in a foreign land, and longed to be back home. It was rare he left his Italian Silk Quarter, and sought not to do so unless he must. He knew though that the time had come and there were journeys he must make. He needed to think and plan, but first he stared intently at the clock.

The hand had almost reached the hour, and if it were day, a white dove would have flown out from one spire to the other as the chime began to call. As it was night, it would be a small dark owl that flew the route. But there would be something else, he knew, and waited. Each time the hour struck, a different figure emerged from the cloisters or the porch or popped up on the roof. It might be a clergyman, or an artisan, or a curious visitor. There was a dog, which sniffed the steps, a mouse, which scurried behind a pillar, a bat, which circled the bell tower.

He waited and watched but just as the ivory finger reached seven, the door opened and a man entered and called out his name. Involuntarily Castracani turned his head and did not see the small boy run from the sacristy door holding a candlestick under his jacket, watching the watcher before disappearing mysteriously into a hidden hatch.

'There is a message for you, sir.' It was Marco, Bandorello's manservant. He approached Castracani and held out the tray with its small folded square of paper.

Taking it, Castracani glanced back at the cathedral clock, which was still chiming. 'Thank you, Marco.' He was vaguely disappointed to have missed the show, just managing to catch the spire door as it closed on the transient owl, but seeing no other sign of movement.

'Can I get you anything else, sir?' asked Marco solicitously. He watched for an answer from this man, where he sat in his red plush chair looking singularly alone, his hair singed back to his scalp, his eyebrows pale and burnt, his skin still impregnated with smoke tattoos. Even the clothes he wore were not his own and yet, like everyone else in the quarter, Marco knew that this crisp of a man, this saddened stranger, was now the effective Head of the Council, and without the Council, the London Lucchese would be just another influx of immigrants to be absorbed into the stinking city streets, gone in a couple of generations, and forgotten.

Castracani asked for coffee with cinnamon and Marco left, bowing deeply, though Castracani never saw. He was already twitching at the paper in his hands and read the words he did not want to read. So, there was still no word of Aldo Santorelli, whom nobody seemed to have seen this past week. That couldn't be good, and it couldn't be unconnected with their present troubles. His hand thumped gently at the arm rest as he screwed the paper into a tiny ball, then flattened it out again and reread it, just to make sure. His eyes had not been so good since the fire; there was a tendency for them suddenly to blur, and occasionally the tears would flow unbidden. He rubbed them briefly with finger and thumb, which he then left there, his head bent, resting on his hand. He had to think clearly. There were things he must do.

First and foremost he needed to find the girl, but without Aldo, that was going to prove difficult. The only other people who knew her whereabouts were dead or dying – the reports from the hospital had made that clear – and all the Council archives had gone up in smoke. He needed to find Aldo Santorelli, or find out whom Aldo had chosen as his successor to the Guardianship. If he knew he was in danger, maybe he had passed on the girl's name and where she lived. Maybe Aldo had already trained up his successor and the successor already knew all. But if that were the case, why hadn't he come forward? Surely he must be aware of what was going on in the Silk Quarter? Or perhaps he was away – maybe even in Lucca. Many people travelled constantly from London to Lucca, or Lucca to London and back again. He needed to find out this information. First thing tomorrow he would go to Santorelli's house and search it from cellar to loft.

And yet there was something, something tapping away at the back of his head. He knew something – he knew he knew something, but it wouldn't quite come to the fore. It was a like a cat extending and retracting its claws, now here, now gone, but never quite letting go.

He removed his fingers, lifted his head, rotated it slowly on his neck. He was still sore, inside and out, and what he needed most of all was rest. He would think things through in the morning. He would get Marco to raise him at dawn when his mind was at its clearest. Until then, he tried to push everything out of his head. He knew those nagging thoughts – if you nibbled at them they just retreated; if you let them go, they worked themselves out on their own. The answer would come of its own accord – maybe when he was splashing his face with water in the morning, maybe at the barber's when Giorgio was giving him his shave and singing some aria in his terrible tenor, maybe when he was getting dressed, or walking down the street. It would come, he knew. But for now, he would drink his coffee and sit a little longer, watch the cathedral clock and wait to be surprised by the coming of the hour.

It is time, he thought, that is catching up with us. Five hundred and fifty years have passed and taken our memories with them. If only I could lift the lid off that cathedral clock and see down the centuries, walk down the corridors through thirty generations and ask them to tell us what they know. If only Aldo Santorelli would come knocking on my door and tell me everything, we would save so much time and maybe someone else's life.

And then the cat dug in its claws and he suddenly remembered what had been scratching away in his mind. It was something that he had read in the broadsheet several days ago, maybe a week – it seemed longer since so much had happened. But whenever it was, he recalled the gist of it now: the report of a man who had gone into a church and slit his throat. There had been something about the description of the suicide, something about the church itself that urgently screamed out at him. He sat suddenly upright in his chair, his skin feeling tight and cold, his vision swimming slightly.

'Marco!' he cried out, but the word caught in his throat and anyway he had told the man to leave him for the night. He stood up so quickly he felt dizzy and had to stand a second before striding to the door. Wrenching it open, he started down the hallway, heading for the stairs.

'Marco!' he called again, louder this time. 'Marco! Come here! I have need of you!'

Marco, who had been in the process of putting on his hat and cloak and heading off to play dominoes at the chocolate club, came hurrying back up the stairs. He found Castracani in his master's study scribbling furiously on a piece of paper. Marco didn't even have time to open his mouth before Castracani thrust the paper at him.

'Marco, you must carry me a message. It is of the utmost importance. For all of us. For Lucca.'

Marco was too startled to reply, but he took the envelope, glancing at the instructions. He was to go directly to Luigi Golgafoni, the printer on the corner of Caldera Street. If he was not there working, Marco was to proceed directly to Golgafoni's home and demand entrance in the name of the Council. He must elicit the information Castracani needed as speedily as possible or, failing that, drag Golgafoni bodily to him here. Marco was not to stop or dally. Castracani must have the information within the hour.

This done, and the efficient Marco already running panting down the street, Castracani returned to the living room and resumed his chair. His gaze turned once again to the cathedral clock and he waited impatiently for the owl and the information the hour would bring.

18

Between Times, Between Tides

STROOP SHUT THE scullery door and put his back against it. He'd closed his eyes before he had even entered the room. He envisioned another tableau before him that he did not want to see again. He heard nothing. He saw nothing. He put his hands across his stomach and breathed deeply, once, twice. His face took on an expression of frowning calm, every muscle tensed so it would not have to react, and then he opened his eyes. He blinked once, twice, and then he forced himself to survey the room before him.

He saw the range, he saw the table swept clean. There was nothing there but kettles and pans hanging from their hooks, cupboards politely closed, cleaning cloths neatly pegged from a string that hung across the range, a line of scrubbing brushes in descending size on a small shelf above the large white square of the sink. His body relaxed and he levered his back away from the door as he moved quietly around the bare table. There was nothing here. No murdered cooks or milkmaids nor even strangled cats. He hadn't known what to expect, but this perfect quiet was certainly not it. It was so still he could even hear the herbs drying in bunches above the range. He held his hand over the kettle hob. It was vaguely warm but wouldn't be boiling water any time soon.

He moved his eyes across the floor and hit on the door to the pantry. Slowly he stepped across the flagstones, missing the cracks, as he had always done, and put his hand on the latch. He closed his eyes then swung the door open, held his breath, pinched his nose closed. But there was nothing. Darkness. The shapes of hams and cheeses lying quietly on their shelves. Bottles of honey vinegar, rosemary oil, peach preserves, cubes of cheese in walnut oil, marmalades, jellies, jams, a pail of milk. A pail of milk that had soured. The smell reached him faintly as he saw the yellow scum that had risen to the surface, the cream unskimmed, the whey unseparated, the milk unjugged, but no dead bodies, thank God.

He walked back into the scullery and looked again. His eyes swept the floor and the ceiling and the furniture. Nothing had been touched. There was nothing out of place. Until the light of his lantern caught the bronze lips of the service bells, which hung in strata above the almanac hanging from a hook on the blank of the eastern wall.

'December: Year of Our Lord 1805: for England we see a time of peace and for our continental cousins, a time to reflect.'

Below this stark headline, the almanac rambled on with its details, giving gardening tips and recipes and ignoring the world outside itself. Above it, the bell names stood out unsullied, black against the yellow of their labels, which were peeling slightly away from the wall: Parlour, Dining Room, Living Room, B1,2,3,4,5 – which he took to be bedrooms – N for a nursery not used for many a year, WC for the water closet newly installed with a bath and facilities for the ladies who did not prefer the old ways. He himself favoured the earth closet, and it was one of Jack's perks to sell the contents to the vegetable grower at the end of the street. Stroop had only a small garden, which had been left alone of late. He had allowed the parsley to seed and thyme to flower, and failed to stop the fennel smothering the sage, the lovage shadowing the rosemary.

He looked at the glint of the light upon the bells and was reminded of when he had been a boy and first dragged off to church. He had never understood the need for God, could not understand how a man could be both a body and a soul, could not comprehend how two things, so inimical, could be even momentarily adjoined. Didn't the eternality of the one strike out the ephemerality of the other? A rag-and-bone body lasted sixty years if it was lucky, maybe even a little more, but a soul was eternal. How could something not of body be bound to body and for so short a time? For if the soul was infinite, then the life of a man was less than a second, less than a moment, of less substance than the breath that he had hardly thought to take.

But then Stroop stopped his mind from wandering, and realised why he had veered off. He did not want to see what he now saw. He did not want to know that the bells lay slackened in their collars. He did not want to recognise that their wires had all been cut. But despite himself he understood in a moment what that meant, and whether or not he believed in God or souls or something else entirely, he felt his throat constrict and watched his hand move across his body in the sign of the cross. For a second he held the hand where it rested on his sternum, then, cursing what he feared he'd find, he put his hand on the door that took him up from the scullery and into the cold body of Great-Aunt Flora's house.

Oh! How sudden we all die, thought Jack, as he lay on the stable floor with the pitchfork through his neck. He was awake and he stared into the darkened eaves where he could see an owl had made its nest. The dust kept falling on him and he imagined there were lots of little owls in there kicking up their heels because they hadn't been fed. He tried to smile. He grieved for them that their parents were late, that the rumpus might have scared them off with their offerings of dead mice or voles or the little creatures he knew lay under every blade of grass and clump of dock when the sunshine fled. Jack watched the motes as they spiralled in the candlelight, saw the moths begin to find their way through the open door. He tried to remember how he had come to be here, but nothing came. He tried lifting his hands and feet but could no longer feel them; he thought he saw them going up and down but no longer felt they belonged to him. Nothing much had ever belonged to Jack, not until that night Stroop had rescued him. He knew he wasn't a clever boy, knew he wasn't one who would go far. His mother had always told him that.

'You'll never go far like your father,' she'd crooned, 'thank God, though he was a pioneer, the very first boat bound for Australia, and God knows there's been plenty more since. Make sure, my son, that you never go that far.'

And he hadn't. He'd stayed with his mother for as long as long could be. He'd slept in alleys and drains and in cellars and under haystacks. He'd picked hops and pears and cabbages and peas, but never stolen, just like his mum had taught him. He'd always wondered how he would end up, and although lying on a hard floor with a pitchfork through his neck was not ideal, he somehow had a happiness about him. There was a warmth spreading over his body, a conviction that he was no longer alone. He'd liked that the girl had found him and looked after him like his old mum might have done. He'd liked that Stroop had treated him well these past years, that he'd met Thomas and that the boy hadn't wanted to leave him alone.

'Don't go, Jack! I'll be back in a moment,' he'd said, and the nice girl had stroked his cheek. It was odd, thought Jack, that here he was, all seventeen years of him, laid out in the dark, dithers of dust falling about his face, and no longer could he move, but he hadn't really been happier in all his short life.

Oh well, thought Jack, everything's for the best, as Mum used to say. And it did feel best, this lying here, knowing that any minute now, Stroop would come and pick him up in his two arms and rescue him all over again.

Stroop had climbed the scullery stairs and emerged on to the first-floor hallway. Ahead of him the carpet rolled lazily down a corridor broken on the right by three doors and on the left by a magnificent staircase, which curved up towards a pink-stoled landing before splitting in two to reach the upper floors. The lack of noise was alarming. At least his shoes had kept him company up the uncarpeted wood of the servant-steps, but now the richly papered walls seemed to suck all sound into their flowery depths. Pictures of girls on swings or gathering shells or having picnics clashed rather badly with the florescent walls, as did the two large bowls of silk lilies installed on their pedestals lipping at the paper with orange-tipped petals.

He began to move softly, letting the liana-lined carpet lead him on. He pushed gently at the first door, which was already ajar. It opened with an appalling screech and swung back hard on its hinges, hitting the wall with a horrible thwump, making the girls in the pictures tremble and shake. Stroop's heart bounced and he grabbed involuntarily at his throat as the reverberations ceased. No one appeared in response to the sudden disturbance, no one called out from an adjoining room. The door stayed back upon its scratchy damaged hinge and Stroop gained the doorway, braced his hand against the jamb and leaned into the room.

In front of him was a sewing table with a machine and trestle like a great iron vine beside it. There were several small piles of coloured squares and others of octagons, another of triangles. The beginnings of a quilt lay over a chair, untrimmed, spider-legs of cotton twine awry at angles, unbacked faces blank within their seams. Over to one side, under the window was a small dresser. Every drawer lay on the floor by its feet. Spools of cotton rainbowed across the floor, skeins of wool tangled and snaggled with every size of needle, some of which had lost their wooden tops, which had rolled under the table into a small silver pool of thimbles and pins. Several of the pictures on the walls had been slashed, severing a milkmaid from her churn, an industrious spinner from her loom, a mother from her child who sat with its thumb in its pink-bow mouth. Stroop hung for several minutes in the doorway, not stepping in but noting everything with its index, making mental notes, fixing the context of destruction. For certainly someone other than a seamstress had been here and not been pleased. Even the hourglass mannequin had been semi denuded of its half-finished dress, a froth of lemon lace bundled at one shoulder, leaving the other bare. The skirt with its hoops had concertinaed to the floor, the middle hoop leaning to one side, breaking the even flow, destroying the harmony of sister circles. Stroop closed his eyes and recalled the scene, stored it away, left the door open and moved on.

The dining room was directly opposite the staircase, and here the devastation was less visible. There was no broken crockery or glass, no cutlery lying like dead soldiers on the floor. Indeed the table looked as if it had just been laid. A silver centrepiece rose up unchallenged, the crystal sparkled, the candle-stumps still flickered half-heartedly in their polished sticks. The only thing that appeared to have been touched was a long dresser, which stood with its cupboards agape, stacks of table mats and serviettes pushed roughly to one side, pieces of sundry silver pulled out and examined. Some lay on their sides on the floor, but most still winked inside the dark caverns of the old cupboard.

Stroop got out his mental pencil and got to work, sketching and cataloguing, taking longer than he needed, ticking off every scratch, noting that the curtains had been closed, that the large mirror hung askew as if it had been lifted from the wall and hurriedly replaced. In truth, he was afraid to move on, though move at last he did. He could hear footsteps coming across the cobbled yard. He heard the scullery door open. He knew he did not have much time to do what needed doing. In spite of the sickness that rose up in his throat and the sweat burning on his skin, he forced himself to move quickly down the hall to the last, large room. He knew this would be the drawing room, and had a fair idea what he would find.

The door had been closed and he quickly turned the handle – but it would not move. He bent down, held his eye to the lock and saw that the key had been half turned. He thumped the lock hard with his fist, feeling the capillaries burst, hearing the slight scrunch of his finger bones. He tried the handle again – still locked. He fisted the lock twice more and this time heard the key fall from the door and hit the parquet of the floor. The handle turned and the door gave. He entered the room and, with dismay, immediately tripped and fell.

Sprawled in front of the door with one arm outstretched lay a woman, her grey hair a tangled nest, her face half upturned and horrid pale, her eyes half open, her lips quite blue. Immediately Stroop righted the lamp that he'd knocked over with his fall and which still glowed in its smoky canopy. He bent down to the old woman, lightly slapping her cheeks, placing a hand on her neck. Her skin was cold and clammy but to his surprise there was a faint, irregular pulse. He got behind her and hauled her to a chaise longue and laid her on it, propping her neck with a pillow so her head hung slightly back. He breathed hard into her mouth, once, twice, three times. Again, once, twice, three times. He knew it to work on half-drowned victims and hoped it would have an effect here.

There was the slightest sound, like a bone-creak in the morning, and he held his hand below her nose, saw his fingers shake slightly, tried to hold them still to feel for any exhalations. Again a small noise, taffeta crinkling, a leaf underfoot, and this time he saw the woman's lips twitch, felt a slight pressure on his elbow where she had leant her hand, trying to pull him down. He laid his ear over her mouth, caught a faint waft of violets, felt the tickle of powder as it lifted lightly from her skin. There were no words, only a whisper, the expiration of air. Possibly the woman had asked for help, possibly she was saying a final prayer. He thought maybe he caught Mabel's name, but he couldn't have been sure. The wind was rising outside the windows, catching on corners, whistling against the panes, slapping old wrappings and sleet against the glass, dissolving the last words of Penelope Witheridge as they dissolved like incense into the chill, dark air.

Jack was dreaming in the shed. His hand had dropped on to the sacking and over the back of Bindlestiff. He made a slight wuffle and paddled his paws, repositioning himself. Jack felt the warm body across his midriff and went back to the night he and his mother had sheltered in a barnyard filled with mothering goats. It was at one of the farms they had stayed, employed for a while hauling soft-hooved kids from unwilling wombs. Jack would be nearby with towels warmed on a small stove to rub the heat back into the newborns if they shivered too much, ready with a flask of sugared milk should the nanny be too feeble to allow feeding. His mother had once had her own flock of goats she said, back on her father's farm when she was a girl. She knew all about swinging a weak kid by its back legs to clear its nostrils of mucus; she knew how to coax a first kidder into relaxing and letting go her load. She knew all sorts of things, did

Jack's mum. She tried to teach Jack, but Jack had a brain that didn't hold very much and after a while she stopped. She never chided him, just stroked his hair and told him never mind, there's people can do one thing and others can do others, and there was something that Jack would always do better than anyone else. What that was, she never told him, and he was still trying to find it out. Perhaps it was always being glad he was alive, because Jack knew that was one thing he was good at.

He thought back down the years, all those good years when his mum was there to take care of him no matter what road they were on or where they would be or what they were doing or where they were sleeping. He'd slept under carts, in ditches, covered by branches, in inns that had more lice than a bird has feathers.

It was only that last one place, when Mum had got so tired and so sad, and they'd bought all that gin because they were too late for the last bread from the breadshop and the market had closed long time since. She'd been so tired, had talked to him about his father living so far away and hoping he was fine and doing well, and wondering if he had ever sent word for them like he'd said he would, once he was settled and served his time and had a bit of land and some proper work and maybe even a house built by his own two hands from bits of Australian brushwood. But where would he find them, his mum had mourned, the tears making her cheeks shine in the meagre candlelight. She'd put the bottle to her lips again, took a sip and grimaced, then squinted at their surroundings. 'Not here,' she had said. 'Not damned well here.'

They had settled for kipping in an old coal shed that night

because it was hidden behind a hedge at the back of someone's house and the house looked empty so they probably wouldn't be seen. It wasn't too cold, and it was fine sitting there, cosy with his mum, and she had said lots of things to him that night as they supped side by side from their bottles. She had smoked her pipe while she lay on their bundles and they had talked of walking to the ports and cadging a ship out to Australia. They would work their way across the seas and weather the storms and find his father and start again somewhere new in the sun.

They had fallen asleep to dreams of better places, but the pipe had fallen too, and all the ancient coal dust had been stirred up by their moving and settling and talking, and the last bottle of gin had rolled on its side and cracked, and as the pipe began to smoulder in their bundles, the gin seeped across the floor and licked at the embers, and the coal dust drew to the tiny sparks like a magnet makes metal dust to dance. The drink had deadened them both and the smoke just made them sleepier and they had the happiest dreams they had ever had.

And then Mum's dress had caught alight, and she was screaming and coughing, and Jack couldn't see through the smoke and the flames, which were all around them, and he was yelling and shouting and trying to bat at his mum with his hands before she became a fireball. But the smoke and heat and flames and cinders were flying everywhere in the air, catching at the old wood walls, snatching at their hats and hair and sleeves and trousers, and even the ground was burning up beneath their boots. His mother had fallen to the floor and Jack was standing beside her, holding her hand, and he was dizzy and sick and fell to his knees and was just glad that he had time to tell her goodbye, not like his dad who had been taken before he was properly able to speak. He didn't know much after that, just felt his head hot against the ground and the crack and split of roof beams falling and dangling like the old black crows the gamekeepers hang on their hedges to keep the foxes away. His mum's hand had gone from his own and there was a rasping lick like a red-hot cat's tongue at his throat.

He didn't really hear the battering at the door amidst the roar and holler of the flames, but then the wall came crashing in and someone was rushing at him through the whirling smoke and all he saw was a hundred thousand fireflies swirling in the air above him and all around him, and then Stroop's hands reaching down into the flames to seize him from his faint, lift the beam from off his neck, skin puckering and blistering in the heat; Stroop's hands bringing him out into the cool black air, which swept over him like water. He looked up and saw the hundred thousand fireflies break and blur as he was dragged on his back through the dark, damp grass. His mouth hung open, sucking at the raindrops hanging in the air, his tongue scorched and steaming, something soft and wet laying across his neck.

Like whatever was lying across him now, keeping him alive, knowing that any minute he would see Stroop's face bending over him saying, 'You're all right, lad, you'll be all right.'

And he was all right then. His mum had gone, but his wounds, like Stroop's, had scarred and healed, and he knew that lying here, if he just kept still and waited long enough, he would be all right again.

19

Sandro, Meet Henry;
Henry, Meet Sandro

IF CASTRACANI COULD really have lifted the lid off of time, he might have seen Sandro Santorelli as he was stepping off the boat on to the slimy green pier. He was the last to go ashore barring the crew, had waited for all the Jerusalem men to disembark before himself, standing still by the deck rail, scanning the busy dock for a face he knew.

He scrutinised with distaste the dirty embankment, which was thick with slurry and rotten fish guts, the hoops of broken barrels whose slats were burning on tawdry fires, tended by men wearing what looked to be meal sacks. There were a hundred makeshift stalls selling ale, wine, ropes, knot-work, wax, candles, wicks, caulking materials, careening knifes, nets, hooks, harpoons, boots, hats, pipes, tobacco, carved horn cups, chests, charts, rigging, sails, soup, pies, and right at the end of the untidy alley was an undertakers. The sign hanging outside showed a man being pickled in a barrel of alcohol. The noise never broke, just changed direction, voices shouting and hawking, old men spitting and talking, gulls squawking, gangplanks creaking, boats barging into tarred pilings, water slopping, slapping between the tight-packed boats, axes split-ting stakes of wood, hammers swinging, anvils ringing. And hovering above it all came the sound of a hundred church-bells, reminding those who cared that it was time for Service.

Sandro put on his gloves, scanned the crowds again for the man the Council were sending to meet him, and at last saw him pushing his way through the masses, unmistakably Lucchese from his colour and his clothes, his foppish velvet hat embroidered with the town crest and the scrawl of the word '*Libertad*' below. Sandro waved his hand and came down the gangplank, and the two men shook each other by the arm in the old-fashioned way, exchanging greetings and names of mutual acquaintances, verifying which family members had married, given birth or died.

They wove their way out from the portside and found a small shop where they could be comfortable and have break-fast and discuss plans. If all went well, Sandro would be in Westminster that very evening and the deal would take place. There was no going back on it now. They ate slowly, discussed the news, the state of the silk business, the latest cuts of cloth most popular with the London market.

The man was the brother of Buono Roncino, one of the most influential Lucchese merchants living in London. He had intimate ties to the Court, and to the King himself, who bought exclusively from Buono to supply his court and ecclesiastical needs, which were many. It was through Buono, confidant of the King, that Ricardo his brother was able to act on behalf of the Lucchese Council in this most important of matters. He and Sandro talked hard throughout the day, finalising the arrangements, which had until now only sketchily been made.

Ricardo took Sandro to his home, on the Via Caldera in the Silk Quarter, introduced him to his wife, who was embroiderer to the King and had been so for many years, and who was cognisant of the situation. Though English born, she came from a family of embroiderers, and as such her family was intimate with the silk traders from whom they purchased their materials and with whom they had intermarried over several generations.

After they had thrashed out the details, Ricardo took Sandro to meet the other members of the Inner Council, and from there, they rode straight into the city and Westminster, left their horses at the inn in which they were staying, and proceeded on foot to the abbey. As they neared, Sandro made out the scaffolding skeletons that crawled over the body of the original buildings. Ricardo expounded on the King's great devotion to the abbey and its church, and how he was personally overseeing its restoration and expansion. To Sandro, it made the place look sinister, a half-eaten carcass shrouded in unexplained shadows, everything coated in stone-dust from the preceding day's work. He struggled to keep the foreboding from his bones, reminded himself of the glorious task that lay ahead; strode forward with renewed vigour, leaving Ricardo panting in his wake.

Sandro Santorelli sat in the newly completed Chapter House of Westminster Abbey, feeling ill with awe and anticipation. The huge pillars towered over him like assassins, and the great glass windows were cowled in darkness, like mirrors palled over after a sudden death. High above him the vaulted roof hung as if the sky itself had turned to stone. The brands burning dimly against the walls made shadows seep and sieve their surroundings and the wind wound through the towers and roofs, the scaffolding boards lifting and dropping, the new stones and arches easing and soughing; they made the chapel sound like a cave buried deep inside a sea-crashed cliff.

Sandro wished Ricardo would return to keep him company. Every few seconds he compulsively felt the pouch tied tight about his waist, then went to the small vial he held around his neck on a thong. The letters were in a satchel slung across his shoulder, but he felt vulnerable in this enormous space where every creak and flitter echoed and grew as it bounced from flagstone to pew to tomb and vaulted sky. He flicked his eyes again and again at the marking candle. It showed he had been here almost two hours, having stayed after nones, when the main doors had been barred to the public and all the monks had gone off to their nights of flagellation, meditation or sleep. Only the old curate could be heard sweeping down the floors with the bristles of his broom, dusting at the shrines and tombs, his ancient knees cracking as he knelt before the bones of King Edward, which once had moved and walked and built this abbey and this church.

A light rain began to fall, tapping at angles on the bare windows, a squall coming in from the east. The eerie sound made Sandro more nervous still and he suddenly stood, feeling he could wait here no longer. At that very moment, he heard the door from the refectory open and footsteps approach behind the Pyx Chapel, along the short walk to the Chapter House, and up the several steps. His hand went to the hilt of his dagger and his heart began beating hard. And then there he was, a small man, plump, covered head to foot in Benedictine garb. Behind him stood Ricardo, his hand flapping as if he were patting a large dog, motioning to Sandro to get down on his knees.

Sandro's hand left his dagger and clutched at the vial, and down he went on to the hard, cold floor. The man came towards him and laid his hand gently upon Sandro's bowed head. The gleam of sweat on his brow gathered into a single drop and fell, silently staining the stone by the foot of Henry, King of England, fanatical collector of relics, soon-to-be-possessor of a portion of the Holy Blood of Lucca.

20

Alien Amidst the Corn

S TROOP RETCHED VIOLENTLY, then worse, he vomited over the pink carpet, his bile yellow, sinking into the fibres, making an unpretty flower amongst the many. He quickly backed out of the door, which took less than a second, having only taken a single step into Great-Aunt Flora's room. He slammed the door shut, but the action released a further waft of fetid air, and Stroop was down on his hands and knees, heaving like a dog that has eaten too much grass. Minutes before, he had heard Mabel and Thomas enter the scullery and the sudden fear had made sweat prickle all over his body. He smelt himself and was repulsed, but the awfulness of the situation overtook all else, and he wasted no time.

He had still been in the drawing room, the woman on the couch. He saw the devastation within: the writing bureau had been turned into splinters, its drawers bottom up and broken on the floor, every picture hung askew or had been turned face in and slashed across its back. On the table by the window, the tea things sat untouched on their cloth. Two cups, he noted, two side plates, a cake stand, a small heap of buttered bread, the edges hard and beginning to curl, the butter a deep unpleasant yellow. He had leant over the table, put out his hand and gently lifted the tea pot. It was full. The hot-water jug was almost empty as were the two cups, so the pot had been refilled prior to pouring out a second cup of tea. He did not need to figure out the implications consciously before his body was running out of the door and down the hall, and heading frantically up the central staircase two steps at a time. His speed was sudden and filled with panic. He knew what that table by the window meant, its quiet tea-time interrupted, its pot still full, its cakes half eaten. It meant that of the two people taking tea, only one was still in that room; it meant that there would be a maid somewhere nearby to wait on them; it meant that there had been a cook shortly before, icing cakes and cooking biscuits.

Stroop's stomach was already in his mouth when he bounded from the landing up the last few steps. The door just to the right was slightly ajar, and before he had time to think he flung it wide and stepped inside, his eyes wild and staring, his hand shaking as it moved to guard his mouth. Too late. Every muscle in his body revolted at the sudden flight and what it had brought him to see. A heap of discarded coats piled on the bed, whose eiderdown was so steeped in their blood it had lost its own colour. His head did not even try to disengage the maid from the cook from the mistress. His vision blurred and he could no longer keep his balance as the bile surged through his body and sought release. He turned and managed to reach the door, slammed it tight behind him.

Mabel and Thomas heard his vile retching and came hurtling up the stairs, Thomas reaching him first, Mabel just behind, her face without expression, her skin the colour of buttermilk, tight, translucent, her hair dark and dishevelled despite the band she had tied around it to keep it back.

My God, thought Stroop, she's so young. But there was no time for more. Her hand was on the handle of the door and Stroop yelled from somewhere deep inside himself, his voice hoarse, its coarseness cutting her into immobility.

'No!' he cried. 'Thomas, tell her no.'

Her hand rested on the handle and she looked directly at him, saw, perhaps for the first time, the pallor and sweat of his skin, the marks of watery vomit on his chin, the slight tremble of his limbs as he forced himself backwards from the floor and knelt before her.

'No, Mabel. You mustn't.' His voice was quiet, imploring. She gazed at Stroop, and he felt she was looking right inside him, that at any moment, she must see what he had seen, imprinted inside his head, and he turned abruptly away.

Mabel's hand quivered on the handle. For that moment, there was nothing else in her world but that handle. Stroop did not see the movement, had closed his eyes, was breathing fast and deep. It was Thomas who ducked right underneath her arm, just as he had done with many a market stall holder and shopkeeper, and put himself like a cross against the door.

'You shan't go in,' he said, his arms braced against the door-frame, his feet jammed across the base. 'I shan't let you.'

For a moment they were all completely still, Thomas strong and wide and barring the way, Stroop on his knees, his cold forehead cradled in his hand, Mabel with her arm outstretched, her fingers feeling warm on the dinted brass globe of the handle. There was not a thought between them, just a fixity,

171

a void, a complete stillness of body and mind, and then Mabel took her hand from the handle and reached into a pocket. She took out a small lace handkerchief, licked it, and leaning over, softly began to dab at Stroop's chin. He caught her hand and took the lace square from her. Thomas released the door-frame, took Stroop's elbow, and he and Mabel helped him up. They turned their backs on the door and Great-Aunt Flora and Elsa and the cook, and stood irresolute at the top of the stairs.

'Jack,' said Mabel, appalled she had forgotten him even though it had been barely a minute since she and Thomas had gained the stairs.

'Where?' said Stroop.

'In the stable,' she replied, 'but I think he might—'

Stroop interrupted, ordered Thomas to go and sit with Jack. He had regained his possession and he had used a voice with which you don't argue. Thomas, assured that things were right as they could be in this most bizarre of days, legged it down the staircase without a backward glance. Mabel and Stroop heard him clattering down the scullery stairs and running out across the cobbled yard.

'He must have left the back door open,' said Mabel as they listened to his retreating steps.

'I don't think it matters,' said Stroop, and actually smiled. He took Mabel's hand gently in his own. 'I think that's the worst of it over, but there's still something we have to do.'

'I know,' said Mabel, 'but I can't think what . . .' She didn't continue, and they made their way down the corridor. There was a room between Great-Aunt Flora's and her own and a small boxroom just beyond. They glanced into the middle room but it had barely been touched. It wasn't often used, and apart from the bed and a wardrobe and an escritoire, it was obvious there was nothing there to be sorted through or searched.

Mabel's door stood open and, side by side, Stroop and Mabel looked inside at the devastation. There was nothing, absolutely nothing in the room that had not been touched or turned over or destroyed. There was not a square inch of carpet to be seen. Every last one of her clothes had been ripped out of their drawers and cupboards, the hangers stark and bare, every last inch of every corner of every piece of furniture had been searched and discarded. Her bed linen was scattered, the cases torn from their pillows, the mattress pulled from the bed. She looked with dismay at the tortoiseshell-backed brushes, thinking of that first day she had arrived. Cursing herself for the destruction she had brought on this home. Tried to push the thoughts away, but felt tears flooding down her cheeks.

Stroop squeezed her hand gently. 'Is there anything else? Anywhere else something might have been hidden?' He knew it was almost hopeless, that even if they knew what they were looking for, chances were it had already been found and removed. The people who had done this had been thorough to the point of obsession.

'There's just the boxroom, and then there's Cook and Elsa's rooms in the attic. The others all live out. I don't suppose there's anything—'

Mabel stopped suddenly and let go Stroop's hand. She moved swiftly to the boxroom and couldn't stop herself from crying out.

'Oh, no! Not that as well! They were my . . .' she swallowed, then looked at Stroop as he came up behind her, 'it's my trousseau. It was my mother's. Dad sent them on a few months after I got here. It's just shawls and things, and her old wedding dress.'

She looked down at the open chest and the jumble of precious linens littering the floor. She stepped in and started picking the things up one by one and folding them, replacing them in the chest. Cotton tablecloths and napkins, a swaddling wrap, a christening shawl, the long wedding veil, the satin dress that had once been her mother's and her mother's before that. Some of the items were very old but they had spent most of their years wrapped in paper and carefully packaged with herbs to keep away the moth-worms.

Stroop stood in the doorway, watching the girl pick things up and fold them, replace them in the chest. He didn't stop her. He understood this was a way of putting some order back into the intolerable chaos that had been thrust upon her. The fact that the house was piled high with dead bodies seemed irrelevant. He just watched her hands as they touched and smoothed and folded, touched and smoothed and folded, and Stroop standing there, intrusive, feeling like a voyeur.

'I'll go and see to Jack. Come down to the stable when you're ready.' Mabel didn't reply but he saw the dip of her head as she nodded. 'And, Mabel, don't go in—'

'It's all right, Mr Stroop,' she replied, her voice a little stronger than before. 'I'll come straight down.'

'All right then,' said Stroop, and started back slowly down the corridor.

Something was niggling at him, but there was so much turmoil going on in his brain there was no place to pursue it.

It was just as he was starting down the scullery steps that he suddenly stopped stock-still, then turned and raced back up the central staircase and along the corridor. Mabel, alarmed at the noise, was standing by the door, looking scared but defiant. Stroop came into the room and started rummaging in the chest, undoing all the pretty folding she had done.

'Mr Stroop!' she protested, but Stroop ignored her and dug down.

'Aha!' he cried. 'I knew it!' He was brandishing a length of double-sided silk, pulling it from the shredded paper Mabel had so carefully rescued to wrap it in.

'Be gentle!' chided the girl. 'That's very old—'

'I know, I know,' broke in Stroop. 'What exactly is it?'

Mabel looked puzzled, but answered, 'It's a christening shawl. You're supposed to use it when the first girl of the family is baptised. It's one of the few things I remember my mother ever talking about. I think Dad mentioned it once too. My mother loved it, he said, and I should love it too.'

Stroop was holding the shawl out at arm's length, then bringing it in close, staring intently at the embroidered hem.

'Have you ever looked closely at this?' he enquired.

Mabel was beginning to get huffy. 'Of course! Well, I mean, not really, I suppose. I had to repack the chest once a year, replace all the herbs and everything, make sure everything was fine. When I get married it'll all come in useful. I've even added some things myself.'

'Never mind all that.' Great-aunt Flora would have been scandalised, but Stroop was no longer listening to ghosts. 'I think this is what we want!'

He stood triumphant, handed her the shawl. 'Here, get this all folded and stowed nice and neat. Put it in a bag or something and keep it safe. Bring it with you. I'm off to see what's to be done for Jack. Don't be long, Mabel. Hurry, hurry. That's what we need to do now. I need to get home and do a little research but, by God, I think we're getting somewhere at last, I really do!'

Mabel took the shawl and gathered it to her chest for a moment as she watched Stroop go. She held it out and looked hard at it, but couldn't see what Stroop must have seen. It was old, she knew that, one of the oldest things she owned, but it was just a christening shawl, for goodness' sake! Still, she did what he had told her and found a small draw-string bag in which to put it, wrapping something sturdier around to keep it safe.

She looked at the mess all about her, everything she had packed returned in a mess to the floor. She didn't care now to put anything away. Even the wedding dress, distorted in a heap by her heel. Home, Stroop had said, and standing there ankle-deep in a snowdrift of linen, she knew she no longer had one, not here, nor at Epping. She had nowhere to go. She looked into tomorrow and saw nothing. Her life had been emptied and she had been cut adrift. I'm just like Thomas, she thought, and for some reason felt mildly comforted. If he's managed, I'll manage, she thought, and clutching her bag she started down the corridor.

She stopped briefly outside Great-Aunt Flora's room and almost put out her hand. But there was something not quite right as she stood there by a puddle of Stroop's vomit, and she dropped her hand again, and suddenly, strongly, felt the urgent need to get out of the house that was no longer her home and breathe deeper than she had ever done of the open air.

21

Discoveries

BANDORELLO'S HOUSE WAS no longer his own. It was crawling with men, all of whom he knew by face if not by name. His tobacco supplies were dwindling fast and Marco had been sent out yet again to fetch supplies. Marco himself seriously doubted he would ever have the energy to play dominoes again; he'd been up and down the Silk Quarter for what seemed like hours, giving the message to every family of Lucca he could find. The men Marco had fetched stood around Bandorello's drawing room, leaning on mantelpieces or bookshelves, standing in tight clusters talking quietly. Nobody wanted to sit. Nobody minded that it was almost midnight. Nobody cared that they had been dragged out of their beds or their clubs or the tavern. Some drank the wine Marco had provided, others downed small cups of strong, dark coffee to wake themselves up or speed sobriety. Smoke hung below the stucco ceiling aided by the oil lamps, which had all been lit, an event that was unusual. Bandorello generally preferred just two lamps burning, the one by his chair, the other by the bookcase.

When he was sure that all that were coming were gathered, Bandorello went to alert Castracani, who was in the writing room next door. He found the man head down on the large leather table, his hand still holding a pen, a long line of ink drying illegibly on the page. He cleared his throat and immediately Castracani opened his eyes and lifted his head.

'Are all here?'

'All we can find,' answered Bandorello. 'Some are in the city on business. Several are at the silk mills. Some still in the hospital. Rosso and Alvaro are, er, somewhat incapacitated.'

Castracani nodded. 'They have good reason. It was Rosso lost his boy, was it not?'

'And Alvaro his wife and two daughters,' added Bandorello. 'Sad times indeed.'

'Indeed, and they will be the sadder if we do not get to the bottom of this,' said Castracani, easing himself to his feet with the help of the table. Bandorello leant forward and handed Castracani the cane, which had fallen to the floor.

'Well, then. Let's begin.'

Castracani picked up some notes and placed them in a folder, then left the study with Bandorello at his back, proud to lend his house to such a cause. He might not be a member of the Council, but he was Castracani's oldest friend, and everyone knew it. His house was Castracani's, and for the moment, wherever Castracani was, there was the Council.

The instant Castracani entered the main room, the whispered conversations died away, and there were several clinks as cups and glasses were put down, several gulps in the silence as their contents were surreptitiously finished off. The men cleared a way for Castracani, and he sat once again in the red plush of the chair by the cathedral clock, only this time the chair had been turned out to face the room and not the fire. He looked at the men who came forward: the remnants of the Council and the heirs of those who were unable to attend through death or injury caused by the fires. He knew each one, had eaten with each family, shared their food and wine, done business with others, yet he had a suspicion that not only was there treachery in Lucca, but that possibly there was a thread of it here. He must guard his words with care, he must watch for reaction or recognition, or lack of such, or signs of anger, nonchalance or guilt. It did not come naturally, this suspicion of his fellows, yet someone had known where to lay the fires, which houses were vulnerable in what particulars, which time the most propitious. On the basis of what he discovered here tonight, he must elect several to be his aides and in these few, he needed perfect trust.

Castracani began.

'I have already told you some of this when we gathered in St Thomas's, but we were not all present then, nor were things so clear as they are today, now that the smoke and the cinders have been swept away along with many of our houses and most of our possessions. I have been honoured by your trust in ceding to me the temporary leadership of our Council. We must have time to mourn those members we have lost and go through due process to elect a new Inner Circle. This situation is unique in our history but, make no mistake, we shall rise again. Those who seek to exterminate us shall not succeed.'

Castracani scanned each face as they vocalised agreement, slapped their gloves together, chinked the sides of their glasses with the inner rims of their rings.

'You will all know the old legends of the London Lucchese

– how the true relics of Lucca came into our keeping and have accounted for our success. How they were never returned to their true resting place in Lucca but have remained hidden in London for all these long years.'

Most smiled, some laughed, a few looked serious as death. Castracani waited a moment, looked at a piece of paper and then lifted his head.

'I am telling you here tonight that those legends are true.'

At once there was uproar. Shouts of disbelief, some cursing, general hubbub, a great deal of expostulation saying, 'I knew it!' or 'What bloody nonsense!'

Castracani let his eyes linger a little, then tapped at the side of his glass with a spoon, watching each face as it turned back towards him. When silence fell again, broken only by some fidgeting feet and the glug of liquid as cups were refilled, Castracani waved a sheaf of papers at the assemblage.

'Yes, yes. I know we all thought it a fairy tale, something to make us feel important, something to give our children pride in their heritage. We know our very own Volto Santo is only a replica, though it has blessed us all the same and is sacred to pilgrims in its own right, but did we ever think that the true relics could possibly still be here all these years later? That is life, my friends; that is the way of things. They were brought from Lucca into our safekeeping at a time when the Republic was under threat. Our history has always been filled with assault by enemies. They have always wanted what we worked hard to have. They were jealous of what we made of our city and there are some who always will be. Napoleon is outside the gates at this very hour and it is time for us to help in whatever way we can. But first, there is the past, there are the tales, there is the truth to be discovered. I know it is hard for us all to believe in childish stories, but we must believe if we are to help our homeland.

'But how, you will ask, could it come about that the Lucchese did not reclaim the things most sacred to their city, to our city? Why did we not return them as soon as we had the chance? It is simple really, sadly very simple indeed. Since the relics came to London, Lucca has been under constant siege, so at first the Council thought it best to leave the relics here and hidden, where they could not be stolen or defiled. After all, the city-state was doing well despite the relocation of its most sacred possession, or indeed because of it. Every enemy was defeated and the Volto Santo continued to bring pilgrims and prosperity to our town. Perhaps it did not matter that it was the Lucchese in London safeguarding God's holy relics; perhaps it was enough that the Lucchese were looking after them no matter where. Time goes on, people die, one family succeeds another, one Council is followed by another, and so it has been for hundreds of years. There was no design or grand plan, no sneakit scheme that meant the relics remained in London. It was simply that things carried on as they always had and no one really thought to ask or took the time to remember. It was the forgetfulness of faith, my friends. Lucca and London got on with their lives and both of them simply forgot. However, there comes a time when a man has need of his treasure, no matter how long it has been hidden, and for Lucca and for us that time is now. It is time to take possession of a forgotten memory. It is time to return to Lucca that which God gave and which is rightfully hers.'

Castracani began coughing loudly and Bandorello came

forward with a glass. This had been prearranged between the two of them and Bandorello spoke his lines.

'We have tired him, sirs. He is still not well.' Castracani waved a feeble hand in protestation. Bandorello leant down and put his ear close to Castracani's lips, then stood again and turned to the expectant crowd.

'We must disperse and give our leader his rest. There are some of you we have tasks for and I will ask you to return in the morning. As for the rest, we will gather again tomorrow night and tell you what news we have found.'

The men didn't need much encouragement; it was late, the revelations had left them thirsty, excited, eager to talk things out, to wonder about what would be done. To know if they had been chosen for a special task. Castracani reinforced the charade with another chest-cracking cough, though in truth it wasn't difficult to conjure one up. The pain had subsided somewhat, but his insides still felt done over by a plough-drill and sprayed with hot tar. It was with sincere relief that he let Bandorello take his arm and guide him to Marco, who was waiting patiently outside. He had, of course, had his ear to the door the whole time and had heard every word.

Hardly had the door closed when the room behind erupted with ebullient chatter and the clink of glasses, the spills being lit from the lamps to reignite pipes or cigars. Marco took Castracani from Bandorello's care and helped him up the stairs; when they rested briefly halfway up, Marco could constrain himself no longer, felt the flush of excitement on his face and blurted out the question that everyone in the room below must, even in the short space of time it had taken them to climb six stairs, have asked at least a dozen times.

'Is it truly true, sir?' His voice was soft and quick with the thrall of it all. 'Are the legends not lies after all?'

'Indeed, Marco.' Castracani nodded, and with sudden fear he felt the weight of expectation upon himself to prove what he had said and to act on it. The responsibility of it all hung like a lead collar around his neck. He hoped he would prove himself well. If he had been told last week that the fate of the Council and perhaps of Lucca itself would be his alone to dictate, he would probably have laughed and yet rubbed his hands at the prospect, secretly wishing it were so. But now that it was, he dearly wished the stories were lies and the truth could remain buried until some other came along to bear its weight. Of course he said nothing of this, and such thoughts could not make his face more weary than it already was. But he leant a bit heavier on Marco's shoulder as he gave his reply.

'Believe it, Marco, the legends are true and, God forgive us, they have cost us dear.'

Mabel would have echoed that thought if she had known it was being said, but thankfully at that time, she was deeply asleep on a bare mattress in Stroop's house, the soft pink twill of a candlewick bedspread tickling her chin and reminding her body of better days. The sheet and blankets he had left for her lay untouched on the dresser. She had been too tired to even pretend to make up a bed and had simply lain down in her clothes and gone to sleep. When Stroop had looked in half an hour later, knocking gently on her door, bringing her in a badly made-up meal of cold bacon, bread and cheese, he had seen her curled on the damp ticking, her head resting on a cushion she had taken from the small divan, her limbs wrapped around her body as if she were trying to make of herself a knot. He had been embarrassed seeing her there, looking so young and vulnerable, shuddered to think that for the moment there was no one else to give her care, thankful at least that she was not dreaming, knowing what awful things she would see when she did. He had placed the meal on the bedside cabinet, covered her with the bedspread and gone away.

He couldn't remember how many years it was since he'd even been in that room. Once upon a time it had belonged to his sisters, whilst he and his brothers shared the small room next door. His father had built a three-tiered bunk bed to fit them in and they'd passed messages to each other during long summer nights, or made up ghost stories in winter. But that was a long time gone, as were his entire family. One by one they'd died of scarlet fever, pneumonia, typhus, diphtheria, and only he, Whilbert Nathaniel, middle child, thinnest child, quietest child, had survived to bury his parents when he was seventeen after they fell from an overcrowded ferry and died of whatever combination of diseases were swilling in the Thames at that time.

He'd become very friendly with Dr Halliday, who had seen the entire family through from beginning to end. And when he was the only one left, Halliday would still come and visit out of habit, and they would sit in Stroop's study compiling Halliday's Masterwork: *The Nomenclature and Nosological Etymology of Diseases*.

When Halliday died, he left all his books to Whilbert Nathaniel Stroop in the hope of his pupil finishing off his great work. And Stroop had. It sat in its manuscript box next to all the other boxes containing all the other lists and essays he had compiled over the years and which no publisher had ever expressed an interest in. Once a year he touted his intellectual goods again, but Murray and Dale, Winbeck and Stroud, or whoever the latest publishers were in town, were never keen, and Stroop didn't mind. As long as all his lists existed, he told himself, there was order in the world. Maybe he too was only folding tablecloths, but at least he used all his work, he really did, or read them sometimes, just for the fun of it, just for the satisfaction of knowing it had been done.

When he had left Mabel to what he hoped would be a dreamless sleep, he opened the door to his own bedroom. Jack's lanky form was outlined under the blankets, his head propped up on the pillow roll, his neck still rounded with a length of girth-strap, stiff enough to hold the blood in and keep him still. He hadn't really needed the laudanum Stroop had given him, but Stroop had hoped it would dull the pain.

He couldn't stop hearing the awful wetness of the noise as he had taken hold of the shaft of pitchfork and pulled it clear. Poor Jack had convulsed forward, drawn by the tines, eyes wide open, his throat gurgling, the skin stretching. And then the fork had suddenly pulled clear and the skin slipped back into place, Jack's head hitting the ground with an awful thud that had thankfully knocked him out of consciousness. Thomas had been quick with the girth-strap, having considered the problem of what to use while waiting for Stroop to arrive. Of course, Stroop should have brought something from the house, but it never occurred to him. He hadn't known what had happened to Jack until he got to the stable,

185

and to see the poor boy pinned to the floor after all he had seen in the house . . . He didn't think anything; a rage he had never known overwhelmed him and he surged forward and had a grip on the fork before he even knew what he was doing. His body didn't want him to stand and consider, just pushed him on to do what had to be done. There was no time to sit contemplating life from the sidelines. He'd seen Jack, he'd seen the fork, he'd removed the fork.

The most surprising thing had been the dog woofing up from under the sacking and he had almost stabbed the thing through as his momentum pushed him backwards then forwards as he tried to keep his feet. He flung the fork aside and grabbed the strap Thomas held out for him, wound it tight around Jack's neck, checking for signs it was too tight or too loose.

It had been the scar tissue that saved him, from all those years ago when the burning roof-beam had fallen and caught him across the neck, seared him raw, the roasted skin falling from him like crackling from a piece of pork. It had forced his skin to grow again in thick coagulations, crisscrossed with scars where the fresh skin had broken again and again as he made the slightest movement of his head, or opened his mouth to eat or speak. Or laugh. Stroop had always been amazed at the amount the boy had laughed. Maybe that was why he had let him stay, although the boy had never asked. It's just that Jack never left, and Stroop never told him to go, and it was only tonight that Stroop had even paused to wonder why.

22

Unravelling

ALL NIGHT, STROOP stayed up, the shawl draped delicately over his table, surrounded by books and dictionaries and pads of paper on which he scribbled note after note. He was careful not to get candle-wax drips on it, or have it marked by the oil lamp he kept lit and moving from one spot to another as he worked.

The more he studied this square of lightly padded silk, the more he marvelled at it. If the date was to be believed, it had been made in the latter half of the thirteenth century, being begun in 1257 and finished two years later. The material was in remarkably good condition, partly because of the outstanding quality of the original cloth and the threads with which it had been painstakingly stitched, partly because it had obviously been very little used, and great care had been taken during its storage. Still, it was a thing that astounded.

It was approximately four feet by three, of a plain design consisting of self-coloured cream stitching that kept the two sides and its wadding together and described a pattern of flowers and arabesques. It spoke eloquently of purity and was perfectly suited to swaddling infants at the baptismal font. Several small stains could be detected under his magnifying glass, and these Stroop took to be splashes from a long line of ceremonies down through the centuries. It was with awe that he held such history in his hands.

However, that was not what had been occupying his attention throughout this long night, nor what had originally caught his eye back at the house on the square. It was the curious stitching, which circumscribed the shawl at every edge. Done in a delicate shade of purply blue, enhanced at intervals with gold, it took the form of a linear pattern, which looked at first to be a rather ornate form of blanket stitch. On closer inspection, Stroop had noted that it was regular in its irregularity, and closer still, working with his magnifying glass, he made a great discovery. The embroidered lines had distinct shape and form. They were marked in blocks by the gold stitching; they were squared in places, rectangular in others, broken in parts. The blocks of patterns differed in length, though some were repeated at intervals. There were particular small blocks that occurred far more than others. Stroop spent his first few hours doggedly following the edging with his glass, copying down block for block what he saw.

Only when he had finished this tedious task did he allow himself a glass of strong wine, and a smile lifted one side of his mouth. He could not stop himself, and smacking his lips he exclaimed out loud, 'Ha!' and then again, this time with a small snort of laughter, 'Ha indeed!'

There was no one to hear him. Both Mabel and Jack were sleeping soundly upstairs. Stroop had dragged some covers down from the blanket box to put on the floor for Bindlestiff, who seemed to do nothing else with his life but sleep and occasionally wag his tail or make a wheezing woof. Next time Stroop had looked, Thomas was curled up next to the dog, his arm around the old shoulders, his back against the warmth of the range, which was miraculously still lit when they had arrived back.

Stroop had been awake for almost twenty-four hours by the time he had finished, and at last he draped his aching body into an armchair and pulled a quilt over himself. The shawl lay carefully folded in a square in the middle of the table. He had stacked the books into towers waiting to be reshelved. The piles of notes had been tidied and one note-book took pride of place. On the first page, written out neatly in Stroop's meticulously neat hand, was a heading, which he had underlined once, precisely aligning it with the letters above. 'This', it read, 'is the story of Lucca & my small part in its history.'

London lies quiet like a knot, the river flowing through it. Far off in the Cotswold Hills, a thunderhead has built and blown, flinging lightning streaks across the grass and bracken, and the rain hitting hard and fast. It pushes aside stones, slides between boulders, swimming like an eel down the sides of the hills. It breaks then races, drags against the scree, leaps ledges, joins and splits, joins and splits, hits the river hard, making the surface boil. Through towns and fields, under bridges, under trees, under hills, night and day, night and day, not pausing in its flow.

Stroop is kneeling by its side, watching his reflection break and flow, break and flow. He leans forward, his arm outstretched, the cup in his fingers dipping at the surface. He sees deep beneath the green and the water is tanned by peat and clear and cool as ice. He watches the morning light trace the current as it goes. The sense of the river is so strong and real he knows he must be dreaming, and just at that moment the bank gives way and Stroop is sinking below the surface, unaware which way is up and which is down, flailing, gasping, lungs beginning to bleed for lack of air. His hands scrabble at his throat as if they can break through the skin and then there is a voice which whispers in his ear.

'Don't struggle, sir. It will only makes things worse.'

And then Stroop was suddenly awake and the bag was over his head, tied tight about his neck by a cord that someone was pulling. He breathed quick and fast, felt the rough burlap scratch at his dry lips, felt the moisture already forming in the fibres. His fear was all the greater because he could not see, though his eyes were wide and open. The panic lent no time to let his mind work. His skin prickled all over, his fingers trembled, he tried hard not to urinate.

'You are a very interesting man, Mr . . .' Stroop tried to work his lips. There was no sound, except that of the man moving around the table, flipping at papers and books. 'Strroooopp.' He dragged out the Rs and Os, pronounced the P a little too hard. 'A name as indecipherable as its owner.'

He had an accent – it was the first thought Stroop had been able to make, and he clung hard to it. He had an accent, Spanish maybe, or Italian, quite strong, yet no foreigner would use such a word as 'indecipherable'. The reability to think calmed him. He tried to relax his fingers, let them lie

190

still on his chest, then dropped them to his lap. His elbows were pinned to his sides.

'My colleagues tell me I am not a patient man, but I do not agree.'

His steps were soft upon the rug, his voice very low. Stroop understood that this man wanted to remain unheard, except by him, but he couldn't understand why and was about to shout, to raise the household; Jack wouldn't wake because of the laudanum, but Mabel was only up the stairs, and Thomas in the kitchen just down the hall. He slowed his breathing, drew a deep breath, which brought the wettened burlap with it, then kept in the breath and made not a sound. Suddenly he understood what would happen if he yelled and called the alarm, and the images of Great-Aunt Flora's bed flooded before his blind eyes, and the farmhouse, and Edward and Jack in the shed. These images could not frighten him any more than he was already frightened, but again he felt an unaccustomed anger begin to burn within him, a rage he had never thought himself capable of.

He tried to concentrate. He heard the man move back around the table. He was picking something up; Stroop heard pages being turned. He felt a draught at the back of his head and knew the window must be open, knew this was how the man had got in. For a few moments there was absolute silence, except for the sounds of night outside, or rather, not night. It had to be the brink of dawn. He heard a blackbird begin to sing several gardens down, and a distant clop of hooves as the draymen began to lug their loads around the streets.

'Ah, Mr Stroop.'

The voice was suddenly right at his ear again. He felt the

man's damp breath mingling with his own, smelt a faint scent. Perhaps of bluebells. His mind began to make its notes. It was always taking notes.

'Do you know how long I have been standing outside your window, watching you work? Did you know my colleagues followed you from the old woman's house? They wanted to break down the doors and do what they do best, but you have me to thank that they didn't. I tell them you do not have to kill the bird to take its feathers. And if you're clever, you can get the chicken to pluck itself. Just, my friend, as I have been. And you have done the plucking.'

Stroop wriggled roughly in his chair, realised there was rope binding him across his chest, another around his feet.

'Ah, ah, Mr Stroop, you do not need to fear. I am not going to string you all up by your necks and slit your throats.' A small puff of laughter tickled Stroop's ear. 'I have come by myself to watch you work. The lone wolf steals silently down from the hill to take the new-born lamb. He does not need his pack to slaughter the flock. And see? I have found it. I have what I need right here,'

Stroop heard the man tap his fingernails against the leather surface of a book. His notebook. The one he had left open on the table. The man had moved behind him, and Stroop's neck felt clammy and cold. Something came to rest against his head, something round, small, hard. Stroop closed up his eyes, and a small tear escaped the corner of each, regretting for him everything he hadn't done. A last soft whisper in his ear and then all he heard was the wind scratching the curtain against the window. The blackbird was still singing, closer now. A cat miaowed to be let into someone else's house.

'If I have need of you, any of you, I will be back.'

He heard the curtain fall, the soft sloop of it as its foot regained the floor. And Stroop realised he was alone. And still alive. This time he didn't try to stop the tears, and hated the scratch of the burlap against his skin where the tears were flowing wildly down his neck, and the more the tears fell, the more the knot began to loose its grip and the sacking began to sag as it parted from the cord, until, of its own volition, it began to open.

23

Not Far, as the Owl Flies

A T DAWN, BEFORE early mass, Father Ignatius knelt at the altar of St Anthony's, his head bowed in prayer, or rather, in pretend prayer. He had long ago ceased to have anything to say to the Almighty on a daily basis and tended to spend the time mulling over small worries, such as what he would have for his dinner, or what had been said in Confession and whether the penance he had proscribed was just. He wondered if other priests felt as he did, as if the sacerdotal sacrament had slipped into the ordinary, the rule of the Church becoming the rhythm of his life or perhaps the rut of it. God knew, he still believed, but over the years he had begun to wonder what exactly it was he believed in. Certainly not the roll call of the saints. A man who allowed himself to be griddled alive or skinned like a rabbit was less a martyr than an idiot, and Father Ignatius couldn't help but compare himself to such people. He knew he wouldn't last a minute under torture but would recant in an instant. He hated physical pain. He hated the cold. He hated the harshness of the world and the wickedness of men. He felt a moment of despair as he often did when such thoughts came flitting through his mind like bats unbidden. He hoped God would forgive him the weakness that forced him to think such things. He hoped his love for his church and the true care he felt for his parishioners would in some way compensate for his secret heresies. He thought of the great owl, which had slept silently on the eaves while the drama of Thomas and the girl took place below. He hadn't seen either of them since, and he and Stanley Izod had exchanged several glances over her empty pew the past few mornings. They wondered if they should tell someone about what had happened. But would anyone care about the disappearance of a rapscallion boy? And by tomorrow the entire population of London would have heard what had happened at her house, which stood emptied of its inhabitants right opposite St Anthony's on the other side of the square, accusing him with its blank windows every time he glimpsed furtively in its direction. Stanley had asked him confidentially that very morning if they shouldn't mention something of it and he agreed he supposed they should. After all, Mrs Brackman knew as much as they did, and being a woman, and worse, a widow, it wouldn't be long before her tongue started flapping. It would be best to get the whole thing out in the open, and he and Stanley had agreed that Father Ignatius would take a trip over to the house as soon as possible and have a quick word with the man put there by the Authority of the Borough to guard the entrance and stop looting and sightseers. He'd been sitting on a folding wooden chair just inside the railing by the front steps. From here, the man could also keep an eye on the gate to the yard, which had been bolted now, but wasn't so high that someone sprightly couldn't get a grip on it and leap over the top. There'd never been so much fuss in the square, even more so than when that suicide had been brought out of the church the week before.

Father Ignatius shuddered and felt the breath of evil pass over his bare neck. It surely seemed curious that two such strange things should happen so close together and not be seen as partners in a pair. He'd once been present at the birth of a boy who appeared to have two heads melded together like a double nut. Thankfully, his birth had also been his death and he'd never taken even a single suck of earthly air but had gone straight from one dark place into another. It had given him this same feeling of foreboding, an impulse of urgency that made every small occurrence take on great import, the constant suggestion of whispers around every corner, murmurs emanating from every wall.

Because his church was the closest to the locus of the tragedy he had been called in to bless the dead, although none of the household except Mabel ever attended his church. Presumably, if they went at all, they went to St Mark's over the other side of the street away from the square. St Mark's was Church of England, unlike St Anthony's, which had kept to the Catholic faith. Whatever the circumstances, he had been called in. As soon as the two out-living maids had arrived at the Midweather-Etherington house for duty soon after daybreak, they had found what they had found. Their screams had pierced the early morning quiet and though there were no immediate neighbours adjacent to the big Etherington house, it hadn't taken long to rouse Dibbleworth, the caretaker of the Innocent Martyrs, who had set about calling the authorities and calling James the footman from home to guard his employer's house.

The authorities had wanted to remove the bodies as soon as possible since, despite the bite of frost that had crept over grass and pavement as soon as the sun began to lower in the sky, the smell of spilt blood was spreading from the upstairs room and hampering any attempt at investigation. First thing was to get the corpses out and all the bedding with them. The rug would have to go too. Apart from the blood, it was covered with various people's vomit. Even out in the open, the sight of those five bodies stiffening on their crude white stretchers in their strange rigor-rigged positions, had made Father Ignatius retch helplessly before he had even come close. When at last he had emptied his gut and made his way across the yard to where they lay in a line by the water pump, his mouth was bitter as gall and the smell of freshly coagulated blood was just like the stink of the butcher's stall without the small comfort of sawdust.

He simply couldn't believe what had happened to these people, who of course he knew, though maybe not well. And despite that, he had a hard time actually recognising them. Death did so many different things to a body: changed its colour, the consistency of skin, rearranged hair and clothing and limbs, gave all a weirdness of position they had not possessed in life. These ones were worse by far than anything he had ever seen. The body that was Edward seemed to have doubled in size and the visible parts were swollen into over-boiled eggs, where the yolk has hardened and is ringed around with a dull and bleeding black. The friend, Penelope Witheridge, was the least marked and looked almost normal, though her face seemed to have been moulded in yellow wax. The others, with their throats all sliced open, he couldn't even bear to look at.

He had closed his eyes and murmured his prayers and sprinkled his holy water, then backed away home before his legs gave way beneath him. He had managed to note that Mabel was not amongst these tattered and broken things. He couldn't call them people. He hoped he was right about God, and that if there was anything left of them, He had taken their souls to Him before the agony of dying had set in. Seeing their faces, he rather doubted it, but all his life he had been taught that faith was something you cannot see, and right now, the raggle of faith that was left him was all he'd got.

Several miles to the north at Erith, Castracani had just set off with his two companions and driver. First, they arrived at Aldo Santorelli's house. Opening the door released a strong odour of mildew and mushrooms, the stale air hanging along the corridor leading to the kitchen. Halfway there, by the entrance to the big downstairs room of which the door stood open, Castracani poked at the boards with the ferrule of his stick.

'This looks like blood,' he commented almost absently, stepping over the stain and entering the room. He had never been here in this room, or in this house; had barely heard of Santorelli before the night of the fire. That was when Sandrini had told him the real tale of the relics of Lucca and the race to stop the treachery before it ruined all their lives. That was the first time he had learnt the truth of all those old tales. How he knew that Aldo Santorelli was the holder of an ancient guardianship of which only six people, the Inner Circle and Santorelli himself, had been aware existed. And now him. The Inner Circle was entrusting this secret to him, confident that he was the right man to do their bidding and stop the threat to their heritage, the whole Lucchese heritage. All those years ago the ancient relics had been brought to London for safekeeping: the nails and hair of Christ, the veil of Mary, the vial of blood. And somehow they had remained here ever since, safe, undisturbed, forgotten, until now, when Lucca had need of them back. But before they had time to get to the archives, unbury the ledger that contained the secrets of their hiding, the Silk Quarter had gone up in flames, and the Inner Circle and archives with it. Aldo Santorelli was the only man alive who had the key to the mystery. And although there was one other way, as Sandrini had told him that night, Santorelli was by far the better option. But Santorelli had vanished and there was blood on his floor, and signs of disturbance in his rooms.

Castracani's men searched the house, forced the hatchway into the attic, went through every scrap of paper, shook out every book, looked behind the precious tapestry that told the history of their hometown, pulled out every drawer, lifted every picture, checked every plank below every carpet for signs it had been disturbed. They found nothing. Except a small square of torn paper lying under the desk by the over-turned chair. It had a name and address on it; one scribbled out, one underlined.

Castracani wasted no more time. He knew what this meant. He left one man to continue the search, gave instructions as to where he would be and, holding that scrap of paper tightly in his hand, he strode out of the musty house and on to the street. At last he had somewhere he could go, a scent to lead him along the trail, cold as it might be. He knew the revelation he had had the night before had been right. He was sad he was right. He knew that Aldo Santorelli was no longer in this world and that whatever had happened, he had not gone willingly.

Castracani called up his carriage and told the driver to take him to Bexleyheath. Specifically, to the church of St Anthony's. The driver didn't need to be told to hurry. Like everyone else in the quarter, he knew that something big was going on. Even before the fire, it had been noticed that the Inner Circle had convened several times and had sent out certain missives. It was generally known now that Aldo Santorelli was missing. He had no immediate family, but his closest relatives had been summoned before what remained of the Council. People were worried, getting a little paranoid. Sometimes when they saw a stranger on the street corner, they switched their conversations to Italian as they passed him by. Just in case. The young men of the big families were all stoked up and went about in little knots and gangs, tight-lipped, knives and pistols on ostentatious display. The few Council members who had been out and about had looked worried and refused to talk; only Castracani seemed to be in control and now here he was on some kind of mission, starting with Santorelli's house and ending at a church in Bexleyheath.

Guido, Castracani's driver for over twenty years, knew Marco, Bandorello's manservant, played dominoes with him, drank with him. Marco heard things and usually passed them on. This time, Marco would say nothing, wouldn't leave the house. Now Guido was driving the most important man in the community on some urgent errand. He licked his lips and thought about where they might be going and what they might be doing. They lurched a little as they went over an uneven paving stone, but it wasn't that that had made Guido's stomach turn over. He was nervous, he was sweating more than usual. It occurred to him that perhaps he didn't want to know what was going on at all. He had a sudden desire to be sitting in his lodgings, perhaps with the backgammon set laid out all neatly before him, waiting for someone to throw the dice, the smell of risotto coming from the kitchen, a carafe of decent wine ready to be poured.

He shivered as the sky, without warning, let loose a cascade of sharpened rain. Within minutes, the squall had hardened into hailstones, and he had to tip his hat forward and pull his scarf up over his nose to continue seeing where he was going. The streets cleared as children and women ducked through doorways and men hunched their shoulders against the sudden cold. The discarded hailstones bounced from roofs and overcoats, huddled in small heaps against gutters and pavement faces, or rolled into dark, thin puddles and disappeared.

From inside the carriage Castracani noticed them too, rattling briefly against the stiff tarpaulin roof. The two men with him pulled their capes about them; Aribert, the older man, had been a soldier and seen and done too many things to be startled by a hailstorm. Still, he noted his companion bodyguard was jumpy as a cat in a cannon and he withdrew a flask from his pocket, offered it to the younger man who refused, and instead took out a box of snuff. His name was Antonio and he was cousin to Aldo Santorelli. He had begged this mission, though plainly being unsuited and untried, but his pleas of kinship had been heard, his keen feeling of duty to his family's honour acknowledged, his service admitted.

Castracani watched them, no expression upon his face, then closed his eyes. He hoped they would reach St Anthony's quickly. There was so much that needed to be done, to be unravelled, to be reravelled. His shoulders sagged and shivered. He tried to sleep, but saw only the insubstantial darkness of smoke.

Thomas woke slowly, sleepy and warm, the dog snoring quietly under his chin; for a while he did not move and did not want to move. His eyes moved lazily back and forth though he did not move his head. He saw the sand-dog, pushed back slightly from the door, the prickly mat, which was bald in one corner and missing another altogether. He saw the legs of the small table and its set of chairs like children, unruly, untidy, set at angles, standing where they had been left and not where they were supposed to be. The floor was quite dirty, he saw, though the teeth of the broom, which stood behind the door, were obviously well used, and there were neat little ridges of sand and dust here and there where someone had swept them like miniature waves upon a sea of black and white squares. Bindlestiff suddenly twitched his paws and yawned, and even though Thomas's head was behind him, it was hard not to recoil from the sheer awfulness of dog-breath. He'd smelt rotten fish before, and this was worse.

He gently pulled his arm out from under the dog and sat himself up, his back against the stove, still warm. He blinked several times, yawned himself and stretched, then stood up, shook the kettle and found it full, lifted the plate cover and set the kettle down. He tiptoed to the back door and opened it, urinated copiously out into the post-dawn light. There was a slight frost on the stalks of fennel, which though dead were still standing, the clusters of their heads slightly bent. He yawned and stretched again, did up his trousers, wriggled his shoulders back into his coat and started opening cupboards and drawers, trying to find mugs and pots and sachets of tea. It was fun, this opening and closing of hidden places, seeing tins of strange things and cartons and bottles of mysterious ingredients, which no doubt mixed up into wonderful things. Not like checking under the old crate for the bit of cheese from the baker's bin, making sure it hadn't been pinched by some bloody thief of a rat.

A picture of the old bridge came suddenly to his mind, with Toby still sleeping, and Thomas standing beside him eating their last apple right down to the core but only on one side. Leaving half carefully wrapped in a scrap of paper until Toby finally woke. Thomas shook his head angrily, swatting the memory away, slamming the cupboard that he had just opened without even looking inside.

He heard the door open, saw Stroop standing there watching him. He looked awful – big grey patches under his eyes, bristle striking up through his chin, scratchy red marks around his neck where he could see it sticking out like a cabbage stalk from his unbuttoned shirt. On the stove, the kettle began to hiss with steam.

'Can you make tea?' asked Stroop. His voice was hoarse and cracked.

'I think so,' said Thomas, 'with a pot and everything?'

'Yes,' Stroop said, 'with everything.'

Then he turned away and closed the door. Thomas had been feeling happy when he first woke up. Happy and warm and safe. He'd slept like a stone that's been dropped down a well, not being dragged to the surface every few minutes, just feeling protected and deep and warm. Now, as he tried all the cupboards again one by one, he felt worry and care creeping all over him again, taking him over, turning him inside out. But the time he had found the pot and the tea, all the water had boiled away and the kettle was dry.

Father Ignatius was just finishing the recital of the Te Deum when the door was gently opened and three men stepped inside the church. He had heard the hailstones that had battled for a few minutes against the glass windows before subsiding into a gentle droop of drizzling rain. He could hear rivulets of water gurgling along the tilted gutters, eddying down the drainage pipes, past gargoyles and gluts of rotting leaves, finally slewing away into the rain barrels at their base. The man who had initially entered stood back against the wall and allowed a second man to pass under his protective arm as he held the door wide. This second man looked sick and grey. He leaned a little too heavily on his stick, the metal ferrule sounding loudly on the flags as he creaked into the furthest pew and eased himself into the hard wooden seat. He seemed not to notice that every head had turned to stare, and there were plenty of heads, far more than usual.

Father Ignatius' services had never been so well attended. Some had come for comfort or protection, having heard what had happened over the square and of course what had gone on in his chapel. Others had come so they could have an excuse to poke about the church before strolling casually about the square, stopping hopefully in front of the House of Death, as the local crier had dubbed it, adding, for a few extra pennies, details that he could not possibly have been privy to. God knows, thought Ignatius, what they expected from the abandoned building. Did they expect to see blood oozing out over the balconies or corpses staring at them through the windows? If they'd seen what he had seen, they would regret it. He would be having nightmares for years to come.

He suddenly realised his mouth had stopped saying the words and he coughed quickly to bring his congregation's faces back to himself as he finished reciting the hymn. He couldn't help rushing through the responsories and being a little short with the final prayers. Like everyone else in the church, he had noticed that these men weren't like the others. They weren't the only strangers, to be sure, but they were the only ones who looked so strange. Their manner of dress was slightly at odds with the rest of the company, their skin was sallow, their features more defined, their demeanour somehow serious and with a touch of menace.

Father Ignatius saw Stanley Izod out of the corner of his eye. He was sneaking away with the offertory bowl, leaving the body of the church, taking sanctuary in the sacristy from which he could dash at a moment's notice if need be.

Ignatius finished the final blessing, holding his hand high

above his head to include the many extra bodies who were here. He thought he saw the seated stranger mouth the proper words along with him and nod his head as he said, 'Amen, and peace be with you,' but perhaps he didn't. The light was bad, having dimmed with the coming of the rain. He glanced up at the eaves but the owl wasn't there. He hadn't seen it since that last morning. He hoped it had found itself somewhere else to stay, somewhere dry and quiet and warm. He hoped it would come back. Hoped he would be here to see it when it did.

Mabel suddenly opened her eyes. The shutters to her room had been closed and it was still in darkness. She stared for a few minutes at the ceiling, unsure of the time. Then she saw that daylight was streaking through a shaft at the top of the left-hand shutter where the wood had warped. She rolled herself to one side of the bed and sat with the eiderdown around her shoulders. She couldn't remember going to sleep, but she remembered the room. It was a pleasant room, plain and comfortable. It looked as if it was, or had been, a woman's room, and she paused briefly, thinking about Stroop.

She had assumed he lived alone, but there was no reason he shouldn't be married. Have children even. But somehow she knew that he wasn't, and didn't, that there hadn't been a woman in this house for a very long time.

She got up. Her feet were cold and she wriggled them into her boots. She felt in sore need of a wash and change of clothes. She opened the small wardrobe that leant crookedly to one side, one of its feet having broken off or been eaten through by mice. Sure enough, there were dresses here, all small – a girl's dresses, she thought. She put out her hand and touched one of them, drew it to her nose. It felt damp and smelled of mould. She let it go and watched it swing back into darkness. She would have to be content with the clothes she'd got on now, for a while at least.

She went to the window, opened the shutters, was surprised at the depth of day that was going on outside. How long had she slept? She had absolutely no idea, but she felt rested and, more than that, she was happy. It was as if a shutter had come down in her head overnight and separated off one bit of her life from another as definitively as with the blade of a guillotine. She could recall all the images she had seen, but now they were as if they had happened a long time ago, and happened not to her but to someone else. She felt a slight remorse, an empathy for the child it had all happened to, but was equally glad that it hadn't happened to her. She knew who she was, of course, and where she was and what had happened, but the paradox seemed irrelevant and she didn't even allow herself to think of it.

She went out into the corridor and tiptoed into Jack's room next door. He was still sleeping, but he woke dreamily as she started to unwrap his neck-bindings. She took the flannel and bowl of water from the cabinet and began gently to soak his wounds. He flinched a little from the cold but otherwise it was amazing what little damage had been done, at least on the outside. The scar tissue seemed to have sucked itself back together, and though a trickle of clear liquid seeped from the wounds, there was very little blood. Mabel went back into her room and riffled through the drawers of the wardrobe. She found a linen stole that wasn't quite as damp as the other things, and came back to Jack, laying it gently over his wounded neck, tying it off at the back.

'Feeling all right?' she asked softly, but Jack had already closed his eyes and, with a large smile on his face, had gone soundly back to sleep.

What goes on in there? thought Mabel, watching him wriggle back into sleep. Is it better in there than out here?

She shook herself and got to her feet. She already knew the answer to that question, but luckily, it was on the other side of the shutter, and for a while at least, there it could stay. Just for this small part of the morning, she would shut out the worry and care she knew would be waiting for her downstairs.

24

There Are Times When . . .

IT WAS A day for worrying, as Father Ignatius was also finding out. He was standing at the church door, shaking hands with his newly flourishing congregation, trying to persuade the newcomers to soon return. He knew that the swollen population would have had a good effect on the offertory bowl, and that perhaps he and Stanley might celebrate with something special tonight: a hot veal pie perhaps, with mustard sauce, and maybe a couple of bottles of decent port rather than the cheap church wine that he sipped as little of as possible, even during communion. It was down to the bottom of the barrel and getting sour. The bells had gone silent as he shook the last few hands, and he saw the bell-ringer trotting down the street by the river to go and launch his precious boat. If he wasn't on the end of one kind of rope, he was at the end of another. All he did was go fishing, and all he ever caught were rancid roach and perch that had been in the river too long and had spent the time sharpening their bones into needles. God knew, he'd been given enough of them. Still, that was not his main worry of the moment.

All the while he had been shaking hands, giving people a final blessing or a little chat, he had noticed the strange trio out of the corner of his eye. Only one of them was sitting, and though his back was to Father Ignatius, he could see by the bend of his head that he was tired, very old or perhaps penitent, although the latter didn't seem likely. The two others stood behind him, obviously bodyguards. The older one was at ease, confident, he had the bulk and build of a soldier, one hard hand resting on the pew, the other hooked into his belt buckle, a fraction of an inch from his dagger. The other was jittery, his colour high, his eyes flittered around from one side to the other, never at rest. It was plain, even to Father Ignatius, that this man wasn't used to the job. He was nervous, inexperienced, probably dangerous.

When the last of the congregation had left, Father Ignatius could put off the confrontation no longer. The three men were still there and obviously had no intention of leaving. The church doors were still open, and Father Ignatius wondered for a moment whether he shouldn't just step outside and leave. It wouldn't take him long to scuttle across the square; he could visit a few sick people, or maybe go to Widow Brackman, who was always ready with a cup of tea and a cake. The wind had veered to the east and was pushing the rain in through the church door. It streaked the flagstones at his feet, brought him back; he knew he couldn't run away, despite his fear. Sighing, he closed the doors. It could be worse, he thought, at least he knew Stanley Izod was still in the sacristy. He would have put the offertory money in the cupboard by now and was probably standing with the door ajar, listening. Father Ignatius had no doubt that Stanley had seen these strange men come into the church. Everybody had craned their neck for a look; perhaps it made up for not having a fresh corpse in the chantry chapel. He closed his eyes a moment, cleared his throat, and spoke.

'Is there anything I can do for you, sir?'

He addressed the seated man, even though he was behind him. The man seemed to know it was him who was being spoken to and he began to get himself to his feet. Father Ignatius heard the tip of his stick scraping on the stone. By the time Father Ignatius had come level with the pew, the man was standing. He seemed to be having some trouble moving, was stiff with arthritis perhaps, although despite his earlier observations, this man wasn't particularly old. His skin was oddly discoloured, slightly mottled on one side, and as he steadied himself, Ignatius saw that the man's knuckles were scraped as if he had been in a fight. Father Ignatius couldn't imagine what had caused such injuries; a man like this did not get into idle games of fisticuffs. Besides, didn't he have two bodyguards to do all that sort of thing for him? It was obvious this was a man of authority; it was equally obvious that though normally a strong man, for some reason he was at the present moment in a state of weakness. Father Ignatius wondered what on earth could drag such a man out of the bed in which he patently belong, and bring him here, to his church, of all places. It wasn't a grand place, it wasn't well known; it was old, of course, but most churches were. He had a foreboding, eyes glancing over to the chantry chapel on his left, couldn't help seeing the large stain that he could not erase, no matter how many times he had Stanley scrub the stones. Every time he looked, the stones still looked wet with blood, even if no one else could see it.

'Can I be of help?' he repeated, tucking his hands into his sleeves, feeling the goosebumps on his flesh, the coldness of his fingers. His voice, after years of practice and preaching, sounded far more calm than he felt, its monotone heightened by cadences of lift and fall, modulated to enhance the most boring biblical reading. The stranger forced a smile, which made him look wearier than ever. His eyes were sad, a little bloodshot. Father Ignatius was used to reading people, and it occurred to him that this man was not the threat he had initially supposed, that perhaps this man needed help and guidance, that perhaps God had not forgotten him after all and had brought this stranger specifically to him.

'My name,' said the man, offering Ignatius the hand that was not holding the stick, 'is Petrus Castracani, and I wish you well. Excuse my intrusion,' he waved his hand slightly in the direction of his bodyguards, 'but it is imperative I talk with you.'

Ignatius was apprehensive still, but no longer fearful. He motioned Castracani to follow him to the sacristy where they could sit. He was too embarrassed to offer his visitor his bilge-wine, and settled for offering nothing. Once Castracani had been seated, the two other men remained standing by the door. Ignatius removed his liturgical garb without hurry, folding each piece with care, until he was once more down to his bare black cassock. He felt the tension easing as he always did when he removed the fripperies of his office. He liked things simple and plain – that way they were easier to understand. As he sat opposite this Castracani, he noticed that Stanley was nowhere to be seen; he also noted that the side door had not been quite pulled to, and wondered if Stanley was standing out there in the rain, waiting. He hoped so.

'I need to ask you a few things,' said this Petrus Castracani, 'about a certain incident that happened here a week or so back, and perhaps also of a girl, a young woman of whom you may have knowledge.'

He coughed a little, and Ignatius stood and got him a carafe of water. Castracani thanked him, then went on.

'Please understand, you are not obligated to tell me anything. We are of the same faith and I honour the seal of all the sacraments, but this is of the utmost importance. Particularly concerning the girl. Or woman. I am unsure of her age, but I do know that she is, at this moment, in very great danger. I am here only to help her as I am hoping she can help me. As you can see, I have protection and I can protect her too.'

He was about to continue but he started coughing again, violently this time. When he had finished, he sipped at the water, clutching the glass with both hands. One of his body-guards, the soldier, came forward, placed his hand on Castracani's back, then retreated to his post. Father Ignatius watched the lines on the man's face. They were impregnated with something – with what? It looked like soot. He could see also that as the man coughed and his hat tipped slightly to one side, that his hair had been singed back to his skin. Realisation made his scalp crawl. This man was from the Italian quarter. The whole town was gossiping about the dreadful fire raging through houses, rampaging down the streets. People had terrified each other with old tales of the Great Fire, and some had started packing away their valuables in case the wind changed, and caught at the old ashes, carried sparks across the streets and hamlets into Bexleyheath. Of course, it was nonsense. There had been no danger to anyone else. It had been quite clear in the reports he had come across that the conflagration had been localised. Perhaps too localised, thought Ignatius. And all this tragedy had happened within the boundaries of a week. He couldn't see how which was connected to what, but he didn't doubt there was a connection. He made a decision – an unusual event, for ordinarily he was a man who preferred to let things take their own course – and while Castracani was still dabbing at a black-spattered handkerchief, Father Ignatius spoke.

'The girl, the young woman you are talking about, is called Mabel Flinchurst. She lives in the house across the square. Or rather, she used to. No one knows where the poor child is now, only that great misfortune has visited her home.'

Castracani looked puzzled. 'What misfortune is this? We are not talking about the man who killed himself in your chapel?'

Ignatius kept his sharp gaze on Castracani. He had known that this would come up sooner or later. He hoped that someday someone would explain to him that suicide; so much interest in the unfortunate man, not unnaturally, considering the manner of his death, but so much mystery too. Ignatius was used to knowing people's secrets and he saw that there was a secret here. He also saw that no one was going to tell him anything very much at all. He was chary, wondered if he should exchange information now rather than just provide. Father Ignatius was a man who was curious about other people's lives. He heard so many bits and pieces, confessions from one or another, pieces of puzzles he tried to fit together from what people said. His interest was not salacious, but he derived a satisfaction from knowing he had fitted two things together correctly. The adulterer with his mistress, the victim with the thief, the sinner to his crime.

'Mabel lives, lived with her great-aunt who owns the house just across the square behind the church. Yesterday, no one knows when or why, a gang of murderers broke into the house and killed everybody there. Even the stable-boy who, God knows, was no saint, but no one deserves to die like that. He was stabbed, I am told, and not only once.'

'They were robbed?' asked Castracani. He had kept his eyes downcast, but Father Ignatius, who was studying his guest intently, was ready to swear he saw a tear drop on to the table. His fear had left him completely and now that he was speaking of it, all he felt was an overwhelming sadness for Mabel, and he wondered what she would do now. Return to her father's farm, he thought, which, who knew, might even make her happy.

'There was much destruction in the house, I gather, but the valuables do not appear to have been touched except to have been destroyed. It is a most odd occurrence for which there seems no explanation . . .'

Ignatius left the sentence hanging in the small hope that this stranger, who plainly knew something about the affair, would give him an answer. But the man was silent for a moment, then he turned to one of his guards, the older one, and told him to go over the square and find out as much as he could. The younger man was itching to accompany him, but Castracani did not give him leave and he was left hanging half in the sacristy, half out of the door, a look of mute frustration covering his dark features. He was a handsome lad, thought Ignatius, though God help the girl who fell for his charms without first chaining him to an altar.

At that moment the outer door to the sacristy opened fully, and Stanley Izod stood on the threshold. The younger man lunged across the room and stood in front of Castracani, fumbling with his clothes, finally removing a pistol, which he had kept in some concealed pocket, and pointing it at Stanley's head. Stanley stood absolutely still, except for very slowly lowering his raised foot back to the floor. Father Ignatius stood up and the pistol swung round, almost knocking into him, it was so close. Ignatius saw panic in the young man's eyes as he swung his arm back again, keeping Stanley in his sights. It was plain he wasn't used to handling firearms, but if he somehow managed to find the trigger, there was little doubt he would hit at least one of them in the confined space of the sacristy. But before anything could happen, Castracani put out his hand and rested it on the young man's sleeve, forcing him to lower his arm.

'It's all right, Antonio, it's all right. These people are not our enemies. It is their help we have need of, not their blood. God knows, there's been more than enough shed already.'

The boy – and he looked very much like one at that moment, sweat beading his forehead, wetting the short dark curls into commas – did as he was told and stepped back behind Castracani. There was a feeling in the room that some boundary had been passed, the boy's hand trembling as he resecreted his pistol, and Stanley walked solidly, slowly, into the room.

'This is Stanley Izod,' said Father Ignatius.

He pointed Stanley to a chair, but Stanley stayed standing,

twisting the rim of his hat in his hands. All the while he had stood there in the doorway, he hadn't twitched; the expression on his face hadn't changed. There had been no fear in his eyes, no terrified tics of movement giving away his concern. It occurred to Ignatius that Stanley had had no concern. There had always been a certainty about him, that absolute belief in something bigger than himself. He has more faith than I will ever have, thought Ignatius sadly, and he is the better man.

'I took the girl to Mr Stroop's house.' Stanley said what he had come to say. He had indeed been waiting outside the door, the raindrops spitting from the gutter on to his head. He had been ready to barge in if Father Ignatius had been in trouble, had taken the time to lift a hammer from his tool-bag and tuck it in his trousers. He was not generally a man of action, he knew his mind was not sharp, that it took him longer to think a thing through than it did for other people, but when he'd seen those strangers coming into the church – into his church – he knew that he would not let them bring their trouble in here with them. And he would have done anything to get that trouble back out on the streets where it belonged. He had grown up in Bexleyheath, only two streets over. St Anthony's had been his special place of sanctuary and peace for over fifty years. He had known every priest, every elder, every deacon who had ever knelt before its altar. He knew every brick, every window, every crack of this place. He would sooner have burned down his own home than have harm come within the walls of St Anthony's. But as the visitor had talked, Stanley had heard something in his voice. It was authority. It was need, it was also empathy. He knew that his man understood far more about what was going on than he ever would. He also understood that this man, this stranger, was strangely familiar. He was very like Father Matteo who had been at St Anthony's when Stanley was just a lad. Father Matteo had been just that — a father to Stanley when Stanley had no one else. Whenever he had troubles, he would go to Father Matteo and Father Matteo would do whatever he could to lift the burden from Stanley's shoulders and take it for himself. It seemed to Stanley that Castracani was that kind of man also. It was something about the way he spoke, the words he said, the manner in which he said them, the quietness of his body as he sat almost crumpled in his chair. The crease of silent mourning in his face. This is a man who has seen bad things and knows how bad things can be, thought Stanley. This is a man like Matteo, who will gladly take our troubles from us now, if only he can. And then he made up his mind and spoke.

'I took the girl to Mr Stroop's house,' said Stanley. 'I can take you there,' he added hopefully. 'You'll find her there, I'm sure.'

They were all looking at him. Father Ignatius still stood with his hand on the back of his chair. He wondered how far outside Bexleyheath Stanley Izod had ever been. He wondered if going to Stroop's house that time had been the furthest he had ever gone. He was a man who knew where he belonged, and Ignatius suddenly pitied him and envied him, and had to turn his face away.

25

Knots Within Knots

IT HAD BEEN a hard day for Antonio Santorelli, from the moment they'd set foot in his cousin's house that morning, to where they were now, in this musty sacristy. His heart was still beating fast and his skin felt clammy. He had an awful feeling that the walls were tumbling in and had an urgent need to get out. He was glad the sacristy door was still open and he could feel the cold, wet air blowing in, see the supple back of the river gliding on regardless under a bridge as it rounded the bend. All that water, he thought, where does it all go? He guessed he was still in shock from earlier, when they had gone to see that dreadful undertaker, Dismal Cobbett. Somehow Castracani had known to go there; he'd had messengers out all the previous night. So they'd gone from his cousin's straight on to see Cobbett, who had obviously been annoyed he was being interrupted.

'Taking the stinkies to the suicide pit,' he'd grumbled. 'Got no time to sit and chat.' But he'd got down off the trap anyway and walked round back to where they stood. He didn't like the look of these men – bloody shifty foreigners is what they looked like – and he could tell straightaway that they would know that body that had been lying in his hammock all week. Same colour skin. Same pointy noses. Same shit-black hair. They'd want to take it away with them and that was going to cause him problems. Ruin his schedule. Still, they'd asked, and when the man in charge opened his mouth, Cobbett was surprised it was pure English that came out. No accent, nothing. So he'd pocketed the coin without comment, undone the rope holding the old sheets together at the top and roughly struggled with the layers until he'd got them down from the face. It was a bit sticky inside where the skin was beginning to go, and all three of the strangers involuntarily gagged and covered their mouths with their hands.

'I told you. Stinkies,' said Cobbett, not bothering to hide his smirk. There weren't many perks in his job, but this was one of them. The two older men only took a quick look, but the young one went pale as porridge and all that draining blood must have made his boots awful tight. No doubt about it, the young one recognised the stinkie. Course, it could just have been the smell and he had to admit it didn't look pretty, but all the same. The one who looked like a soldier put his hand on the boy's shoulder, led him away. The older one, the one in charge, closed his eyes and crossed himself.

'Where are you taking him?' he'd asked.

'Over beyond the green. Got a pit out back of St Andrew's, only place we're allowed to put them these days,' sighed Cobbett, as if in the good old days he would just have buried them where he stood. 'Suppose you want to take him your-selves then?'

There was a note of irritation in his voice, but Castracani didn't notice. He was thinking of the garden he was going to grow when all this was over. It would have to have a lot of trees, he thought sadly.

The undertaker's voice creaked at him again. 'So you taking him or what?'

Castracani shook his head. 'He's a suicide.' His voice was worn and grey as his face. 'We've nowhere to put him. Perhaps I'll come and visit him when . . .'

He didn't finish his sentence. An olive for Aldo, was what he was thinking, if only I can get it to grow.

'Suit yourself,' mumbled Dismal Cobbett, launching himself back on the trap. The pony, which had stood motionless throughout the whole exchange, started forward. Its head was still down, but its feet knew where to go.

'Giddup,' said Cobbett unnecessarily, and the three men watched him go, the trap bouncing on the uneven ruts of the road, the shrouded bodies lifting slightly with the move-ment, Aldo's face still uncovered, green as melon skin. Castracani found himself mouthing a prayer. Antonio was struggling not to cry. Aribert sighed inside and thought to himself, ah well. Another good man gone, as he brought out the small talisman around his neck and touched it to his lips.

Around the time Antonio last saw his cousin at Cobbett's, Mabel made up her mind to face the day and descended the stairs. Later, when Jack was up too, they all sat around Stroop's study table, which dwarfed the chairs they had dragged in from the kitchen and which had been made for a table much lower. It meant that Thomas and Mabel and

Jack, his neck tight bound but otherwise unhurt, were uncomfortably low, with the edge of the table far too high. A good interrogation technique, thought Mabel; easy to hide grub, thought Thomas; it makes us all look funny, thought Jack.

Stroop was standing by one of his bookcases, slotting another book back into its place. He scribbled something furiously in a notebook, then dotted it with a flourish, underlined the last few words, a thing he very rarely did. He didn't like to stress syllables and meanings. He thought that words worked perfectly well on their own and didn't need extra pushes or prods, at least not if you've got them in the right order. It was a mark of how tired and excited he felt. Feverish would be the word. All morning he had locked himself away in the study, another notebook open in front of him, writing, writing as much as he could remember of the previous night's work. Trying to get things exactly as he had had them before. And it was while he was doing this that certain other things occurred to him, about the way things had been written. There were clues here, he was sure, and he had been rushing up and down consulting this book and that, accumulating another large pile next to the one that was already there.

Now he had written the final word and had asked the others to come in. They had been sitting in the kitchen, chatting quietly, eating the soup Mabel had managed to make from the dregs of ingredients she had dragged from the cupboards – quite obviously Stroop rarely cooked, a surmise Jack confirmed.

'We usually goes to the pie shop,' he volunteered happily, 'or sometimes he sends me to the tavern for stew. We have fish too, but I don't like that very much so we don't have it very oftcn. I always gets bits of bone in it and I don't want to choke so I usually have to leave it after that.'

It was the longest sentence Mabel had heard him come out with, and it made her smile. They were like a little family sitting around this table, Thomas slurping at his soup, Jack picking out the bits with his fork and eating them first with great care and deliberation.

She'd taken a bowl in to Stroop, but it was still sitting untouched on the table when he called them in. He isn't looking well, she thought; I wonder if he's ever had anyone look after him? For some reason the idea embarrassed her, but no one noticed the slight flush creeping up her neck.

'I have managed to translate the writing that had been embroidered on the edge of your shawl, Mabel.' He looked at her, and she looked around the room, wondered for the first time where the shawl was. Last night she had seen it right here, on the table, with Stroop rootling around in a drawer mumbling about magnifying glasses.

Stroop carried on, 'It tells rather an unusual story, and a very old one. And she has your name,' he nodded across the table, 'Mabel.'

That got them going: Jack and Thomas started jiggling in their chairs, Mabel merely looked startled, her hand arrested halfway to her mouth.

'I told you how old it was last night. That was the one bit of the message that was fairly easy to decipher, it being numbers not letters. That shawl was made many, many years ago and took the seamstress a long time to complete. From 1257 to 1259. She was probably doing it in her spare time

and she probably didn't have much of that. She was embroiderer to Henry the Third, King of England, and I have
consulted my books. She is quite well known in certain
circles and much of her work has survived to the present
day, primarily because she embroidered religious or cere-
monial garments. Mostly in royal collections, some in the
abbeys and monasteries to which they were donated. There
are several fine examples in Westminster Abbey, and more in
Bury St Edmunds. But then there is your shawl, Mabel, and
this is what it says.' He tapped his notebook.

There was absolute silence.

'It contains the instructions to find the lost relics of Lucca.'

There was no time to say anything, for anyone to react,
because just then came a loud knocking on the door. Nobody
moved. Stroop blinked, then said in an urgent whisper, 'Mabel,
Thomas, upstairs now. Go into my room. Pull the bed away
from the wall. There's a small door there in the panelling.
Jack, go with them. Push the bed back as soon as they are
in, then you go and hide in the big blanket box and cover
yourself over.'

The knocking came again. It wasn't so loud as to be intim-
idating, but it was insistent. Mabel and Thomas and Jack went
swiftly and silently up the stairs. Stroop stood for a moment.
He didn't believe it could be the man who had been here
earlier that morning returning to find out more. Although
the only thing of him he knew was his voice, it was enough.
That was a man who could read between the lines; it might
take him a little longer than Stroop had taken, perhaps a
little time to get his hands on the right books, but he had
no doubt that he would get there. So who could be at the

door? He reasoned that if it were a gang of seasoned murderers then they would have the back door marked by now, and it wouldn't be long before they started to break it down. The idea upset Stroop. He hated the thought of leaving his house open and unlocked; they were going to come in anyway, so he might as well let them in. He tucked the notebook behind his trouser band, pulling his shirt over to cover the top, then he left the room, moved down the hallway, tried not to think what there might be on the other side of that door.

26

This Is the Story of Lucca . . .

THE CHRISTENING SHAWL was three feet by four, the embroidered glyphs small and hard to read. It was written in Latin, medieval, a little clumsy, mistakes made in grammar and tense, words truncated, vowels excluded to increase the space, though with fourteen feet of hemming, there was adequate length for what had been said. And what it said, as Stroop had discovered and transcribed throughout his long night, was this.

I am Mabel, wife of Ricardo Roncino, member of the court and embroiderer to the King. Here I lay out the history of Lucca and my small part in its history. In the year of 1247 the most holy relics of Lucca were under threat of theft and destruction by the enemies of the City. Many plans were made but only one was kept, and in that year, under aegis of King and Council, the holy relics of Lucca were brought to this shore. They travelled with brave men and true, who had come from the Holy Land on their own mission, seeking help for the

Crusades. They had with them their own relics, and the guard was strong. From Jerusalem to Lucca they travelled and then on to London to be received by the King. A letter from Robert, Patriarch of All Jerusalem and Legate to the Pope, travelled with them, and so too did our man and our treasures went with him. My husband and the Council were welcomed at Royal Court because of their trades and their dealings, and with Henry they had an agreement. For his royal protection and patronage, they would provide this most righteous and pious of kings a portion of the Holy Blood of Lucca. It was a goodly time. The messengers from Jerusalem had brought their own relic, a worthless thing, manufactured to suit their purpose and in which no true man of God would have believed. But Henry saw true our purpose and our gift and blessed us with his protection. With his own hands he carried a portion of the gift of Lucca's Holy Blood with him into the Abbey of Westminster where still it lies. For the other relics, he granted us his seal and we had leave to hide them as we would, and we chose to leave them under the protection of our Patron Saint, our Little Sister, and the Thirdmost Holy Face of God. We had promise of the Royal Seal of Silence, and though records were made and laid in our archives, the King himself gave instruction to lay down a message on the hem of his commission, a cope which I embroidered and which Henry gave in its entirety to the shrine at Bury. In this manner, he had always in mind the true nature of the Blood at Westminster, which would bring with it the Blessing of God Himself though nobody knew it but the King and our few of the Council here and in Lucca. In privy with the Council, I have made here my own copy of the secret of Lucca, for walls may fall and kingdoms come and go, but this I will leave to my daughter's daughter and hers to hers. With it I will bequeath my name, so that both my history and Lucca's shall be passed on in perpetuity, and so that my heirs shall have benefit and right to the Guardianship of Lucca who will forever oversee their wellbeing. The lives of my daughter and my daughter's daughters shall be as one with mine in their sharing the most sacred of secrets of Lucca and they will be precious, the one to the other. Thus has it taken me this time to complete, in the years of our Lord 1257 and 1259. God willing I shall live a long life, and our secrets shall live much longer than that, though it take centuries. This is the work and will of Mabel Isabella Roncino, embroideress to the Court and person of King Henry the Third of England, whom she will bless, as will her husband and his homeland, unto their last breath. God bless and protect all who take part in my story, and my daughter's and my daughter's daughters. Amen.

The man closed Stroop's notebook and placed it gently on his knee. This was the eighth or ninth time he had read it through. He needed to think. He knew he was missing something, yet knew he almost had it, as if some part of his mind had got there and was waiting for him to catch up, the way his horse, without it knowing it, calculated the fence long before he made the jump.

He poured himself another glass of wine. He'd stopped drinking in the morning since he'd got to London. He'd been here before many times, and had suffered badly from the surfeit of beer, the lack of crystal-clear wine, the thick clag of cider. But today he needed to relax. He had sent his servants, his companions, his men-at-arms away. He took a slow draught of the wine, reflected that it was not as warm as it would have been in Lucca. The very body of it seemed thinner, the taste shriller. He knew that if he could not succeed then he would never return, and what he wanted most in the world at that moment was to return home.

The sudden image of his parting raced through his mind like a tidal bore. He saw again his father who had levered himself out of his bed and had himself dressed for the occasion. He looked old and weary as he stood by his desk. His body was weak and thin, yet he retained that strength of presence he had always had. His father had beckoned him over and he had trotted obediently across the carpet, only to be met by a stinging blow across the face. He'd still felt a little woozy from last night's wine and the shock left him unable to speak. His father had turned away from him, sat heavily on the chair guided at the elbow by one of the two men with him. He had turned his back to his firstborn son and signed the document on the desk in front of him, as had the two men. Without moving he had pronounced his judgement.

'Boy, you have been a bad son to both me and to your mother, God rest her soul, and you have had your last chance. You are disinherited. Your brothers shall reap the reward they deserve. They may find it in their hearts to give you a roof over your head, but from me, and while I am still alive, you will receive nothing. And when I finally depart this earth and my family, I shall thank God that you are not a part of it.'

He had remained standing, shocked into immobility. His father's back shook slightly but he didn't move his head. He only extended his arm and shooed his son away, and away he had gone, moving backwards across the carpet, everything hazy and unreal. Then once outside the door he had stamped his foot, shaken his fist. He had gone out into the narrow alleyway behind the house and screamed. He went to the nearest bar but was disinclined to drink. He squeezed the bottle hard by the throat until it broke in his hand. He felt nothing, just sat there picking the glass shards out of his skin, watching the blood staunch and flow, staunch and flow as he flexed his fist. He knew looking down at his soft fingers that his father had been right, but that did not alleviate the overwhelming humiliation and anger that surged through him, making his head throb, his blood feel like it had been fed by scorpions.

A man caught him by the shoulder and as he wheeled round he saw it was one of the men from his father's study. He knew him. His name was Benedetto Gadi and he was high up in the Council, his brother was part of the Inner Circle, he had links with London and Venice, part-owned several of his family's business ventures. His father had sent him on errands for this man many times, to Italy, to England, several times to France.

Taraborrelli brought his fist up, bleeding as it was, but the man caught him hard around the wrist, pinioned his other arm to his side, brought him sharply round until Gadi had his elbow crooked around Taraborrelli's neck, leaving him gasping, tears of rage pouring down his cheeks, Gadi like an iron fetter behind him.

'I can make this better for you.' Gadi's voice was a gruff whisper, hard against his ear. 'I can give you power and wealth. I can give you what your family has taken away. And there is only one thing I need you to do . . .'

Taraborrelli realised as he sat here, a continent away from home, that something had changed in him. The anger was still there, but it had hardened within him into permanence, the humiliation had passed briefly into guilt and then dissipated. He realised for the first time that right up until now, until this adventure, this quest, his life had been illusion, all shadows and puppets and a changing cavalcade of masks. He smiled grimly as he reflected on this new-found purpose. His father might even take pride in his former son if he was still alive on his return. And he would return – that he swore. He would succeed. He would not be thought a failure. He would not tolerate having lost, being seen to have lost.

And he really had nothing left to lose. His brothers already had their hands on his inheritance; he might be older, but they had made the most advantageous marriages, linked lands, made contacts without whom the whole estate would collapse. He had been left behind as usual, or sent away. He realised that all those times he had been dispatched to London or Venice or Rome 'on business' it had simply been to get him out of the way. He'd wasted his years and youth riding horses, playing cards, travelling, while others slipped in and took control. He had shown no interest in the family business and now his brothers had grown up and taken what should have been his. And without this, they would succeed.

This venture would be his making, or else it would leave him undone. But he wouldn't think of that. He must concentrate. He would not admit defeat. He had got this far. He had found the Guardian; good God, he had beaten the Guardian half to death! What did that say about the London Lucchese and their pathetic secrets? They had no secrets, they were lost to their homeland. He had found the Guardian and the girl. And now he had the secret of secrets, if only he could unravel it.

He had too much pride to return to the scholarly Stroop, although that was the only reason he had left him alive. He must recover the lost treasure and return to Lucca with the power in his hands; he who had the relics had Lucca; and he who had Lucca could give Maria Bacciochi what she wanted and she would give he who had Lucca whatever he desired. He did not want it known that he had needed help, would not admit to himself that he could not solve the puzzle of a needle-wielding wench who spent her life braiding silks and threading threads hundreds of years ago.

He closed his eyes, squeezed out the image of his father's back bending over that desk, of the warm, dusty streets of Lucca, which smelled of oranges and oleander blooms and new-pressed olive oil. He banished these images from his mind, rested one hand on the little book, which still lay on his knee, rubbed his eyes with the other. He would find the answer, he was sure of it, he needed it. He took long, deep breaths and let his thoughts wander at random amongst all those words.

At almost that exact same time, Stroop put out his hand and opened his door to whatever lay on the other side.

27

Ports and Storms

THE TWO GREY men faced each other. Behind Castracani's
shoulder, a sift of snow whispered down upon the roofs
and gardens, melting upon contact as it would upon one's
tongue. Stroop felt panic rising in his throat and his limbs
twitched as if for flight. For a dreadful moment he wondered
if he would ever walk again beneath the arced afternoon of
a London sky, if he would ever feel rain upon his skin, wind
upon his face. His eyes blurred slightly but he drew deep
on his resolve, his hand holding the door handle as a man
who has been tipped overboard will grasp at the slightest
piece of wood that comes floating by. He wetted his tongue,
cleared his throat, thought of Mabel and the boys upstairs,
felt the notebook tucked in his trouser band.

The movement of two black rooks dancing through the
branches of a bare tree, their nests clearly visible as knots
against the silt-dark sky, caught his eyes, calmed him.
Everywhere, the world was going on as normal, oblivious to
the dramas unfolding in its creases and crinkles, hidden away
from the rest of life. Stroop of a sudden felt ridiculous

standing there, gripping the door knob, thinking dark thoughts. He cleared his throat. He spoke.

'Yes?'

Castracani had stayed silent when the door had opened, watching the man before him contain himself. Obviously he was nervous, looked like he hadn't slept for a week, and yet there was a resolve in his tight mouth, a lack of fear in those dark grey eyes, which gazed past him for a few seconds into the distance. His voice when he spoke was steady, not loud, but quite firm. Whoever he had been expecting, it surely was not Castracani.

'Mr Stroop, I assume.' Castracani spoke, leaning on his cane. He could feel the snow falling from the sky, the heavy stillness of the air, noticed the robin in the next-door's tree had ceased singing. 'You need have no fear of us. We are here to help you, and to help the girl.'

Stroop unfroze his hand from the door. He noticed the man had tipped his head slightly as he spoke. He saw the skin around his neck, deeply lined with soot, noted how bloodshot was his right eye, how hard he leant upon his cane. A quick glance at the two men with him showed their hands ready to grasp this man if he should suddenly fall. One was young, a little fidgety, the other was heavier, taller, his skin tough and scarred. A soldier, certainly. These were not men who garrotted milkmaids and massacred old women with less thought than it took to crush a bird's egg or stamp an ant underfoot. In fact, now he took stock of the men before him, their hands away from their weapons, though clearly they carried arms, a less murderous gang he had yet to see, and he grasped at last who they were.

'You are the Lucchese.' A statement, not a question; the slight undertow of singe and smoke, the pallor of the old man's skin, the solicitousness shown by his companions. He recalled, when they had left Aldo Santorelli's house, how the Silk Quarter had been in uproar with people shouting and the heat of the burning houses had singed at their skin even as they turned away from it, cinders falling through the sky like fireworks.

'You had better come in.'

Up in the cubbyhole behind Stroop's bed, where the roof sloped down and met the floor, Mabel and Thomas sat squashed and hunched, rubbing shoulders and backs with corners and bumps and surfaces of old mouldy objects they could not see. Tiny pinpricks of light slotted through the joists and tiles of the roof, but once the door had been closed and the bed pushed to, they sat in absolute darkness. The air was stifling, filled with must and dust and a century of powdered mouse droppings. Evidently next door's cat hadn't been hired out yet this year to keep the population down, so the sharp odour of fresh mouse-nest caught in their throats, and their knees where they had crawled in were stained with droppings. They held their breath as long as they could, pulled their clothes up to cover their mouths and noses, strained their ears to hear what was going on downstairs. Mabel's blood sounded like seashells in her ears and she hugged her knees close to her chest, battening down her body as far as she could, shrinking into the claustrophobic space. She felt Thomas's hand squeeze her arm, and she groped with her free hand to clasp his, and so they sat, sweat sucking at each other's palms, their breaths short and moist through their clothes, or stuck with motes when they breathed freely of the air. Both had their eyes open, though nothing could be seen save the small points of light above their heads, which flickered like distant, dimming stars.

Outside the room, in a small alcove at the top of the stairs, Jack had burrowed himself a nest in the blanket box, pulled the lid down over his head and fastened the rope pull around his wrist so it could only be opened with difficulty from the outside. It was warm, if cramped, and the closeness of the air made his chest heave a little, and the extra strain made his wounds ache. He clearly remembered lying in that shed with the fork tines puncturing his neck, as completely night-time as it seemed now, as completely quiet except for his own breathing and rats scratching in the old hay at the back of the stalls. Then, as now, he did not feel alarmed. It was squashed and lonely in here, but it would only be for a while. He closed his eyes and hummed a little tune to himself. He heard Stroop walking down the hallway to open the door and, taking deep breaths, Jack willed himself to fall asleep, knowing everything would be all right again when he woke.

Stroop showed the three men into his study where Castracani introduced himself briefly and sat down. The younger man also sat, but the soldier stood behind his master, where he could see both the window and the door, his back against the wall, his hands flexed, thumbs looped in his belt.

Stroop brought them some spiced wine, which he heated with a bit of water from the kettle. As he leant over the stove, pouring the steaming water into the wine jug, stirring in some dried lemon peel and a little angelica to sweeten it up, he had the absurd notion to laugh. He tried to stifle it, but couldn't keep back a short snort. The thought of Mabel and the boys upstairs, cowering in blanket boxes and attic spaces seemed suddenly absurd. He wanted to shout out, to bring them all down for the party. He felt light-headed, a little dizzy. Lack of sleep, he thought, a little logic getting into the stream of thoughts as it swept on by, and possibly being half-strangled in a meal-sack by some stranger who has crept in through your window in the middle of the night.

The rush of enfeebled intoxication left him as quickly as it had come. He replaced the kettle, leant for a few moments his back against the stove, savouring its warmth, its solidity and strength. It was so old, he remembered his father telling him, that when the old house fell down, they had to build the new one around it because it had sunk its feet into the earthen foundations, and little short of six oxen wrapped around with yokes would be able to get it to shift. He tried to drag some strength from its resilience, and indeed, felt a little firmer for its very presence, the fact that it had been here so long and remained immovable. He felt steadier as he carried the tray through to the study, but he would not call the children just yet. He would make sure. Too many mistakes had already been made and if blood were to be spilled in this house also, he would make sure that it was only his that stained the carpets and seeped into the floorboards below.

★　★　★

Castracani watched Stroop as he poured out the wine. He was curious about the scarring on the man's hands, the raspberry-red scratch marks ligatured around his neck, more curious still about the apparent loyalty he had in common with his own men of Lucca, though he knew from Stanley Izod that a week ago Stroop had probably never known of their home-town's existence.

He appreciated the fact that so far Stroop had kept his silence; it showed caution and patience and restraint. He was a man who, like Castracani himself, had the control and judgement to wait. He watched as Stroop took his seat, leant back, hands tight around his cup.

Castracani sipped gently at the tepid wine, which he could not taste, had tasted nothing but the damp of ashes since the fire. He saw in Stroop a reflection of himself: sombre, care-worn, a man who had seen too much in too short a time. He replaced his cup, wiped his lips with a serviette, decided it was time to tell Stroop the truth.

Castracani's narrative was concise but complete: how at the time of Lucca's greatest prosperity, in 1247, plans were hatched for its Holy Relics to be stolen in the hope that without them and the immense patronage brought by its pilgrims, Lucca would fall. It was a time of intense religiosity, and every man who had power had a reliquary. Louis IX of France had built the Saint-Chapelle for his Passion Relics, which was the splendour and envy of all Europe. Men of all stations were flying off to the Holy Lands on Crusades to crush the Moslem beneath the Christian heel. Lucca was famed as far as London for its olives and particularly its silk, but the intimate flux and flow of its wealth and power came from its pilgrims, who came from all over the world. The Volto Santo and its relics had unimpeachable provenance, having been brought to Lucca by God Himself. Kings and queens came to kneel at the foot of Lucca, and they brought gifts befitting their positions, and better, mercantile contacts, lucrative contracts. Even the poor, everyday pilgrims needed food and drink, somewhere to stay, souvenirs to remember their pilgrimage by. Without the relics, Lucca was just another town rising and falling with the centuries. If they betrayed God's trust, allowed His Gifts to be purloined and sold to the highest bidder, would God not withdraw Himself from their streets, leave them foundering, allow their city walls to be breached and broken? With God's Grace they had been so strong for so many years, it was unthinkable now to allow the town to betray its treasures.

And so the Council had charged Sandro Santorelli to take the relics to London for safekeeping. He went under guise of the returning Crusaders who carried a message to Henry, King of England. Even at that time of great belief and devotion it was generally acknowledged that the patriarchs of Jerusalem and Acre and the other city-states of the Holy Land had despatched so many relics in their constant quest for money and men to bolster the Crusades, that if all the splinters of the Holy Cross and nails were gathered together, they could build a ship and sail themselves back home. They were bringing this time to Henry III a portion of the supposed Holy Blood. Henry was devout and desperate for relics to enhance the reputation of his great cause, the Abbey at Westminster. Matthew Paris, royal chronicler, maker of the map of Britain, monk at St Albans Monastery, was among the many who puzzled over Henry's fanatical devotion to a portion of Holy Blood whose provenance was shaky, to say the least. It was also noted that despite his apparent utmost belief in this relic, he forwarded no help to the man who had supposedly sent it, Robert, Patriarch of Jerusalem.

The Lucchese, however, understood. They had traded a portion of the Lucchese Holy Blood, whose origins were unimpeachable, their efficacy proven in two centuries of Lucca's prosperity and pilgrimage. Henry agreed the substitution and gave his protection. It was perfect. He had his own Holy Blood, which would raise his abbey to the greatest shrine in the kingdom. Whether people knew or not that the Blood was really Holy was beside the point. It would soon prove itself in miracles and blessings. And so came the relics to London.

Of course, records had been kept. Sandro Santorelli had hidden a sealed document in the archives before he left, scratching a crude maze upon the cathedral wall to show its location. But he hadn't known then the ultimate hiding place of the relics.

Once in London, and the decision made, three records were made. One in the London Lucchese archives, now a drift of cinders blowing over the North Sea; a second commissioned by Henry himself, an embroidered cope, which he donated to the abbey at Bury. Of course Castracani had sent a delegation to Bury, but there were problems. First, the delegation could not explain directly the urgency of their need to access the cope nor tell the Abbey of the secrets inscribed upon its edging. Secondly, the cope was very old and precious, and like many such things it would not be on permanent display but kept in storage, which meant more time before the Lucchese scholars could petition the Abbey and gain access to study the meaning and the tale the cope had to tell. Thirdly, there was the distance of Bury. Time to get there and time to get back. And they had none.

Mabel had none.

She was the last thread they could follow, and what made it so urgent was that they were not the only ones.

The preceding night, Castracani had discovered the full extent of the treachery that had engulfed them. After the meeting of the men of the Silk Quarter, when Castracani had sat alone by the cathedral clock, things had suddenly taken shape. He had sent Marco to Luigi Golgafoni's, the printer of the quarter's weekly broadsheet. He had asked for all the man knew on the death of the suicide in the church. Marco had returned within the hour and had confirmed what Castracani had feared. Golgafoni had gone through his copy, had summoned the boy who originally filed the story. All the details they could remember had been written down. The description of the man, of his clothes, of his death, of the church, of the chapel, the way in which he had died, the place he had been taken to be stripped and swabbed, robbed and disposed of.

Castracani had wasted no time. Antonio Santorelli had been sent for. He recognised the description of the dead man's height and build and hair colour, the buckled boots. There was still doubt, of course, though Castracani already believed the man to have been Aldo Santorelli. The church was the church of St Anthony, and when they'd discovered that slip of paper in Santorelli's house, the girl's address had been given as St Anthony's Square. What room there for coincidence?

And then there had been Dámaso di Rudini.

Castracani had noted the man's strain at that meeting. The sweat had shone on him like a pilchard just pulled from a jar of oil. Marco had not needed to go far to find him. He'd not gone to the tavern with the others, had not gone home. He had been in Siccardi's Café, the small one on the corner of Via Canale and Via di Tessitóre.

He had confessed straightaway, had been frightened, had constantly murmured, 'I knew I should have said something, but I was drunk! I couldn't remember properly. But this man, he had been asking where all the Council lived. I shouldn't have said anything, but what was the harm? I was going to come and tell you in the morning, but it was my cousin, Veza. Veza Gozzoli, and who wants to get his family in trouble . . .'

And the name had confirmed what Castracani had already known. Gozzoli was well known to him, had been mentioned by Sandrini at their meeting. He had an associate, one who was suspected of dark things by the Inner Circle in Lucca. He was in the direct employ of the traitor, and though they knew not the traitor's name, they knew his. Aribert had brought the name with him. He was Piozzo Taraborrelli and had been the friend to whom Dámaso had been introduced. His arrogance hadn't even let him properly disguise his name: Pietro Tarrabombi, the so-called reporter from their home town, the man who had been so interested in where the

Inner Circle members lived, the man whom Dámaso in his pitiful state described as best he could. There was no Tarrabombi. There was only Taraborrelli, the man in the pay of those who would betray Lucca, who had brought destruction on their homes and families right here in London, who had taken so many lives with as much thought as throwing salt over his shoulder. Piozzo Taraborrelli. No one had seen him here but Castracani could feel him as if he had been a thundercloud, casting oppression and dis-ease wherever he had made his steps and his moves. And he wasn't far behind him now, Castracani knew. Just as he must now know about the girl. And Stroop knew about her too, and knew where she lay hidden, like the lost treasure of Lucca that she was.

Castracani looked at Stroop. Stroop looked steadily back. Castracani paused in his tale, sipped his wine, wiped away a thin accretion of black spittle that had formed at the edge of his mouth. His chest creaked with the effort of all this speaking, but he had almost done.

'We must take the blame of what has happened,' said Castracani sadly. 'We forgot about our own legacy. We treated it merely as a tradition and forgot the truth of it, as I believe had Lucca. It was all so long ago. How could it possibly matter to us now? And then,' he raised his hand, extended a finger to where the soldier stood stiffly behind him, 'and then Aribert here was sent galloping to London because Lucca had fallen to Napoleon along with the rest of Italy. It was discovered he had made a gift of our city to his sister, Maria Elisa Bacciochi, a most religious woman; maybe she requested Lucca for that very reason – our fame has long been wide. A contingent of Napoleon's soldiers came to Lucca and told us we had been bartered and sold as if we had been nothing more than an ancient ox or a field of poppies. With a garrison at our gates, we could do nothing but acquiesce. We were told we could go on unhindered, that our lives would not be changed. The name of Lucca was a mere title on a worthless deed, but it was prudent to pretend acceptance.

And then we received a missive from our new princess. You must understand that this Maria Elisa Bacciochi is a very devout and religious woman. She believes that what is God-given is absolute and sacrosanct, and there are no exceptions. The missive was clear. There was to be no disagreement. She asked to be shown the relics.'

Stroop rocked slightly on his elbows. He understood that at last the logic he believed in was about to make itself plain. An epiphany, he thought, when all the things you have seen finally become clear. Castracani's eyes had dropped. Stroop could see the grey lines the soot had etched around his eyes, his mouth. He wondered what this man might have been before; if he would ever be the same as he had been. The man creaked and his shoulders stooped. Here was no mystery. This man had suffered and was trying to suffer no more.

'The Council met. Of course, they would agree. She had sent her missive and they would comply. What harm in a religious woman viewing those things that are sacred to her and which at this moment she believed she owned? A date has been set. She is to visit Lucca on the sixth day of January. Epiphany.'

Stroop started at the word of which he had just been

thinking. Castracani didn't notice. He cleared his throat, carried on.

'The day which celebrates the Divine Being of Christ investing himself in our human world. But then come the doubts and the problems. Someone mentioned the old legends about the removal of the relics to London all those hundreds of years before. There was laughter at first, but when the Council asked at the cathedral, no key could be found. The back of the Volto Santo kept its secrets like a tomb. Scholars were sent to the archives, but no mention of the relics could be found. Five hundred years of dust were brushed from the back of the Volto Santo and the lock was picked. We know what they found. They found nothing. The relics are not there, because they are still here, in London. All they found was a piece of silk.'

Castracani was no longer looking at Stroop, as Stroop was no longer looking at him. Castracani's eyes were fixed on the table. He saw every grain and knot of the wood. He saw before him the empty body of the Volto Santo, he felt the dust of the centuries in his throat as they must have felt it, that other Inner Circle, breathing constricted by the awful news. Without the relics, they were worthless to Maria Elisa Bacciochi. Lucca would become the byword for a lie. She would cast them out as hypocrites and blasphemers. She would say they had traded on the Holy Face of God for monetary gain. Without the relics it was supposed to entomb, the Volto Santo itself would come into doubt and all the years of miracles and pilgrimage would count for nothing. Did he say it out loud? He wasn't even sure. But what he did know was that she would see the city-state of Lucca as anathema. She would call upon the Pope of Italy to excommunicate the place and the land on which it was built.

'At worst,' this time he knew he spoke aloud by the ghastly grating of the stone within his throat, 'she will call upon her brother to have us obliterated street by street, stone by stone, man by woman, child by child.'

Castracani looked at the edging of the table as if the vision of Lucca lay within its wood, as if already he could see it being dismantled splinter by splinter. He knew that at the very least, the reputation of Lucca would be destroyed. At first the Council had talked of substitution. How would she know? Couldn't they replace the holy relics? Couldn't they imitate what was lost with a few bags of fakery? It had been a short suggestion at the Inner Circle meeting, for there was not one of them could live with such a lie. This was Lucca. This was the essence of Lucca. This was what had kept them and secured them all these years. The Holy Face of God had not deserted them. It was they who had led their God into the wilderness, and it was they who must bring Him back. God had kept faith with them throughout these many years of goodness and prosperity, and they must keep their faith with Him. They had the map of silk. They had the maze on the cathedral wall. They had their compatriots in London. They had the Grace of God to bring back to Lucca what belonged to Lucca. The Holy Face of God had protected them all these years. Surely it would protect them now, in this final quest.

'But,' said Castracani, lifting his eyes from the table, from the wood, from the overbearing weight of history that keeled his shoulder like someone holding bark to the flame to make it bow, 'there is a problem. There is great power, political power, to be had. Whoever holds the relics and their story holds the fate of Lucca in his hands. The silk we spoke of, it was left by the original Santorelli as instructed. He took the relics, and left this little map in its place. For those who are able, it leads to the maze carved into the cathedral wall, and through the thread of archives to London. When the Council opened the Volto Santo, the silk was still there. But it had been disturbed. The creases of centuries were out of line as though they had been unfolded one way and folded back another. Outwardly, there was no sign of disturbance, no fingerprints in the dust, though perhaps they should have guessed by the ease with which the lock mechanism moved that someone had been there before them. Someone who knew the Bacciochi woman's plans. Someone who must be privy to the secrets of the Inner Circle. We wondered why they didn't take the map itself, but we think they need us. They need our knowledge. They are at our heels. These men are enemies of Lucca and must be stopped. They will sell our secrets to the highest bidder. Maybe they will sell the relics to Maria Bacciochi directly. Maybe they will sell them back to Lucca for some exorbitant price. We do not know. What we *do* know is that for Lucca, it is disaster. If Maria Bacciochi does not destroy us, they will, whoever they may be. If Lucca falls, so does our whole community in London. It is about power and who has it and who will buy it.'

The smoke that blackened Castracani's lungs began to choke him. The noise came from his chest like a fox barking on a frosty night. He said these words, but they seemed distant. He couldn't understand how someone could do what

251

they had done. He couldn't understand the man whose name he was about to speak, who would sell his homeland and its dependants as if their history was nothing. As if the Grace of God was nothing. As if the future of Lucca was little more than the bag of gold he was already seeing in his hands. It was hard for him, all this speaking, but he knew that now, around this other table, which had not been made by Sandro's grandfather, which had not stood here for more than five hundred years, that nevertheless what he said here would mean the first and last of his life: it meant Lucca, it meant what the Lucchese had built in London, it meant his life and the lives of all those who had already been destroyed. It meant far more than he could ever say. He sipped his wine. He tasted nothing. He wiped his chin where the wine had dribbled because his skin was swollen and no longer did his bidding. He coughed again and went on. He was almost finished, as was Lucca, unless something here around this table could halt the awful things that had come to pass.

'They have sent a man and his name is Piozzo Taraborrelli, a vicious young man who has great ambition and reason to seek gain by underhand means. He is a wastrel, but clever and cunning; he knows people here in London, has been here many times, has friends with connections in the Council. We have our suspicions of who has hired him and the Lucchese will carry out their own investigation.'

He did not mention that in Lucca, Inner Circle Member Tomaso Gadi had a brother Benedetto, that Benedetto Gadi was friend and business partner to Taraborrelli's father. Neither did he say the words he knew to be true: that Gadi, if he was indeed the guilty man, would surely hang for what he had done, maybe not by the public execution he deserved, but softly, quietly, with no secrets spilled. Nevertheless, his neck would see the inside of a noose and his body would be buried outside the city walls. These thoughts only took a moment to flicker through Castracani's mind.

Stroop noticed the slight hesitation, leaned over, poured a little more wine. Castracani closed his eyes, opened them and sighed.

'As for here, we know what he has done to the girl's family and we are sorry for it. We cannot guess what he did to the Guardian to make him do what he did, but we know Santorelli did it to protect the girl. We believe she is now in your care, and you must believe it is imperative we get to her before he does.'

Castracani stopped briefly, then repeated, 'It is imperative, Mr Stroop. He is here, in London right now. It is only a matter of time before he finds her, as we have found you.'

Stroop had closed his eyes and a faint smile ghosted his lips. The room was utterly steeped in silence except for the slight creak of Castracani's breathing and the nervous tap of the younger man's fingernails upon the table. Stroop at last understood the final pieces of the puzzle. With perfect clarity he saw the tale unfold across the centuries. The tapestry on Santorelli's wall became alive and lived and moved. It was a microcosmic story encompassing the best and worst that men had to offer each other, travelling, unravelling down hundreds of years, right to this place, this room, this table, these few men. Himself. Oddly he felt no fear but a great relief, a happiness even, that an end, long groped for, could finally be seen. He opened his eyes and smiled; at Aribert the soldier who had hightailed it from Lucca; at the younger man, Aldo Santorelli's cousin, too young, too inexperienced to bear the familial duty. At Castracani, a man who appeared, like himself, to have seen better days.

'I think,' said Stroop, getting to his feet, pushing back his chair, 'that there is someone you should meet.'

28

Different Threads, Same String

PIOZZO TARABORRELLI WAS cursing himself for having finished off all the members of the Inner Circle, which hadn't quite been his plan. Destruction of the archives and widespread disruption in the Lucchese quarter was his compass, as well as ridding himself of one or two of the Inner Circle members. He hadn't counted on them all being caught out at once. He had expected at least one of them to have survived so that he could, if necessary, squeeze him for further information. He'd heard that there *was* still one, but he had fled the town and would be heavily protected. Whatever. The Inner Circle was gone one way or another. Gadi at least would be pleased. He had two cousins over here in London, and one of them had been most anxious to help Taraborrelli at his task. Gadi had promised this cousin a seat on the London Lucchese Council when all the hullabaloo was over, and Gadi was a man who kept his promises.

Taraborrelli didn't care about the cousin one way or the other. It had crossed his mind that perhaps the man should be quietly disposed of in some backstreet or gaming house.

After all, he knew Taraborrelli's face and his name and his purpose, and that was something Taraborrelli didn't like. And quite recently he had come to appreciate what he did and didn't like. He had found the interrogation of Santorelli quite invigorating and had surprised himself at his talent for torture. He hadn't supposed he could be quite so callous and insensitive to another human being's pain, but there it was. At last he had found something he was good at. Perhaps a talent he might practise on Gadi's cousin before demonstrating it personally to his father, assuming he was still alive when Piozzo returned. If he wasn't, well, good riddance, and there were a few brothers he could work a way through instead.

He thought again about Santorelli and his spectacular exit from this world. He had been surprised the man had managed to drag his bruised bones as far as he had, had assumed he would make his way either directly to the girl or to another contact. His demise in the church had been entirely unforeseen. He supposed it to have been an empty gesture to kill himself practically in sight of the girl he was supposed to protect. It was a puzzle that niggled at him, but he soon dismissed it. He had more important things to think about. He needed to know where the relics had been concealed, and the only person who could tell him was himself, of that he was sure. He now had the only record, the only accessible record of their whereabouts, at least for the present, and he would find them. If he didn't, he vowed he would destroy the Bury cope as well and then the secret would be lost for ever. If not him, then no one. He looked down at Stroop's notes, at the sentences he had underlined. The answer was there, he knew it; he hadn't spent his life playing cards and backgammon and chess and a thousand other games without learning something of strategy and bluff and concealing the truth with false gambits. He understood a code was at work here, which of course was why he had been chosen for this particular task. He might be slandered behind his back and even to his face, but when it came down to the nub of it, those who mattered knew it was Piozzo Taraborrelli who was capable of picking free this knot. He stared at the words he had underlined.

'. . . the protection of our Patron Saint, our Little Sister, and the Thirdmost Holy Face of God.'

He furrowed his brows, rubbed his eyes, took a bite of bread he had dipped in a bowl of wine. He needed to think harder. He needed books. He stood up abruptly, shouted for his men. He gazed out of the window, saw the snow slowly scatter across the afternoon horizon, saw it linger for a moment on tiles, on tips of icy trees, saw the clouds coming in from the north, heavy and dark, a hint of yellow on their bellies, the menace of ice and cold. He shivered, turned from the window, knew he must complete his task no matter what. He would not be exiled to this dismal island where the soil was black instead of golden, where the wine was piss and perry instead of full and warm, where the sky scowled on you for half the year and wept weak warmth and showers the rest. Damn the lot of them, he thought, and damn his own pride. The sooner he was out of here the better, and he no longer cared for the means.

His men arrived from the kitchen where they had been drinking and playing cards. He told them to saddle up and get ready. They would force the hand of their foe and win the game. They would hie back to Stroop, and if that didn't work, well, as Piozzo Taraborrelli had always known, you could skin a cat one way or you could skin it another, and both of those ways he well knew. As he turned from the table his eye caught the glistening satin of Mabel's christening shawl. Which Mabel, it didn't matter. The innocence of that ancient secret maddened him and his head was filled with a boil of black thunder that he couldn't stop. His mouth grimaced and his hands reached out for the precious thing. He took his dagger from his belt and thrust it through, ripped the thing from top to bottom, twisting as he pulled like one would tear the skin from a new-born lamb. It was done. He threw the pieces in the fire, watched five-century-old stitching catch and burn, sending shivers of blue and green into the ascending flames as they licked their way through the blackened chimney and out into the dreich and drab of London air.

Aidan Wethelbridge was leaning on his broom smoking a cigarette. It was rough tobacco, cheap, cut in long hard strings that jagged at the thin paper, letting languid juts of thin smoke escape, making Wethelbridge work hard sucking the rest of it into his lungs. He took quick, deep drags, closing his eyes with the effort, pinching the cigarette closed with thumb and forefinger, both of which were yellow-stained and cracked, revealing a rawness underneath like the skin of new-born rats. He threw the last gasps of cigarette on to the floor, shuffling it under his boot, then dislodged the broom from the crook of his arm and began to sweep. He sneezed frequently as he always did when he got to the chapel. They used a different kind of incense in here and that was what did it, far worse here than in the main body of the church, although that was bad enough. The broom-bristles dragged across the stones; he liked the sound, found it comforting, liked the regularity of it, how it never changed. He got satisfaction from the minute mountain ridges he made of the dust, mini-molehills dotted with squashed fag-ends or owl-pellets, the occasional glimmer of foil or a small coin. His back ached as he took the long-handled shovel and began to destroy his creations, whole geographies undone by a single sweep of his brush. He emptied the shovel into an old tin pail, which he dragged around the church with him, and when he had finished going up and down the transepts and crisscrossing the nave with his broom, he sat down by the altar rail and rolled another fag, sat there smoking, coughing, gazing at the inelegant stained glass of the windows, clumsy in their execution, colours faded, the lead casings splitting or in some cases missing altogether.

The parish council talked about it every year – getting the repairs done, getting the paintings retouched. The one time they had actually done it had been badly. Instead of doing the job properly, they'd paid a local sign painter a pittance and he had gaudied up the window of St Frigidanus himself, making a mockery of the hermit-bishop who walked his way from Ireland to spread the Word of God.

It galled Aidan Wethelbridge each time he saw it, but just of late he'd noted with satisfaction that the cheap paint was beginning to flake off and he took great pleasure in sweeping below the window, getting rid of all the fakery, tipping it into the bucket with all the other muck, where it belonged.

He took out the old watch he kept in his top pocket. It was heavy and the face was all cracked over so he could hardly read the dials of which there were two – one for the days of the year, one showing the cycle of the moon. He'd been given it when he'd left service after fifty-two years, man and boy in one place just like his dad before him, steady as a tree as his dad had always been. That great big garden he'd taken care of for all those years, tending the beds and lawns, clipping the hedges, planting up new copses and orchards. He'd been with his dad when they first put up all the new beech standings along the driveway, after the big storm had knocked half the old trees down back in '71.

'Them'll still be here hundreds of years after you and me is gone,' his dad had told him. 'Hundreds of years, maybe three hundred, maybe five hundred, but they'll still be here when you and me is turned to dust and scattered across the earth. We're just small things, you and me, lad, but when you work a garden right, you'll still be right there in it a thousand years on.'

Aidan smiled and tapped the watch. It was beginning to get a bit rusty on the inside, just like himself. He'd heard dipping it in vinegar helped, but he hadn't tried it yet. Didn't want to ruin what little he had left. He always thought of what his dad said when he looked at the watch, thought of the garden and how his dad had been right. He could still see his father's hand in that garden, and his own, and was glad to think something of him would go on for long after he was gone. He sighed, stamped on the fag and put it in the bucket.

Late again, he was thinking. Why is that father always late?

He snapped the case of his watch shut and set it back in his pocket.

I'll give him this watch when I'm gone, thought Aidan, his old bones creaking as he pushed himself to standing on his broom. Not long now, though. No, it won't be all that long.

It didn't sadden him, this feeling of impending death. It had been with him ever since the snow had started falling late last night. He'd hobbled his way home just up the street from the church, the snow lacing the tip of his hat. He'd felt it cold upon his old skin, melting among his chin bristles, a breath of wind caught a flake, emptied it down the back of his shirt, making him shiver as it caught him on his neck. He'd felt it then, the finger of God, telling him it wouldn't be long. And that was all right, he'd thought, that was how things should be. Winter would see him in the ground, he was certain of it. He hoped he'd see the snowdrops up before he went, wanted a brief yellow wink of aconite, maybe get to see an early cherry blossom. But if he didn't, well, that was all right too. He'd seen it all before and knew he would remember. He stopped a moment in the street, his knobbly hand on the gate. He closed his eyes and held his face up to the clouds, felt the snowflakes gently pattering on his face.

'Yes,' he murmured, 'not long now. Not long now.' Then pushed open the gate and went in to make his tea.

Aribert rode like the devil down the darkening streets, hooves cracking the ice as they passed, cloth and cloak dappled by the snow, froth steaming from the horse's mouth and nostrils, flicking backwards into its mane. Aribert's eyes narrowed against the cold flakes that masked his vision, created phantoms and shadows lurking in the mouths of alleys and doorways. When he reached the gate he hit the ground running, leaving the horse to snort and stamp and wait for the return of his master. Pounding up the path, heart and lungs hammering like a blacksmith's forge, Aribert didn't knock, just flung the door open, hurled his way down the corridor, knife and pistol already in his hands, shoulder vicious against the study door, quick jab to the right as the wooden frame gave and he crashed into the room. Castracani still sat where he had left him, arms folded on the table in front of him, head slightly tilted to one side. Stroop and Santorelli had leapt to their feet, chairs scraping hard across the floor.

Aribert checked the room, saw the windows were tight, saw no alarm apart from at his entrance, his eyes quickly clipping from one face to the next. Castracani calm, almost somnolent, Stroop standing swaying, hands gripping hard at the table edge, Santorelli pale and sweating, a vein pumping spasmodically at his temple. Three children turning white faces towards him, two boys, one girl, dusty, unkempt, her eyes wide open but oddly unalarmed. He'd seen that look before in the wrecked faces of war-weary men who knew that whatever was coming, it couldn't be worse than what had gone before.

'You are all right?' He spoke his native tongue, fast, punctuated by short breaths. 'I have just come from the meeting as arranged, and Taraborrelli's hideout has been found, but he has left it. He is on his way here. He will be here any minute. We must leave. Right now. We must leave,' Aribert repeated, sheathing his knife, replacing his pistol, already moving to help Castracani from his seat, 'right now.'

★ ★ ★

When Castracani had set off for Dismal Cobbett's with Santorelli and Aribert, he had sent scouts out across the city looking for Piozzo Taraborrelli and the men who were working for him, including Veza Gozzoli from Lucca and Fillip Gadi from right here in London. No doubt by now the three of them would have several local ruffians in tow, but at least Castracani's men had good descriptions of Taraborrelli, Gozzoli and Gadi, particularly Gadi, whom all of them knew. And Castracani knew they must have been somewhere near the Silk Quarter, watching and waiting, or how could they have known exactly where to set the fires, the movements of the households, how to find Sandrini at Castracani's own house? They must also have been in the area by St Anthony's where they had snatched the boy from under the bridge. They had been at one time to Epping, to the Flinchurst Farm. Taraborrelli had also been to Stroop's, as Castracani had not long ago found out.

When Stroop had first brought the girl out from her hiding place, Castracani had almost laughed. Her unpinned hair was netted with cobwebs, her dress was torn at the knees and filthy, the big boots made her feet seem enormous. She was accompanied by a boy who might have been scraped off the corner of any street, and another who had a stiff cloth around his neck and the dazed eyes of a cat coming from night into day.

'Well, well,' Castracani had said, levering himself up, walking around the table to greet her, 'you must be Mabel. It is an honour, an honour,' and then he had taken her hand and held it to his lips, despite the grime and rime of dirt that ringed her fingers, was caught underneath her nails. 'It seems,' he had remarked once he'd regained his seat and had been joined by the others, 'that we have all been having a hard time of it.'

They had talked then, of Mabel's heritage, of her family, of her great-aunt, of the fire, of Toby, of Jack, of Stroop's attack in the study not twelve hours since. On hearing this, Mabel and the boys had got suddenly to their feet, fluttered around him, demanded to know why he had said nothing until now. Mabel went out and made tea. Thomas followed behind to help. Jack just followed. They had sat in the kitchen, waiting for the kettle to boil, Mabel washing cups in a pail, Thomas getting down the caddy, Jack sucking at the corner of the towel with which he was wiping a tray.

'Do you think he can help?' asked Thomas, spooning tea into the big pot.

Mabel nodded. 'He seems at least to know what's going on, and I think he's probably a kind man.' She looked at her hands and grimaced, remembered the crack and crinkle of his lips, wondered what it would be like to have your house burn down around you, have the flames licking at your heels while you ran and choked in heavy smoke, your hair singeing a halo around your head, leaping into the black well of the canal far, far below.

Jack was still sucking at the towel. 'What do you think, Jack?' she asked him as she filled the pot, the steam filming her skin, making her think of long hot baths at her great-aunt's; tried not to think of her great-aunt's, closed her eyes quickly, jammed the lid on the pot.

'It's an adventure,' said Jack, 'and when Mr Stroop reads them, they usually end up quite well.'

Mabel and Thomas had glanced at one another, raised eyebrows and smiled. Between them they had loaded up the tray and took it back into the room. They felt safe in here with Stroop and Castracani, and the soldier man before he had left, and Santorelli, even though he seemed more nervous than all of them put together.

They had drunk their tea and discussed what had happened and Stroop had told them of the shawl and his translation, and how after Taraborrelli's visit – for there was no doubt that was who it had been – how Stroop had struggled feverishly to remember it all over again, get it all written back down. How, as he had been writing it a second time over, certain things had come to mind, certain threads had started winding together. He had got up and taken a couple of books from a stack leaning haphazardly against a lower shelf, taken down a box-file labelled 'CH4 A–F', and extracted a few sheets of hand-written notes, a sheaf of drawings, laid them in front of Castracani, who had then handed them over to Mabel, the boys pressing round her shoulders as Stroop explained his reasoning. Between them they had consulted maps and worked out a route, passed round a glass of wine, made their plans. They vaguely heard the horse hammering up the lane, the clatter of someone charging up the path.

Oh, no, was all that Mabel had time to think as the door flew open, and in ran Aribert, breathing hard, his voice fast and firm and insistent, his eyes going this way and that, from Castracani to the window to Stroop to her, settling on her like cold mist, and once again the ice began to freeze and claw at her skin.

29

Symbols and Riddles

THROUGH THE NIGHT streets of London pounded horses' hooves, the lit lamps flickering as they sweated by, the watch men cursing as snow-sludge flew up and splattered their thick-weft cloaks. It was just gone nine, and men and women straggled out from the mills and workshops, funnelling past the oyster-sellers, buying rag-ends of pies, pots of eels, hot potatoes, warm gin whose fumes prickled through their mouths and noses, cleaning away the dust and the dirt of the looms, of the cobblers' lasts, of the itch of spinning ropes and sacks, the stink of woad-mixers, the metal spindrift of the die-casters that cut your skin, the heat and burn of the foundry. The taverns were loud and busy, noise coming and going, doors closing and shutting as people came and went like an indolent sea.

They kept the horses to the back lanes, the carriage scraping at the brick as it swayed from side to side down the narrow alleys, round tight corners, wheels catching in the gutters where piles of sludge kept their silence under the snow.

Santorelli rode at front like the devil, his cape flapping

high above his shoulders, his heart thumping in his ribcage with the rhythm of the horse. Every few hundred yards he'd have to pull the reins in tightly, wait for the carriage to catch up, looking back into the night, feeling his skin shrink with fear and anticipation. Up until this moment he knew he hadn't really been alive at all. His whole life had become blurred together, a long streamer dangling uselessly in the wind behind him. He tried to picture his father's face, his mother's long and golden braided hair, his sisters sitting in their sitting rooms embroidering at their hoops, stitching scenes in silken threads – men at hunt, women at work in the kitchen, social gatherings, London landmarks. It was his job to frame these pictures up and they sold in the little gallery for a handsome price. It was their family trade, always had been, and yet as he rode headlong into the night, his teeth and forehead frozen, the snow dancing all around him, he had forgotten it all. It was as if he was looking at his past through darkened glass, through an image he saw whichever way he turned his head, a single spectre a veil before his eyes, whether closed or open.

He saw Cobbett's cart again. More: he smelt it, felt it, saw the roughly bundled corpse, the sheet peeled away from the face, the ghastly green of skin beginning to decompose over nose and eyebrows, lids half-closed, eyeballs sunk and yellow and looking so much of dead things that they repulsed and fascinated in equal measure. And his cousin's lips a taut unpleasant grin of purple that hid his nature so completely there was no need for burial to know that Aldo Santorelli had truly gone forever from his body. Every few minutes, the vision came and went, sending Antonio's hot blood racing through his body as he was racing through the streets. He was afraid, he was elated, he wanted vengeance, he wanted more than anything to see his cousin's face as it had been the last time they'd played chess at Giorgio's tavern, talked about girls, drank too much wine. He remembered Aldo trying to talk to him about the old legend of a lost Lucchese legacy. How he'd waved it to one side, got up to get more wine, laughed that Aldo took all that old stuff seriously. If only he'd known then what he knew now maybe it would have been him rotting from the inside out on Dismal Cobbett's cart, although he doubted it. He never did have Aldo's strength or resolve, could never have done what he had done, assuming Stroop was right about the chapel – that he'd struggled to that place for a purpose, to try to send a message, to warn the girl, make the only hint he could about the nature of the treasure in her keeping. The chapel in St Anthony's where Aldo had split his head half off his shoulders. The chapel of St Clare, patron saint of embroiderers, who had spent her life sewing gifts for God.

In the carriage, Mabel, Stroop and Castracani bounced and rebounded like beans in a rattle, bruising shoulders and elbows against the carriage sides, knocking each other's elbows and knees, heads bobbing back and forth as the wheels flew and slew along the narrow lanes. They had long since given up attempting to talk and were clinging hard at the straps hanging from above the doors to try to give themselves some control and rigidity.

It was hard going. Stroop looked as if he were going to be sick at any moment, his Adam's apple bobbing up and down with alarming speed, his head ducking and dipping like a pigeon at seed. Castracani's face had gone sheet-white, apart from two sharp high points of red on his cheekbones, his eyes bloodshot when he opened them, which was not often. His mouth was clenched hard, he had already bitten his tongue twice, and the warm blood stained his teeth, which felt like they were being shaken one by one from his gums. He tried to concentrate on the problem in hand, but his thoughts were jangling all over the place, peas in a sieve, nothing coherent coming out of them at all. Every now and then his eyes were jolted open and settled briefly on the girl who was sitting opposite him, her thin wrist caught hard in the strap, fingers clutching at the leather, a look of grim determination on her face, her gaze constant on the window as if she were counting the snowflakes racing by outside.

In fact, Mabel was in a strange state of rest. Her body was so shaken that there was nothing to do but hang on. All the images of the past few days were at first just jumbled one into another any old way, racing along helter-skelter, losing definity and outline and individuality and then altogether gone, and she was just floating, staring at a distant point in the darkness outside, all thoughts melted away. It was for her a kind of dreamless sleep despite the constant motion of her body, and had she been aware, she would have been glad of it.

So were the carriage occupants: separate, silent, estranged, the noise of the flight filling the space between them. The iron-rimmed wheels scraped and sparked, the walls of the trap creaked and groaned as it was swung from side to side on its chassis. There were yahs! and hahs! coming from the man above, controlling the horses with a whip. To each side of him, Thomas and Jack clung to the guiding rail for dear life, the wind and snow plastering their hair to their foreheads, eyes wild and alive, the laughter of fear and exhilaration squirming in their bellies. Thomas kept opening his mouth to let in a blast of frigid air, swallowing the snow that landed on his tongue, shaking his head to shift them from his eyelashes, the corners of his mouth drawn back in the grin of a devil riding hard through the wildest of nights.

Aribert took up the rear, constantly looking behind him, twisting his body till his ribs ached, eyes squinting, searching the black alleyways as they closed behind him for a sign of the enemy. He knew they couldn't be far behind, knew that when they'd got out of Stroop's, running up the road to the waiting carriage, that Taraborrelli's men were only streets away. His scouts had found the house and listened at the windows. They'd heard Piozzi bark his orders out that, damn the time wasted waiting, it was back to Stroop's and beat the rest of the riddle out of him himself, force him to its conclusion even if he hadn't found it yet himself. Not five minutes later and the horses were being wrestled from the ostler up the road, who had been caring for them overnight as he supposed. A few more minutes to get him out of his house and down the yard with the key to the big back doors that guarded the stables from thieves and strays. Then getting tackled up – that would have taken time, and the horses would have been tired, ready for a night of rest, probably full of water and a meal of oat and beets. It was getting dark, there were many people on the streets, other carts and riders returning from markets and work, travelling home, not in a hurry.

It had given the scouts enough time to get word back to Aribert, who had sent for a carriage, headed straight for Stroop's, bundled in his charges and carted them off. He had left a message with the scouts: get back to the Italian quarter, find as many able-bodied men as you can, get them armed and on their horses and out behind us as fast as you can. We're headed for the Borough of Bermondsey, he had screamed at them through the dying twilight, for St Frigidanus and the Church of the Sacred Heart.

Aidan Wethelbridge closed his watch and tucked it back in his pocket. He sighed, listened to the mice scuttling along behind the skirting boards of the sacristy. He poured himself another small glass of wine and waited. It was 13 December, almost midnight, time to start the vigil for the Dark Night of the Soul to celebrate St John of the Cross. It was a private ceremony, open only to the Members of the Mystic Heart, as were he and Father Durandus, and during which time they would recite John's canticles of spiritual purgation and ascent and pray for the Cloud of Unknowing to come over them and unite them with the Sacred Heart of God.

But as yet, there was no sign of the father. Only a few minutes left. He would probably be late again. Aidan had already lit the candles and got the two books out and ready, face open on the small altar in the chapel of St Citha, where they could read them side by side while remaining on their knees. It was for him a night of grace and spiritual reclamation. All over England, Europe and elsewhere, wherever the members of their community happened to be, all of them would be reciting the same words, invoking the same blessing, travelling the same journey from sin to acceptance to unity with the Body of Christ via the Eucharist, and they would enter into the wounds of Christ and for one ecstatic moment, would have a foretaste of heaven. For Aidan, the night seemed more precious than it had ever been, for he felt certain it would be his last, knew somehow that this time next year he would not be standing here waiting. He willed Father Durandus to look up at his clock and know it was time and come hurrying down across the glebe and the graveyard so that they could ring the small handbell, set the spill to the thurible, the sweet perfume of incense carrying their prayers to God.

He went to the small side door and had a quick look out. No sign of the father yet, just a soft, soft sprinkling of snow falling on the headstones, whispering through the black branches of the yew trees, settling like moths upon the grey of the grass. He pulled the door to, made his way down the empty church, his footsteps echoing, his breath making a slight mist around his head. He checked the bolts to the outside door were closed although he already knew they would be. He watched as a single bat detached itself from a beam and made its way skitter-skatter down the upturned hull of the cantilevered roof and away off into the belfry, which rose like a mast above the nave. He followed the soft light that led him to the chapel and checked all was in readiness. The bell, the eucharistic offerings, the books, the spills – they were all there, waiting quietly below the pall of white cloth as if the snow had somehow passed right through the roof and fallen here too. He crossed himself, knelt and recited a small prayer. He was interrupted by the sound of the side door being opened. He took out his watch. Three minutes to midnight. He smiled. Father Durandus, for once, was just on time.

There was some slight confusion as to where the church was. Santorelli had pulled up his horse and leapt to the ground. Behind him, Stroop was getting stiffly from the carriage, standing crooked, swaying slightly, holding a piece of paper to one of the lamps set into the carriage corners.

'It should be right here.' He tapped the map with his finger and looked around him. 'We can't be far . . . the river's over there, I can hear it,' he pointed off to his left, 'so it must be . . .' He peered off to his right, hunting amongst the dark squats of buildings for one that might be a church. The flutters of snow fell in a constant screen around him, making it hard to distinguish one shape from another. He scanned the rooftops, looking for a belfry or a spire, but could make none out. He held his hand above his eyes like a cap, and methodically swung slowly from right to left. There was the river, the bridge, that flat expanse must be the green, and there . . . yes . . . there! He could just discern the solidity of a tree where the snow was beginning to settle on it like skin and separate it from the darkness, shining slightly.

'Leave the carriage here,' commanded Stroop, and instantly Santorelli was by his side, helping Castracani out of the carriage, Mabel, knees cracking, jumping down as soon as he was clear. Thomas and Jack, their collars pulled up, their noses going blue, were capering nearby, tired, excited, unaware of the cold, throwing snowballs at each other even though it was the wrong kind of snow and fell to bits before it left their fingers.

Aribert appeared out of the whirling night, two of his men gathering up the horses, tethering them to a short railing, which appeared to guard nothing at all under the snow.

'The rest of our men should not be far behind,' he said quietly, taking Castracani to one side. 'Would it not be wise to wait for them?'

Castracani had already started out to follow Stroop as he strode off into the night. 'We are here, Aribert, if our enemies are behind us we would do better to be inside. If they reach us before our men do, we will have a better chance of defence.'

'But if we waited . . .' Aribert was anxious. Blasting into battle without your army was a bad plan in his opinion. Caution was the better part of valour; courage without the means to back it up was a waste of resources.

'If we wait,' Castracani gasped slightly, trying and failing to keep Stroop's pace, 'it may be that Taraborrelli will get there first and that we cannot allow.'

He had to pause for breath. Mabel and Thomas hurried past him. Jack was just behind him, head craned up, looking at the snow falling out of the sky, wondering where it all came from and if it would ever stop. Aribert took Castracani's arm and weight, and propelled him on.

It was true that Taraborrelli was no fool. Their trail would be easily followed in the snow if their pursuers were not too far behind. Besides, if Stroop had worked out where they were going, it would be a simple thing for Taraborrelli to follow his lead. Stroop's house was laid open with no one to guard it. Aribert realised now that this had been a mistake. He'd never been much of a one for reading and books, but he recognised that Stroop had sniffed out some trail in the pages lining his study, and if he could do it, so could Taraborrelli. Maybe not so quick or reasoned, but the relevant books were still stacked on the desk, and apart from the box-file that Stroop had brought with them, it was all just lying there waiting.

But by now, they had entered the churchyard, the great yew a black hole at its centre, angels looming out of the darkness, fancy grille-work grinning on the frontage of marbled tombs, snow softening every edge, dulling every sound, causing the man in front to disappear, his footsteps covered almost as soon as his boot left the ground. A slight breeze whisked across the surface of the snow, making every-thing seem to sigh and shift. The pale face of half a moon appeared for an instant as if the snow had taken a sudden breath and before them they saw quite clearly the side of a church, its denominational sign obscured, with only several letters '. . . f St . . . rigi . . .' visible in their mottled gold.

'We're here,' whispered Stroop, stopping so suddenly that Thomas bowled right into his back. Stroop steadied himself, listened to the hard beat of his heart for a moment, then put out his hand and lifted the latch from the door.

30

Midnight, Between One Day and Another

TARABORRELLI HAD MARCHED up Stroop's back garden as if it had been his own, stood to one side of the step while he motioined his man on. Quickly, quietly, the man slid a jemmy in the frame by the lock and struck it once with an iron block made for the purpose, grooved on the sides to fit his fingers. The noise was slight, no more than a metal-tipped boot missing its step, and the door swung inwards. Had they tried the handle, it would have opened anyway for no one had thought to bolt the doors before they left. Taraborrelli spoke softly to his companion, gave his instructions.

He had sent two men off immediately after the trail laid by the carriage tracks and horses at the end of the street. The first man had a small sack of salt. When they had gauged the general direction, the second man would head back towards Stroop's whilst the first man continued after their quarry. At every corner he would drop a handful of salt to melt a marker in the snow. He also had a lump of chalk, which he struck against the brickwork as he passed. The third man set out to meet the second, and a relay was formed. If they lost the trail, if the snow thickened, if the morass of tracks became confused, the markers would show their fellows the direction to proceed.

Taraborrelli would follow shortly, but for the moment, he stood inside Stroop's kitchen, closed his eyes, cleared his mind of thoughts. He could smell soup – turnip, he thought, and lentils. His mouth grimaced involuntarily. He was a man who liked cheese, soft and smooth on the tongue or hard and strong on the throat. He ate chorizo sausage or salami with tomato and garlic, basil and oregano, thick yellow bread crumbled into olive oil, white veal sliced thick and fried in coarse ground pepper, bitter black coffee, a lick of some strong spirit to enliven and cleanse the palate. He thought the London Lucchese a watered-down version of the real thing and despised them for it. He thought of them savouring their hard melons, which had long since left the sun and had no taste of it any more, eating oranges that had been picked unripe, carted overland for weeks to arrive hard-skinned and filled with a juice that had no part of their homeland. The smell of this kitchen made him sick and his thirst for revenge was strong.

He opened his eyes, saw the two doors, knew that one led to the hall and one to the study, opened the right one and walked into the gloam-filled room. On the table he saw a mess of cups. He put his hand out to the teapot (insipid, he knew it without thought) and found it still warm. So, not long gone. He pulled the piles of books towards him, lit the oil lamp on the table, turned up the wick, closed the glass. He straightened the first untidy stack, turned the spines towards him, glanced down them one by one, squinting to read the tooled words or pulling one out to check the cover, or turn it open to the title page.

He found the one he sought on the top of the second stack. He flicked through the pages, found a piece of notepaper tucked inside, extracted it, holding it carefully between his fingers and towards the weak light.

Zita, Virgin, St: Patron of Domestic Servants and of the City of Lucca where she lived and died. Born Montsegradi, a village nearby, from 12 years old served with the Fatinelli Family in Lucca. Since a child, known for her piety; ecstatic visions; humility, honesty, devout, penitential labour; disliked then revered for this; facility for constant mental prayer despite assiduous work; remained with the same family until her death 1272; buried in the church of St Frediano which was contiguous to Fatinelli's house: body incorruptible: miracles; beatified 1696, canonised 1748; figure of veneration even during lifetime, particularly in Lucca but also in London where the cult is thought to have been introduced by travelling Italian merchants. Lost keys.

Taraborrelli recognised Stroop's handwriting and struggled to make out all the words. A lot of it was hard to read, scrawled as if in a hurry, but he lingered particularly over those words that Stroop had lightly underlined in pencil and then repeated at the bottom of the page in the form of a list:

Zita: Lucca: London

P/St. Lucca & Domestic Workers

St Frediano? Frigidian?

Lost Keys?

Taraborrelli laid the sheet of paper out on the table in front of him, staring at it hard. Frustration was beginning to boil within him but he clenched his fists, sat himself up straight and went back to the stacks of books. He flicked through them all. Nothing. He checked each bookmark, of which there were many, mostly scraps of torn paper, a few bits of coloured ribbon. He found nothing that could lead him further. He gripped the last book so tightly in his hands that the cover began to curve and protest. He hurled it across the room, knocking several books out of the shelf, the hole dark and gaping like a missing tooth. And then something switched on in his memory. *She* had said patron saint of Lucca – he had assumed 'she' meant Zita, whom everyone knew to be the patron saint of Lucca. It was practically drummed into every child after the age of three – she was so sweet and perfect and obedient. Why can't you be more like our little sister Zita? Every parent said it to every child at least once a week. But that was now. When the shawl had been inscribed, Zita was still only little sister and not yet saint. So who had been then their patron saint? Taraborrelli didn't even need to finish the thought. Of a sudden he knew it: every year at the procession of the Volto Santo, who was it who led the cortege? Who was held up on high before the Holy Image? Who had graced Lucca with his sanctity hundreds of years before the snivelling sister had even been born? He scrabbled at the little piece of paper before him.

St Frediano? Frigidian?

He leapt across the floor and kicked aside the books until he found the one he had just flung away. A dictionary of English and Irish saints. And from far away he remembered his early teachings of Frediano. Irish monk, came to Lucca, hermit, bishop, parted the waters and so on and so forth. *Irish* monk. *Frigidian.* Men took different names for different times in their lives. Frediano was the Italianised version of his original monkish name, and here in England, would his original name not be used?

His fingers ripped through the pages, trying to find an index, but the book was old and there was nothing but a cursory list of headings. He willed himself to be calm, he put the book on the table by the scrap of paper. He held his hands out until his fingers ceased their trembling. He took a small flask from his pocket and slowly, slowly undid the lid, took a long draught, replaced the lid, replaced the flask, put his fingertips back on the book. He gently lifted the cover, laid it flat against the table, leant over and made his eyes crawl word by word over the headings list. His blood began to increase its speed around his body, his skin tingled, his pulse quickened, he could hear a faint tick-ticking in his ears. And there it was, the clue that he was searching for:

'The Irishman's Churches in the Greater Borough of London . . . pp. 214–218'

He turned to the indicated pages. Not on page 214. Not on page 215. Not on page 216. He turned to the last two pages and there it was. The name might have been back-lit in gold, it leapt so from the void at him.

St Frigdianus, church of, begun 1135, completed 1178, destroyed by lightning, rebuilt in . . .

His eyes gleamed with tears of triumph and he felt he had caught a peach-pit in his throat. At last. *Frediano, Frigidian, Frigdianus.* Three in one. One in three. A trinity. And he knew that now he had them. St Frigdianus Church, Borough of Bermondsey, Greater London.

Taraborrelli took the book up in two hands and closed it, held it, each hand just the other side of prayer. His kissed the faded gilt of the pages, put it back on the table so it covered Stroop's scribbled note. He reached for a goblet that lay over to his right, swilled its contents, smelled it. He wrinkled his nose and threw the sour wine down his throat. That is the last of England that will pass my lips, thought Piozzo Taraborrelli, standing, leaving.

He opened the front door and walked up the path between the sagging plants and tired white-lipped trees he didn't know the names of. He saw how dark it was and didn't care, he didn't know where Bermondsey was but knew he would soon find out. For just a moment the moon was released and shone down upon the earth before the skies closed back in around it and Taraborrelli smiled.

Behind him, the door to Stroop's house stood wide and bare, the snow beginning to settle upon the mat and melt, then a little more, and a little more as the white footsteps made their way down the hollow emptiness of the hall.

31

Under the Thirdmost Face of God

S TROOP HADN'T REALLY expected the small door to open, although he had known where it would be. He hadn't been here for many, many years – almost seventeen, according to the notes in box-file CH4 A-F – and yet he had recognised the stiff black staff of the turret, the spare square plan of the original Norman architecture begun so many centuries ago. During the journey, before the constant hurl and burl of hurried travel had scattered his thoughts like seed before pigeons, he had tried to dredge up everything he knew about this old building.

Church-hunting had been one of his first projects, inspired by a small book he had acquired listing all the churches in London and the outlying regions. It had been detailed and dense, unrelieved by illustrations, and he had made it his business to spend an entire two months travelling to each and every one of the buildings mentioned, and making copious notes on the details of their structures, making sketches and maps of their locations. He had begun at first by scribbling his notes in the margins of the book, but soon he decided this was no good and had purchased various bundles of loose-leafed notebooks, and into these he transcribed all the notes he had made during each day's sojourn.

When he finally completed his project, there were very few that had eluded his attention: three had ceased to exist completely, their foundations plundered for stone, their graveyards and glebes ploughed over into common grazing; five more had been razed and rebuilt, and one had been utterly overbuilt, the land around it raised, the original architecture still extant, but now underground. Most, though, had stayed the same throughout the years, usually with the addition of chapels, buttresses and spires, or with their towers toppled by years of gales and frost cracking at their stones, redesigned and rebuilt using the elderly blocks or replacing every other one of them with something new. It had pleased him, this continuity, this fluidity in something so solid, the way that something can remain the same at the core and yet grow a new body around itself, meld styles and expectations, incorporate architectural adventures and dire mistakes as an oyster retains a piece of grit at the centre of its pearl.

The latch was black and worn with the years of hands that had lifted and closed it, lifted and closed it. It made barely a sound as Stroop raised it from its cradle and put his weight against the wood. He had expected the door to have been locked but instead it fell forward and crashed hard into the wall, small puffets of dust rising from the impact, the sound echoing from the bare stones. Aribert hurried forward and pushed Stroop gently to one side, took a stance in the middle of the small anteroom, one hand resting on his pistol, the other striking a flint between thumb and finger, a skill many had admired but few had mastered. Within moments he had located several candles and a lamp and had them lit by the time the others had straggled into the room.

Santorelli was last in, and when he pushed the door to behind him, closing out the snow and the night, they stood in their positions, completely still, their breath rising around them, eyes wide in the candlelight, the wail of the wind high in the tower, setting the bells humming on their rests. It was Aribert who took charge, shaking the others from the trance of having reached their goal, and finding themselves alone, not quite knowing now what to do or where to go. His English wasn't good, but he made himself understood.

'My men come soon to the front door and by the back. I go up the tower for lookout. You go find . . .' He shook his hand at Stroop and Castracani, motioning them to the small door opposite, which presumably took them into the main body of the church. The soldier was already on the move, seeking out the steps that would take him to the roof or to the belfry where he could set watch, sure that he would see the enemy's approach. He found a spiral staircase set into the wall and ran up it, his boots flying over the stone, his weapons rattling, his breath freezing in the pits of the wall as he passed. He pushed up the trap-lid and was out in one swift movement, skidding slightly on the snow that had gathered on the flat roof. Before him he could see the bells swinging slightly in their tower, nodding in the wind, which was gaining in strength, drawing on the blackness of the night, sending the snowflakes into eddies and tarantellas, one part of the night a frenzy of white, next to it a void of black, blown back by the wind.

Aribert peered intently down the road from which they had come. He could still see the carriage, though it was fast being obliterated, its outlines lost, its contours melting into the white world that surrounded it. He could see the horses moving just beyond it, whinnying softly into the hay bags that had been slung round their necks, the blankets on their backs strangely humped over saddles, heaped with little mounds of snow. He cocked his ear into the wind, listened for the sounds it might bring as it flew and grew its way through the silent streets. He frowned. Had he heard the clinking of bridles, the skim of whip across flank? He dipped his head again, cupped his ear, tried to catch the faint noises as the wind carried them over him, away from him, into the well of a fathomless night.

Castracani caught at Stroop's arm. His breathing was quick, his lungs burned within him, his face felt on fire with fever; anticipation hummed over every inch of his skin and for a moment he felt so weak he thought he might faint. The next second he felt strong as an ox – an old one maybe, but an ox all the same. Something impelled him on, where before he had felt like folding up and expiring where he fell.

'Do you know where we must look, Mr Stroop?' His whisper had the edge of eagerness, though the words were still soft upon his lips. The excitement dizzied him. He was finding it hard to accept that the history of his homeland lay here, within his reach, somewhere close by, sleeping quietly in its hidden grave like a mole within its mound. He clearly felt the heat of fire upon his skin, but it came from within and not without, warmed him but did not scorch him. The impulse to rush onwards was almost impossible to quell.

Stroop gently detached Castracani's arm and placed the box-file on the small table, moved the candles closer. He opened it, gently riffled through the pages, extracting two by their corners, marking their places with thin thongs of leather. Carefully they opened the small door and moved out from behind the choir stalls into the body of the church, Stroop at front, staring at the bits of paper in his hands.

They none of them expected to see the old man, and he quite plainly hadn't expected to see them. He was so shocked, his hand involuntarily loosened and the lamp he had been holding crashed to the floor. He'd thought he had prepared himself, thought he had been ready, but now, faced with it, he realised he didn't want anything to change after all. All that went through his head was, no, no, no, no, no, no . . . He didn't want to die like this, not here. He hadn't expected a knife through the chest or a gun held against his head. That wasn't what was supposed to happen. He didn't want his body to lie broken on this floor, his face against the cold stone slabs, his blood slip-sliding between the cracks into the ancient tombs below, lost to the resurrection. He didn't want to leave unshriven, he didn't want his body to pollute God's house, he didn't want not ever to see the sky again, to die enclosed, already in his tomb. And all that echoed around his head were those small, hard words that denied him to himself and abnegated all those years of faith: no, no, no, no, no, no . . .

He saw the big man tearing out of the gloom and lunging

towards him – it was Aribert, come down from the roof on hearing the crash of the lamp – his knife already in his hand; he saw the second one stop by the pillars and turn, like a ghost upon the stairs. But it was the girl who reached him first, her arms taking his weight as his legs abruptly gave away and his useless old body began to sag to the floor. Mabel's knees hit the flagstones with a hard crack, but Aribert was already there, taking the old man under the oxters, pulling him from her, easing him to sitting on the chapel steps. He stamped on the small pool of oil that still burnt at the old man's feet, crunching the splinters of glass underfoot, the wick drowned and gone out. Who this man was, nobody knew, nor what he was doing here in a deserted church at midnight; what was plain was that he was terrified. His face had kept the same expression, mouth open, stubbled chin quivering, eyes wide. His hand clutched hard at his pocket as if it held something precious to him, as if it were his heart and he were protecting his flesh with his flesh. It was Mabel's voice that came softly to the old man's ears, the soothing tones she used to calm a calf as it wobbled to its feet for the first time, her arm around its trembling waist, her hand stroking its head. A nice voice, thought Aidan, his mind beginning to settle, a country voice, he thought.

'It's all right, sir, it's all right, we're not here to harm you. Please don't be frightened.' She had moved herself to sit beside him, holding his great gruff hand in her own. 'This is Mr Stroop, and Jack and Thomas.'

Aidan saw two boys pop out from behind the other men like those monkeys you get on sticks at the fair. His fear receded, pulling back like the tide; would death make you comfortable and tell you its name? He didn't think so and his relief was so profound that he almost wept. And the girl, she was only young, and rather crumpled, as if she had just been dragged out from the linen bin where she'd been hiding since last week. She had dark brown eyes, kind eyes, hair straggling around her face. She was a mess, but he liked her, trusted her despite it, because of it. She was still speaking.

'I'm Mabel and this is Mr Castra . . . Castra . . .' she stumbled over the name and the thin man beside her supplied the difference, 'Castracani, and this,' he indicated the big man who was putting his knife back in his belt, 'is Aribert, and behind him, Mr Santorelli.'

In the small silence that followed, they all plainly heard the outside latch being lifted, the door being pushed, unable to open against the bolts, which Aribert had drawn behind them. A slight knock followed as of a single knuckle upon the wood.

'That'll be the father,' said the old man, heaving himself to his feet, 'late as usual.'

Mabel stood as he stood, guiding his arm. He released the grip on his watch and tapped at it gently as he walked stiffly towards the choir stalls, the strange group of visitors moving to let him pass, then sinking back into the shadows, Aribert's strong arm motioning them this way and that: Jack and Thomas to the chapel, Stroop and Castracani behind the pillars, Mabel and Santorelli crouching behind the grey marble of a big wall tomb. Aribert alone followed the old man up the altar steps and hid himself behind the lectern, tucked in against the steps of the short pulpit, watching through a tracery of vines, which curled up the step-sides forming a banister.

Aidan had regained himself, his blood beginning to flow back into his feet, giving him pins and needles, making him hobble slightly on the edges of his boots. He reached the door and drew back the bolts. They slid easily. He was pleased he had remembered to oil them the day before. He lifted the latch and opened the door.

The quarrel of the crossbow tore through his throat like a drill biting through wet wood. His weak skin ripped asunder, his throat opened wide to the world, pouring out the blood from him as from an overhanging pool. This time there was no one to catch his arm and his worn knee-bones shattered with the weight of him as he fell to the floor. He couldn't stop himself and his face followed his knees and broke on the cold hard stone. Someone came through the door behind the crossbow, kicked him roughly to one side, pushing his body up against the wall, his life leaking away from him into the snow-dampened dust, his watch shattering, the arrow-hands bending, the dials jammed. The time was five past midnight and the end of Aidan Wethelbridge's long, hard life.

Piozzo Taraborrelli pushed the priest before him, held him close, his lips tickling the top of the old man's head. They had found him in the graveyard, hurrying along the invisible paths, his hands held up over his balding pate, trying to keep the snow from his already freezing skin. He was preceded by two armed men, and flanked by two more. The one on the right held his crossbow ready and braced upon his shoulder, already reloaded. They came from behind the choir stalls and stood grouped before the altar, eyes gleaming in the frail light. Taraborrelli pricked at the priest's neck with his knife. Behind the pulpit, Aribert tensed, ready to strike, assessing the strength of his enemy, tactics slotting one by one through his mind, cold and sharp as the edge of an axe.

'Ah, now,' Taraborrelli spoke. He was smiling. His voice wasn't loud but it filled every crack and cranny and broke the stillness of the silent building. 'Come out, my friends. It is a long way I have travelled to meet you.'

A sharp cry escaped the priest's lips as the knife dug into his skin and the blood began to flow. It was warm, unlike the snow, but felt to him like ice.

'I can skewer him a little more if you like.' His tone was light, but his eyes sought the dark arches, pried amongst the pews, searched the shadows. He had already noted the candle-light coming from the chapel to his right and had nodded its direction to the man who stood by his side.

'When I was in Naples they had a little game we played with a woodcock. You took off its tail with a knife and split it right down the middle. It was a trick to get it all just right and even, particularly the beak, which as you can imagine is the most difficult part. When we had four or five of the little beasts ready, we threaded them on a stick and roasted them quickly on the fire. Quite delicious. Very juicy, though with a slight crunch. Only in Naples.' Taraborrelli sighed lightly and tilted his head as if in reminiscence. 'Of course, only the Napoletano would be such a barbarian, and nowhere else do I see this trick. We could, however, improvise.' And with sudden speed he drew his knife across the scraggy old throat, source of so many sermons and prayers, comforter of the penitent, speaker over graves, over baptisms, blesser of vows, passage of transubstantiated communion wine. Now from it sprung a line of scarlet frothing at the just-broken skin.

The priest yelped, his eyes starting from their sockets, his fear so great that a few drops of urine expressed and ran down the inside of his leg.

Castracani had seen enough, would take no more. He moved forward from his hiding place, stick tapping on the stones, his mouth grim and set.

'There is no need for this.' His voice had lost the crack of smoke and flame and his strength had not yet left him. 'He is an old man, a priest. He does not even know why we are here.'

'That is a conundrum easily solved.' Taraborrelli swung around to face Castracani as he made his way slowly along the transept towards the knee-high railing separating the public church from the priest's domain.

Time, thought Castracani, I must find more of it. Aribert's men won't be far behind. His eyes flickered at the slight shift of shadow under the pulpit steps, saw Aribert's face staring out at him, making some movement of his head but not understanding what it indicated. He knew that of the three men whom Aribert had brought with them, two would be positioned out the front watching the doors. The third should have made his way around the back of the church. How had they missed Taraborrelli's approach? He must have come at the church from the other side, across the glebe field. He must have been right on their tail. Their own man must still have been throwing the blankets on to the horses' backs, putting the feed-sacks on their snouts. It would only have taken a few minutes, the same few minutes it had taken them to wind their way through the graveyard under the shadow of the big yew and up to the back door and into the church. Taraborrelli had been right behind them all the time. He had underestimated this opponent; they all had. Castracani had seen the old man crumple up the moment the door had been opened, heard the dull parting of his bones as his body slumped without grace and hit the floor. He thought of Aldo Santorelli's decomposing sack of skin on Dismal Cobbett's cart, of Sandrini burnt and barbecued, going God knew where, floating down the river buoyed up by his bloated gut, or smothered in the dirty silt of the Thames, fraggles of his friend's sodden flesh separated from his bones, nibbled by crabs and flounder, sucked into the belly of anemones. These were the things that he had seen, and the life that he had witnessed lost. And the girl's entire family had gone too; he didn't know how many. It was an abstract thing that he had been told of, but nothing is as real as the smell of someone else's searing lungs, their rotting bones, the crump of a fallen body that can no longer stand, whose heart is being emptied of all its blood. The smell of that warm blood as it spread upon the cold stone, soaked away into the cracks and dust. Time, thought Castracani, in the end that is all any of us ever ask. And every moment as he approached his enemy, as he straddled the small gate, as he walked up the soft carpet of the altar steps, Castracani felt the weight of eternity pressing against his back, pushing him on and into the arrow-point he knew would come for him at any moment, and pierce and end the unsteady beating of his heart.

★   ★   ★

Pushing the old priest to his knees, Taraborrelli holding his collar like a dog, he watched with satisfaction the nervous gait of the man as he approached. There was still the whiff of the fire about him, an intangible evocation of acrid smoke covering him like a cloud. His frailty would not protect him, thought Taraborrelli, his mind flitting back to his father leaning over that desk, telling him to be gone for he was his son no more. He wanted to stride forward and crack this man across his withered grey face, wanted to feel the arrogance of his cheekbones break like chicken bones beneath his fists. He curled his fingers inside his gloves, felt the tips of them wet with snow, the soft skin-leather stiffening as it dried. He called out into the gloom, pitching his voice high above Castracani's head. The cobwebs on the roof beams shook in the breeze. The back door had been left open. Snowflakes played on the door jamb, drew patterns on the boards, ticked and tocked on Aidan Wethelbridge's ancient boots.

'Mr Stroop, why don't you come and join us? I know you are here. And what about the girl? Where are you hiding, Mabel?'

He laid a stress upon her name, drew it out as one would play a trout upon a lazy river, up the bank and down, in no particular hurry, tightening the line all the while.

Mabel's heart was beating hard, Santorelli's hand resting on her arm, holding her back, feeling the tension quivering within her as she fought to stay calm. She spied Stroop still behind his pillar. He was studying the two bits of paper intently, then carefully folding them one by one, smoothing the edges gently with his fingers, trying to make no sound. He finally had them small and hard enough to squeeze into the crack between the pew end and the pillar, and there they stayed, swallowed into shadow.

Stroop had stared and stared at the pages he had compiled all those years ago. The plan of the simple building, hardly altered since it was first built: the rectangular body of the main church, the two small rooms tacked on at the front, one on each side of the altar, the tiny lady chapel, the sturdy tower stretching its neck from the flat-bottomed roof. He studied the frescos of St Frigidanus, which were still extant in the egg and gesso, having been touched up at regular intervals over the many years since their first conception. They showed the miracle of the river that the saint diverted to save the city of Lucca from drowning in its flood waters. Stroop knew that was the reason this church had been erected: a plea to the Irish saint to protect the little hamlet this side of Bermondsey from the regular inundations of the tributary that watered their fields and animals, powered their mills, fed their soup bowls. There was a sketch of the small stained-glass window set high into the wall. He leant his back against the pillar, closed his eyes, recalled again the drawings he had scribbled of the lady chapel. Built within the church for the worship of Mary, Mother of God, rededicated, after substantial donations in 1248, to St Citha. A simple space, a plain altar made from a single block of stone, a small reredos of oak stained black with age suspended above the candle nook just to the left of the altar, the floor designed from hexagonal slabs, the only extravagance in its make-up. Stroop had studied the words carved into the floor that ran around the chapel's edge: 'Thy body is like unto a honeycombe filled with the sweetnesse of Jhesus, so love me broughte and love

297

me wroughte, love me fedde and love me ledde and love me letted here.' The writing started immediately under the altar and moved round to the right in two tight circle, the first talking of the honeycomb of Mary, the second beginning with 'love'.

He heard Castracani moving, heard the brief exchange of voices, heard his own name being called, and Mabel's. He looked across and saw the top of her head peeping out over the edge of the tomb. He wanted to tell her to stay put, to shrink into the space behind the tomb and the wall, but he knew that it was no good. There was nowhere to hide in this place; wherever they went they would be found. He moved around the pillar, his back still a brushstroke from its comforting solidity. He saw Mabel standing up, saw her pushing Santorelli back into the darkness, pleading silently with him, for Taraborrelli could not know exactly how many there were of them, and a secreted Santorelli with a loaded pistol was better than a disarmed Santorelli in the open. They heard squeals and shouts of protest coming from the lady chapel: Thomas and Jack were being hauled out from behind the little altar, Thomas's legs kicking in vain at his captor, who held him high and away like a rat by its tail; Jack on the other side, a firm grip around his damaged neck, walking straight and silent, his mouth oh-ed open with the harshness of the grip and the rip of the half-healed wounds beneath.

Stroop held out a useless hand towards Jack, this time unable to protect him, and as he did, his eyes were drawn from Jack to the flicker of candles behind his head. He saw the maps and plans he had drawn unfolding out from their crack in the pews, he saw the ancestral Mabel's embroidering hand, he surveyed the layout of the lady chapel, he heard the words of stone being read out loud and at last, at last the key tumbled and clicked and the lock of the centuries fell open.

And then Santorelli burst out from behind the tomb and took the pistol from his belt and fired. The explosion ran like a crack of lightning round the walls of stone, ripping the stale air in two, sparks jumping through the darkness like sprites as the shot went wide, ricocheted and exploded from the lid of the font.

Aribert leapt from his hiding place and rammed his dagger through the throat of the man holding the crossbow, then ran on towards Taraborrelli. But Taraborrelli was too fast. He shot forward and down the steps and twined his hand hard into Mabel's hair, dragging her backwards, hauling her over the altar rail, her boots kicking as she was hoisted into the air, the bones of her neck crick-cracking as he pulled her onwards.

'Where is it?' The words whispered in her ear, his lips touching her skin, his breath cold and moist. '*Where is it?*' He screamed the words, howled until they rang around the vaults of the roof, echoing from the upright tombstones that flanked the ancient walls. Aribert flung himself forward but the girl was out of his reach and another man was on his back, a strong arm coiled around his neck. There was a pounding at the front door as Aribert's men heard the shot and left off spying in the graveyard and checking on the horses and watching for enemy assault, and threw themselves against the bolts, started running through the snow, tight against the brick, trying to find another entrance.

For Stroop, it all meant nothing, and there was a silence in his ears; the whole world stood still and he stood on the brink of infinity. He saw now what he should have seen before: the increments of brutality, the insignificance of human loss, the tiny catastrophes of private pain that had to be ignored for the players to reach this part of the game. He understood what everything was all about. This was not about relics stolen, stashed and since reclaimed. This was not about lost legends, ancient Lucchese lore, the Grace of God invested in the instruments of His Passion. This was ugly. This was sordid. This was not a holy quest, or a repatriation. This was only and all about power, the sharpest knife that cuts the deepest, the peacock-breast of pride. He who held its relics held Lucca in his hand, and all within its walls would be his. This was a battle, a war of wits that didn't care whose families got tortured and slaughtered without knowing the reason why, how many bodies got burned alive on its battle-fields, how many innocent bystanders were snatched from below bridges, beaten and dispatched into the mucky waters of the Thames to drown slowly, in pain and alone. It had no problem slicing old women from ear to ear or skewering old men and leaving them nameless, stiffening in a coulee of their own blood on the floor of a church whose floors they had swept for thirty years. One more body more or less would not make a difference. One child here, one girl there, one more unknown man or woman.

The sweat stood out on his face, which had turned the colour of old tallow. And for Stroop, the way had suddenly cleared. With four quick strides he turned his head away from Mabel and Castracani and Taraborrelli and Jack and

Thomas and Aribert, and headed for the chapel. As he took the steps he saw what he knew he would see, what he should have seen before, saw the crossed keys engraved into the stone of the candle-nook, the symbol of Zita, finder of lost keys, heavenly housemaid, little sister; saw the small dark reredos, the Face of God carved quietly in its midst, black and old as the oak that kept its form; the words of the floor, the first circle dedicated to Mary the Mother of God, the second circle, added later, changing the dedication from Mary to blessed maid, pointing like a weathercock is pushed by the wind, the last word ending at the nook, telling its subtle tale, 'love me letted here'.

Stroop did not hesitate. He went up to the altar, seized the great iron candlestick and swung it across the candle-nook, sweeping all the live and dying candles to the floor. He swung it again, the iron dashing into the surface of the nook. At the first blow, the stone scraped and sighed and sparked; with the second blow, the surface scarred and dinted; at the third blow a small cloud of stone-dust rose and scratched Stroop all along the skin of his bared arm; on the fourth blow the sound rang like storm clouds around the chapel and out into the church, echoing like distant thunder, singing and seeping into the walls. Then the fifth blow, and the sixth.

Behind him Castracani reached the steps of the chapel and fell to his knees, the tears streaming down his face and neck, hands clasped, eyes bright, mouth closed and silent. Taraborrelli mounted the steps beside him, still dragging Mabel, kept his back to the wall, his lips moving without sound, his eyes smarting from the spill and singe of candle-wax where the wicks still floated, smoking on the floor. Up

301

against the choir stalls, Aribert had broken free from his captor, broken his neck with one blow of his hard hand, lunged for the last man standing, despite the knife which quivered in the flesh of his own back just out of reach. The wound slowed him and the man broke his grasp and ran for the door, where he was cut down by the entry of Aribert's other men, who had found this second entrance at last. He breathed hard, turned, heard the seventh blow, and the stone cracking its surface from side to side, and the eighth blow, which Stroop took from the side, sweeping the broken tablet to the floor.

Stroop dropped the candlestick, which clanged and rolled against the stones. He dipped his hand into the hole as into a deep dark well. The ringing of the blows, the falling of the stone, the rolling of the iron of the candlestick, all sound fell away as Stroop groped for a moment, only a moment, then found his quarry and lifted it high above his head. The hard old leather had cracked and dried but still it was intact, sealed and protected by its stone kist, the thong still tight about its neck, its treasures still encased within its skin.

'Is this what you want?' said Stroop softly and to no one in particular. He closed his eyes then opened them, glanced around the chapel, settled on Mabel's frightened face, then without warning, he tossed the pouch hard and high at Taraborrelli. Surprised, arms moving in reflex, he loosened Mabel, sought to catch his prize, fingers grasping, poised to pluck the pouch from the air. Stroop reached forward – she was barely an arm away – and took Mabel by the hand, pulled her towards him, held her against his side.

He looked down at the crash of stone. Beneath the debris

he could still see the last word engraved upon the floor, saying 'Here', and see St Citha's keys. St Citha, St Zita. The English always presumed their own spelling, always had to take something and change it to make it their own. He supposed they were not alone in that. Abruptly he turned his face away, heard a sob in Mabel's throat and led her down the chapel steps. Before him Stroop saw Santorelli broken-backed against the pillar, tatters of blood and bone replacing the features of his face, scraps of shot sticking to what was left of his skin. They skirted him, left him, they saw Taraborrelli's fallen men, the priest dragging the old man from the anteroom, Aribert being helped to his feet, groaning as the dagger was twisted from his flesh, his men moving forward to the chapel to take Taraborrelli in charge. He saw Thomas and Jack, who stood side by side, staring wildly, backed against the choir stalls, holding each other's hands. Stroop brought Mabel up towards the altar, smiled at Thomas, took Jack by the shoulder with his free hand. Together, they left the chapel, left the church, left the awful smell of still spilling blood, left Castracani bowed upon his knees, head cradled in his arms, tears wetting the stone around his knees; Taraborrelli, sliding down the wall, the stones smooth against his back, anger and defeat darkening the shadows on his face, holding the pouch between his hands like a prayer.

Too late, said the wind as it moved through the graveyard, wrapped around the chapel like a cloak, tapped upon its stones, stroked its fingers on the mortar, found a way through the walls, whispered through the candle-flames on their little sea of wax, then slowly, certainly, blew the last one out and drowned the wick, hardened the wax, set its seal as a slow ripple upon the surface.

32

On the Other Side
of the Shutter

STANLEY IZOD SAT on the steps of St Anthony's gazing east over the river. On the other side, just to the right of the bridge, he looked at the walled garden, saw the tops of the trees tipping over the bricks, still young, still supple, only just clearing the height of the wall. He watched the figure coming out of the garden, closing the grille of the gate, coming back over the bridge with the old tin pail hooked on her arm. Mabel was taller now, and he smiled as she waved, touched his cap, nodded his head. He took his pipe out of his pocket and tucked it into his mouth, handed the tobacco pouch to Thomas, who sat beside him, and began rolling a cigarette. The afternoon light shone red and gold on Mabel's hair, made her skin glow.

She crossed the street and came and sat with them on the steps. Behind them they heard the ruckus of the fair going on in St Anthony's Square, but none of them wanted to go and see the jugglers or the men on stilts, or be hustled and bustled by all the people crowding into the square, buying and selling, pushing and shoving, children screaming, men getting drunk, women worrying and picking at the many wares, checking their purses were still tucked safe inside their pockets. They didn't want to see the big house at the back with its new family, trampling on the souls of the dead. They sat quietly on their step, looking over to the east, watching the ducks paddle the edges of the river, the redshanks dipping in the mud, the distant windmills sculling so slow they might have been asleep.

They watched the leaves on the trees in the Graveyard Garden, bought with some of the proceeds from the Flinchurst Farm. There was a tree planted for every person they had lost, a plaque with a name and a date. There were willows and ash and oak and juniper, a holly, a chestnut, some laurel and laburnum. Castracani brought two olives from Lucca, one for Aldo Santorelli, one for Antonio. They had worried that the soft southern trees wouldn't survive the cold and damp of London, but two years later and they had survived and struggled on, as had the sitters on the steps.

The Lucchese Council in London had survived and their streets and houses were being rebuilt. Aribert had returned to Lucca a quiet hero, the relics repatriated to the Holy Body of God. Maria Elisa Bacciochi had repented when they were revealed to her, saw that this was indeed where they belonged.

Aribert had also brought the name of the traitor on his lips and Benedetto Gadi had been quietly dispatched whilst on a visit to his vineyards. It was never clear what had happened to him, as those who knew would not tell, and his body was never found. In the archives, another chronicle was added, as was the Lucchese way, but it would not be read or spoken of for many, many more years.

In London, Taraborrelli and his companions had been tried

for murder and found wanting. They had been hanged in a line on a hill outside Erith, their bodies left to stink and swing in the air until the frost and the wind broke the ropes and what the carrion birds had left of them fell to a heap where their feet had once been, their last remnants carried off by dogs and trampled into the ground by a band of pigs who had broken free from their fence.

All was quiet now, and so they sat, Thomas and Mabel and Stanley Izod, watched the sky turn from blue to indigo, saw the swans sweep low across the marsh, clouds of Stanley's pipe-smoke keeping the gnats at bay. They heard the gentle gyre of feather on tile and looked up to see the owl returning to its tower, then round the corner of the church came Jack, laughing, running. He held a toy in his hand, watching the little wooden monkey dance up and down the stick as he shook it violently from side to side. He pulled a grubby bag of sweets out of his pocket and thrust it at Thomas, took a hair slide out of the other and gently put it in Mabel's hair. He'd put it in all wrong and it wouldn't stay, but nobody minded. Mabel would fix it when Jack turned his back, which he did the moment Stroop came round the corner after him, out of breath from running, but looking younger, stronger, with more flesh filling out his bones.

'Are we ready for home?' he panted, and Mabel stood up and linked her arm through his.

'Quite ready,' she said, and started down the road, saying goodbye to Stanley Izod, hearing Jack and Thomas coming up behind them, Jack telling Thomas everything he had seen, moving his whole body to turn and look about him, the scar tissue holding his head tight and straight.

Thomas was taller than him now, but Jack didn't mind. He knew, like everyone did, that he would never really grow up and that was fine. He didn't want to. He was happy in the house with Mr Stroop and Mabel looking after him, and Thomas too, telling him stories, taking him on expeditions, getting him into and out of scrapes, sleeping in the cot on the other side of his room. Jack knew that at last everything was as it should be, as it should have been all along. He'd soon enough forget those things he wished he hadn't seen, and then they would disappear for ever into the past like a stone thrown into quicksand. He knew that every new day was a world within a box, waiting to be unpacked. He couldn't have said any of these things, but he didn't need to. He was just Jack, and Jack knew.

Mabel turned back and smiled at him, happy that he was happy, happy that the garden was doing well, happy that they were all going home. He waved the stick at her, laughed as the monkey quickly climbed its tree, then clattered back down and started all over again.

Stanley Izod stayed on his step a few minutes longer, watching the odd little family trail off into the distance. He had a peculiar feeling in his stomach as he watched them go, thought about the things that had been, the things they had seen, that he had seen. He wondered again if he had done the right thing in taking the girl to Whilbert Stroop. He had thought about it often.

A cloud of geese rose, far off in the distance. He lifted his head, watched as they furled over the landscape in a wave of noise and wing, over the windmills, over the marsh, over the river, over the spire of St Anthony's. He smiled to himself as if for once his questions had been answered, then he knocked out his pipe, eased himself to his feet and went back in to the cool blessing of the church.

Historical Note

A lot of research goes into any historical novel, especially one going so far back; however, the fictional flesh in *Guardians of the Key* is hung on bones of fact. The Volto Santo and its relics are exactly as described, but, as far as we know, have never left Lucca. However, there was certainly a cult of both the Volto Santo and Zita (Citha, Cytha) in medieval England, two replicas of the Volto Santo being referred to: one, the most famous, in Old St Thomas's, London (though which particular Old St Thomas's I haven't been able to ascertain) and also a second copy on 'The Bermondsey Road.'. Several medieval churches in England still have extant representations of Zita, with her bunch of keys.

Many of the people mentioned are also well documented, perhaps most surprisingly the original Mabel, who was indeed embroiderer to the Court of Henry III, and who is mentioned over a stretch of seventeen years, making her a particularly longstanding employee of the court.

Buono Roncino was a very important Lucchese silk importer, references being made to his direct dealings with Henry III, who, in 1256, presented an embroidered cope to

St Edmunds at Bury which he had bought from Buono Roncino for the sum of 18 marks. Castrucchio Castracani (1281—1328) is still revered in Lucca as the hero who came hot-foot from exile in London to deliver Lucca from the hands of attacking Pisans and Ghibellines. His life was written up by no less that Nicolo Machiavelli. Both were part of the large Italian ex pat community who lived in medieval London, though I have imposed the fictional Silk Quarter on the wholly unconnected borough of Erith, primarily for its geographical position.

One interesting point of note concerns Henry III and his fanatical devotion to the position of Holy Blood brought back by Crusaders from the Holy Land with a begging letter from Robert, Patriach of Jerusalem, for funds. No one understood, even at the time, why he chose to venerate such an obvious fraud, and I am indebted to Nicholas Vincent's *The Holy Blood: Henry III and the Westminster Blood Relic* (Cambridge University Press, 2001) for many of the details in his excellent book.

Lastly, a slight apology for predating the Chapter House of Westminster Abbey by a few years, but its atmosphere was just right.